To the Sweetwater Husbands;

I am looking forward to meeting the women of Sweetwater. Your town sounds like a place I would enjoy living and working. It is exciting to be part of the town's growth and know my experience and knowledge will come to good use there.

I must admit your offer of a home as well as a place to do business, use of a horse and buggy, monthly allowance for living expenses along with a stipend was more than I was expecting. I will be a loyal member of your community and commit myself to the health and well-being of every woman and child living there.

The contract is signed and will accompany this letter to you. I will arrive on the day and time set forth in the contract or if prevented to do so, at the earliest possible date. I know to some of you that time is of the essence and I will make haste forthwith.

Your Obedient Servant,

Mrs. Rebecca Johansen, Midwife

A Midwife for Sweetwater
&
A New Face in Town
by

Susan Payne

Sweetwater

A Midwife for Sweetwater & A New Face in Town

The Wild Rose Press, Inc.
PO Box 708
Adams Basin, NY 14410-0708
Visit us at www.thewildrosepress.com

Publishing History
First TWA Edition, 2020
Print ISBN 978-1-5092-3120-1
Digital ISBN 978-1-5092-3121-8

Sweetwater Book 2
Published in the United States of America

Dedication

The Sweetwater stories are dedicated to my husband whose sense of romance still takes my breath away.

A Midwife for
Sweetwater

CHAPTER 1

Rebecca had her nose practically pressed to the train's window as it pulled into the neat brick station with stylish green trim. Quickly picking up her two bags, she excitedly headed to the steps where the grandfatherly conductor helped her descend to the wooden platform along the entire length of the building. She noted the wide street behind the station and knew it was the center of the expanding town of Sweetwater. It was a good thing it was expanding because that was Rebecca's reason for coming here - to help the young women of the town bring the next generation into the world.

She stood, one bag at her feet, trying to decide the best route to take, when four of the largest men she had ever seen came toward her, each one appearing larger than the man in front of him. The first one to reach her side put out his big paw of a hand, engulfing hers within it and shook it with friendly enthusiasm.

"Mrs. Johansen?" At her nod, he continued, "I'm Ben Greggs, and this here is Seth Harrison and Mac and James Macgregor." The other men tipped their hats and mumbled a welcome while Ben kept hold of her hand. Mr. Gregg finally realized what he was doing and laughed at himself while trying to explain.

"We are glad you could come so quickly. Our wives will probably be your first, um, patients. We put the advertisement in the newspaper and you caught our eye right off. Young enough not to retire and leave us and a fine-looking list of references that all proved to think very highly of you. We feel very lucky to have you here in Sweetwater."

"Do you all have wives who are expecting?" she asked, faintly amazed.

"Mine and Seth's wives are about ready to burst." Then he turned questioning eyes to Mac and James who looked at each other shrugging.

James cleared his throat saying, "Not yet."

Ben went on, "Well, they are practically newlyweds. Seth and I have been married almost a year." As if that explained it all. Evidently, these men didn't waste any time in starting their families. If there is a big population of young families as the advertisement intimated, there will be plenty of births to keep Rebecca busy.

Just then, a shout from behind Rebecca had all of them turning to see another big man only younger coming toward them carrying two large suitcases. "I didn't expect such a warm welcome home, Mac. How did you know I was arriving on this train? I didn't let anyone know I was heading back." Then he put down his cases and hugged the two Macgregor men.

Mac's face broke into the first real smile that morning while giving a big bear hug to the younger man. Rebecca could see the resemblance between the three men and was amazed at how all these good-looking men call Sweetwater their home. And now here was another, only hopefully unmarried.

Taking a deep breath, she tried not to let out a sigh as she watched the homecoming of the three family members. She was beginning to think she was really going to like living in Sweetwater, especially if these men represented the friendliness of the women as well.

Ben Greggs introduced the newcomer to Mrs. Johansen as Jessie Macgregor, home from university.

"Jessie, I can't believe you decided to come home finally. Is this just a visit or are you home for good?" asked his older brother James.

"I plan to make it permanent or until I get bored and hear San Francisco calling me," Jessie teased.

Mac, evidently a man of few words, said, "Wait in the buckboard."

James added, "We'll be going back to the ranch in a couple of minutes."

"That's all right," said Jessie. "I'll run over to Abby's to say 'hello' and you can pick me up there. I'll drop my cases off, though." He tipped his hat to Rebecca and gave her a devastating smile. "Glad to have met you, Mrs. Johansen." Then he strode towards a buckboard at the end of the platform and left his bags.

"Seth and I can take Mrs. Johansen over to her new home. It won't take all of us to see her settled. Is there anything you want to tell her?" Ben waited for any volunteered information from the other men but there was none from the two brothers.

They escorted Rebecca to a buggy and Ben helped her onto the front bench. Seth folded himself into the rear seat and sat there waiting for Ben to get the horses moving. They went right down the main street with Ben mentioning the various businesses along the route.

Rebecca, wide-eyed, tried to take in all the names and types of items available. Sweetwater was larger than the place Rebecca was from and this neat, prosperous looking town was exactly what Rebecca had hoped to find. She noticed the freshly painted main street buildings. There was a lovely looking dress shop as well

3

as a mercantile and dry goods store.

Soon they were at the far end of town from the train station and opposite the little white church with a steeple. Ben pulled the horses to a stop in front of a small white house surrounded by a white picket fence. Flowers filled the space between the fence and the white painted porch. Rebecca held her breath, hoping this was the house promised in the advertisement for her use.

"Home sweet home," said Ben as he helped her alight. "This was the house of the first minister here in Sweetwater. It was just him and his wife but he retired and then passed on. It's been empty ever since. The church parishioners built a new, bigger parsonage next door to the church for the new reverend since he is young and they thought he would need a home for a growing family."

More growing, thought Rebecca. These men sounded like rabbits and she smiled at her own imaginings. The more young families, the more work for her and that meant her contract here in Sweetwater would be extended. The excitement of having her own practice shivered through her body as she looked up at the house that was so beautiful it took her breath away. So unlike the faded white-washed cabin she was used to living in.

"This is just lovely," she said out loud climbing the steps onto the porch as Ben led the way through the front door. They found themselves immediately in a well-furnished parlor heated by a nickel-plated stove. The room had two windows facing towards the street and two windows facing the side yard.

She walked through a wide archway leading into a dining room with the bedroom off it to one side. On the back wall was a door going into a neat kitchen, completely equipped with a cook stove, hand pump, sink and miscellaneous pans and dishes. Off the rear of the kitchen, was a room with a small window to the neat back yard. Rebecca decided to use this room to see her mothers in. She would have to get a narrow bed or cot for now until she could afford a medical table.

"It doesn't look like I'll need anything besides my clothes and, of course, my medical bag." Which she patted since she was still holding on to it.

"Well, that's all Abby and Miss Lily's doing. We men thought it best if a woman's touch was used in getting the place ready for you," explained Ben and for some reason Seth was now flushed a bright red.

"I'll thank them as soon as possible. You told me Abby was the owner of the dress shop in town. Is Miss Lilly from in town, too?" asked Rebecca.

That's when Ben glanced at Seth and Seth simply stared back at him. Ben said, "Miss Lily has an establishment in town just down First Street where she fixes ladies' hair. But there's no need to thank them. Those ladies were tickled pink when they heard you would be moving here and wanted to make sure you were happy with your new place. We, the four of us men, were happy to bankroll them."

Seth, normally quiet it seemed, added, "Miss Abby will be here to pick you up about noon tomorrow and bring you out to Ben's place. I'll have my wife, Callie, there and you can meet both of them then, if that's all right by you."

"That sounds fine. I'll be able to thank Miss Abby at that time then," she said.

Ben said, "Just call her Abby. If you use anything

else, she'll set you straight anyways. But I look forward to seeing you tomorrow afternoon." He tipped his Stetson and turned to leave.

Seth explained to her, "There should be provisions in the kitchen for you until you can pick-up whatever else you need. You have an account set up at the mercantile that we'll see to as the letter to you stated. There's a gig and horse for your use at the livery in town once you're used to the area. Andy is the stable-hand and he'll harness the buggy for you when you need it."

"That may be needed soon if you're right about how close to confinement your wives are. I can handle a gig and I have always had a good sense of direction," she explained to ease their mind about her being where she was needed when the time came.

"I'll probably see you tomorrow, too. Again, welcome to Sweetwater." Seth Harrison tipped his hat and they both left her to bond with her new home.

Rebecca dropped her medical bag on the floor of the small neat bedroom and went to retrieve the other case Ben had set by the front door. Unpacking didn't take long, everything Rebecca owned fit easily into the dresser located in the bedroom.

Going into the kitchen, she found a small pantry built into the wall between the kitchen and the room she was going to use for seeing her mothers. It was lined with Mason jars filled with a myriad choice of foods. She found a meat pie and what appeared to be bread pudding covered by a clean towel in the pie-safe.

Rebecca was tired but it was still daylight so she checked the cookstove and found it had banked ashes. Quickly bringing them to life to warm the meat pie, she heated water for the tea she had also found in the pantry.

After setting the table with a plate and cup, Rebecca went back to the stove and made the tea. She took the pie out of the oven when it appeared to be hot and bubbling inhaling the rich beefy aroma rising from it.

Rebecca took her first mouthful of hot meat pie filled with root vegetables and rich beef gravy. A "M-m-m-mm" escaped as she took another bite enjoying it just as much as the first. If she kept getting fed like this, she would double her weight in no time and that wasn't a goal she should work toward. After all, she was overweight as it was.

Both she and her mother were built like a little round teapot. Rebecca's mother is the same size today as she was at Rebecca's age and it looked as if Rebecca was doomed to the same round shape her whole life, also. She had come to terms with her destiny, letting other women be the svelte, seventeen-inch waisted Aphrodite men seemed to desire. Rebecca had never had a man look twice at her and expected to remain a midwife her whole life. Finding a town like Sweetwater to make that life in was the best she was going to get.

Replacing the rest of the savory into the pie-safe, she took a spoonful of the bread pudding finding it as delicious as the pie but left it there without taking a portion. Rebecca rinsed her dishes and set them to drain before deciding to wash-up and go to bed early. The past few nights had been strenuous for her. She had found it difficult to fall asleep at night and impossible to sleep on the train during the day. Her trip hadn't been that long, at least, but Rebecca felt her eyelids getting heavier by the minute so succumbed to the urge to slip into the neat bed.

Dressed in a long nightgown, Rebecca crawled into

the double bed and pulled up the sheets. She stretched luxuriantly on the smooth fabric and felt the delicate embroidery work along the top of the sheet and at the pillowslip openings. She would definitely have to thank someone for these fine linens. Rebecca was used to having rather rough sheets with annoying little flubs making sleeping soundly difficult. These sheets were going to be like sleeping on a cloud. She almost wondered if they were silk. Not that she would know but if they were silk, she wouldn't be surprised.

As Rebecca lay there waiting for sleep, she went over the day. Meeting the men of the women she will be midwife for was a little different. Most of the time, she never met the husbands. Sometimes they were in an outside area during the labor and birth process and allowed in after the mother and baby were both cleaned up, any sign of blood or the birth completely removed.

She was never actually introduced to the husbands or felt they were concerned for their wives enough to care who was helping during the birthing process. Rebecca was often not even paid for her duties, even at the most difficult births. And here, these men had gone out of their way to find and hire a midwife, pay for her trip to Sweetwater, give her use of this house, a horse and gig all to safeguard their wives and future children. Then there was their generosity and thoughtfulness of getting this house set up for Rebecca to move in and begin her duties as quickly as possible. It was heartwarming to know these men loved their wives so much they would band together to make sure the women would have the best care during their pregnancies. It was the main reason Rebecca wrote the letter in response to the advertisement in the first place.

One of the reasons, thought Rebecca sadly. The other was the retirement of her mother from being a midwife due to the arthritis that had attacked her hand joints. And it was now affecting her ankles and knees so soon movement will be so painful helping as a midwife will be impossible. Rebecca had always been her mother's assistant and more and more she had been the sole person handling the delivery and aftercare of the mother.

But nothing stays the same and the new young doctor coming into their area had a wife who was a trained midwife. There weren't enough births for two midwives and she didn't want the mothers to need to choose between the doctor and her. Rebecca jumped at the advertisement placed by the young husbands of Sweetwater when it came to her notice and luckily the Sweetwater fathers-to-be liked what she wrote in response.

The local doctor in Sweetwater, who wasn't very young, was more than anxious to give up his expectant patients. According to the letter he wrote in answer to her own, he didn't think he had the time to do a lay-in with a new mother going into confinement for hours at a time. The doctor explained he had a large area to cover and ranch hands had a lot of accidents that meant bones to set and cuts to sew. The doctor could see the population growth occurring and wrote he was more than happy to share the workload by having Rebecca take over the female and newborn population.

Rebecca woke up with the birds chirping outside her window in a flowering apple tree. Stretching, she reveled in the feel of sliding against the smoothness of the sheets. Closing her eyes once more, she pulled the covers back swinging her legs over the side of the bed. She used the privy outside the backdoor then stirred the fire in the cook stove to heat water for tea again. Doing all these little homey things in her own house was a secret delight to Rebecca. Ones she had looked forward to doing. She had always lived with her parents but felt as if she was in their way. At least to her father who always had a problem keeping food on the table for the three of them even with her mother bringing in money from the birthing.

She never knew a time when things were flush. When her mother hadn't had to scrimp and buy on account hoping to pay the grocer back later. She never knew a time when she didn't feel as if she were a burden on her parents. Both of them. How she could weigh so much and eat so little was a mystery but it happened. She never knew a time she wasn't hungry and she never knew a time she ate her fill. Maybe that was why her father always looked at her as he did. He was a thin man who seemed to eat what he wanted and never gained weight. Although Rebecca thought his drinking may have had something to do with his staying thin. It seemed men who frequented the saloon tended to be thinner over all.

Enough of thinking about the past. Her parents will be free of her now and possibly she could even send something home to her mother so she could get a new dress or shoes. Things her mother went without so others in the family could have what they needed. Another feeling of guilt washed over her as she glanced toward the dress she had worn while traveling to Sweetwater. She promised herself to send her mother the money to cover its cost out of her first month's salary.

When Abby pulled her buggy to a stop in front of

the white house with the white picket fence, Rebecca was already on the porch wearing her plaid travelling dress with full bell skirt, piping down both sides of the bodice and epaulets on the shoulders. Her hat was a wide brim straw with several silk flowers waving every time she moved her head. She felt grownup and confident as she waited to meet her first mothers-to-be.

Carrying her medical bag in her hand, she said, "Don't bother getting out. I'll be there in a moment. I'm Rebecca Johansen, as you probably guessed."

"I'm Abby and I'm so glad to meet you. I was excited to know you had accepted the position. Ben and Seth were so worried they wouldn't find someone to come to Sweetwater soon enough. You know, married midwives' husbands won't leave their place of work simply so their wife can find better employment. And experienced midwifes are difficult to find yet alone ones who want to move to the western states."

"I found the timing of the advertisement melded with my needs. The local doctor had married a trained midwife from the east and there weren't enough births in the area for two of us. I found the opportunity to move here to a town where the husbands show such concern for their wives very intriguing. I don't know if these wives know how wonderful their husbands are."

"I think they do but for totally different reasons," chuckled Abby as they left the town behind them.

Rebecca realized Abby was the kind of woman who would never have set foot in her old town. This woman was lovely. Clear hazel eyes, dark hair done in a stunning style topped by a hat featuring a faux feather bird. Her dress was of the finest fabric and so stylish Rebecca was reminded that Abby owned the dress shop on Main

Street.

Even though they were opposites, they were two unmarried women of similar age. Rebecca hoped they would become friends.

It was a little over an hour when Abby pointed to a large ranch house sitting back from the road accompanied by barns, corrals, and smaller outbuildings. The house had a neat porch shading the front and side and a wide front door welcoming all visitors.

Abby had barely pulled the horses to a stop before a very pretty, very pregnant young woman stood on the front porch waving for them to come in. The blond-haired woman hugged Abby and looked expectantly towards Rebecca. Abby did the introduction as Julia Greggs smiled, her light blue eyes offering friendship.

Julia said, "Now I know why Ben has been so nervous. He wanted you to be here before I gave birth. He told me yesterday about the men's plan to bring you here to Sweetwater and he's been on pins and needles afraid I'd have the baby before you were in place."

"Well, babies do make their appearance at their own sweet time. This one is letting us have a little while to get better prepared which sounds like a good thing," replied Rebecca mentally calculating the approximate time of birth.

Julia led the two other women into the cool living area and stopped to take a breath. "I get so winded these days. It doesn't seem like I get anything done."

"Do you have help around the house? Someone to do the laundry, at least, for a while after the birth?" inquired Rebecca, already looking after her 'mother'.

"Yes, to both. Ben doesn't want me to do anything but I still do all the cooking and up to a week ago, I worked in the garden. Now I can't seem to get up with any grace after getting down. I was using the hoe but Ben told me not to do that anymore, either."

"He's probably right at this point but I will know after I examine you. If that's all right with you," Rebecca said.

"Certainly, I want to know everything I can before this baby comes. My mother hasn't been much help. She says she doesn't want to frighten me which, of course, frightens me." Julia laughed nervously.

"Is there a private room with a bed and wash basin with clean water?" asked Rebecca. "That would be the best."

"There's my bedroom right off the hallway. We moved down here to be closer to the privy but after the baby I want to move upstairs so I will be close to the nursery," Julia explained as she led the way to the main floor bedroom.

Abby said, "I'll stay here and make tea. I don't think you need me for this." She smiled to let the others know she didn't feel left out in any sense.

Once in the room, Rebecca sat on the chair and pulled out a ledger book with plain pages. She wrote little marks at the top of the blank page and began to ask Julia about her history. The answers help Rebecca know if there were any problems to be taken care of before the birth.

"Well, using this date of your last menses, your baby is overdue. Let me see if the date may be off a little or if we have a baby just a little too content in their nice warm home," she said trying to put Julia at ease.

Julia lay back on the bed and Rebecca washed her hands then pulled up Julia voluminous dress and felt with her palms flat to the abdomen, moving her hands as she went. "The baby is in position to descend which is where we want it at this point. Head down, bottom up so to speak. This may be more uncomfortable for you because now it will kick up into your stomach or back bone. Either can be painful and annoying if you're trying to sleep."

"I wondered what kept waking me up in the middle of the night. I knew the baby seemed restless. I think it might be one of those babies who'll cry all night," Julia admitted.

"A baby shouldn't need to cry all night. They cry to let you know something isn't right with them. Tummy ache, earache, you have to learn your baby's hints but each baby has them. Colic is the worst, but other little things that make us adults uncomfortable makes babies just as uncomfortable. Being aware of your baby is the first step in having a contented infant. I also would suggest sleeping on your side until after the baby is born. Prop a pillow under your belly to keep it from pulling on your back. I think both you and the baby will find it more comfortable."

"Thank you for the suggestion of the pillow, I'll try it out tonight. Anything for a full night's sleep," Julia said earnestly.

"I can check you physically if you want a closer idea of the birth day. But it's your decision. It won't hurt but it is slightly embarrassing for the mother," explained Rebecca.

"Less embarrassing with you then with old Doctor Winters, believe me. He's a nice man and all but I simply can't see him doing anything but catching the baby as I push it out," laughed Julia. "I know that much about the birth. I have to push."

"I can give you a better idea than that but let's see about this little one first." After a quick check Rebecca said, "I expect to get called back here within the week. You've started the process already and the baby's head is right up against the cervix where I expected it to be. You might be a week to ten days overdue."

Julia's face lit up and then went pale. "I'm not ready."

Rebecca, walking back from the washbasin took Julia's hand saying, "You're much more ready than you think. You have been taking care of this baby for the last nine months and you'll be able to take care of it just as well afterwards. As far as the birth, I'll answer any questions you have about the whole thing. Any time you're ready." The ladies left the room to return to the parlor and Abby.

As Rebecca and Julia entered the kitchen, a very petit, pretty lady stood up saying, "I'm Callie Harrison. Another of your very needy patients." She put out her small hand to shake Rebecca's. Callie appeared as if a slight breeze would blow her over but a longer gaze into her deep-green eyes told of a much stronger person. Her bright orange hair indicated a fiery personality that Rebecca felt was the real woman in front of her.

"Yes, I was made aware of that by your husband. He seems very concerned that you're too far from town. We need to make sure you're all right there or if you should be brought into Sweetwater when you're closer for the birth," said Rebecca remembering Seth's worries from the letter.

Julia said, "You're next." Pushing her friend toward the bedroom they had just vacated.

Once back in the room, Rebecca pulled out her book and began asking the list of questions she and her mother used to help determine a woman's chances of complications during birth.

"Seth worries too much. He thinks because I'm so small and he's so big, I'll have trouble. I think I'll be fine," relayed Callie.

"You're right in most instances but we can check to see if we're going to encounter a problem. I did notice the men around here seem to be a little larger than most," said Rebecca as she lifted Callie's dress and laid her palms flat against the abdomen moving them across the stomach feeling for the size of the baby.

"Everything all right?" asked Callie worriedly.

"Looks like you're on schedule and, yes, everything seems to be going fine. I don't see that you're going to have any problems due to your size. Your pelvic, the space between the hips, is a good width so even if these babies are larger than average, it's going to fit fine."

That comment brought a smile and little laugh to Callie's lips but Rebecca didn't ask about it.

"What about my foot? Is it hereditary? Will my baby have a bad foot, too?" asked Callie concernedly. She had the crippled foot since birth which had caused her to be passed over for adoption. Not that it kept her from doing what she wanted but she worried she would bring pain and suffering to her own child.

Rebecca looked at the small foot that turned in and under. "This occurred in the womb but isn't something that gets passed down. As you were forming, growing, this leg and foot was tucked under the rest of your body. Just a chance happening," explained Rebecca relieving Callie's fear of passing on an impediment to her child.

"So, it wasn't because I was breach and they pulled on me?" she asked to make sure.

"Were you a breach baby?" asked Rebecca.

"I don't really know. I was found on the steps of St. Michaels' Foundling Home right after I was born. The nun's thought that I must have been breach and that my foot was damaged due to that," Callie told the younger woman.

"A breach birth can cause the baby to have broken bones but if they are set properly at the time of birth, there is usually no lasting damage. It's the most difficult thing we could run into but it also is not hereditary," Rebecca said, trying to put Callie's mind at ease.

"Thank you, you've told me more about having a baby than I ever knew. Nun's aren't very good at explaining these things other than to say not to get pregnant until after you're married - preferably to a good Catholic husband." And she laughed outright.

The ladies met up together in the dining room for tea and little frosted cakes, each decorated with a pink rose and green leaves which Rebecca was told were one of Callie's specialties.

"I didn't expect such a treat," said Rebecca very impressed with the little cakes and sandwiches she was served. She ate them slowly, enjoying the savory crustless chicken pate' sandwiches and sweetly covered bite sized cakes.

"I know you must think I'm fretting over nothing. I mean almost every woman faces childbirth but what am I to expect next? How will I know the baby is beginning its way, uh, out?" asked Julia, bridging the need to know with someone who could inform her.

Rebecca bent down to take out a pile of pages that

were linked together with small wire rings and began to show the ladies drawings representing the female human form and what being pregnant actually did to that body. How the changes in their bodies, the discomfort, the happiness are all part and parcel of bringing forth the next generation.

"How will I know if I'm 'in labor' then? It sounds like there are so many things happening," questioned Julia.

"It isn't as easy as a check list. Each woman is different and each birth of that woman can differ. It can begin with aches in the lower back that can't be relieved by changing position. They will continue into a pattern of the pain beginning from the back and coming around to the front lower abdomen. More often it starts as muscle contractions in the lower abdomen and commences to cover the whole abdomen with pain centralized in the cervix area as I showed in the drawings."

"How long should that take?" asked Callie.

"Again, there is no set length of time. First time mothers usually take longer and up to twenty-four hours is not uncommon. Stay active as long as you can, walk around the house as that tends to increase the process. Plan on it taking a long time so if it doesn't, you will be happily surprised. If you are in labor, go onto a liquid diet. Only tea and broth, no coffee or milk products. Are there any more concerns? It's what I'm here for." Rebecca watched the expectant ladies and felt confident their questions for now had been answered.

Both of the soon-to-be-mothers shook their heads but she could tell they were going over everything Rebecca had told them in their minds.

"Julia, your mother will be here with you to help care for the baby?" At her agreement, Rebecca turned to Callie. "But you don't have anyone who has given birth? I'll plan on explaining what to expect with your newborn and how to care for them at another meeting."

"I had a lot of practice taking care of babies in the foundling home I was raised in back in New York. Maybe a little help with the feeding? I've never even witnessed that," Callie confessed.

"Then we will go over that when I see you next," Rebecca said. She sat drinking her tea as the other three giggled and laughed, talking about family and friends and what was happening at home. Rebecca knew she would soon be part of these women's lives. Not only a midwife but a friend, as well. She had never thought she would feel so welcomed and included when she had left her mother's home.

Finally, Abby stood and kissed each of the other women goodbye and then Callie jumped up saying, "I almost forgot. I brought Rebecca some sweetcorn chowder, onion rolls and petit' fours." She handed the basket of gifts to Abby to carry to the buggy.

At Rebecca's protestations, the other women hushed her and said it was the least they could do.

CHAPTER 2

As they climbed into the buggy, Abby said, "I thought we would stop by the Macgregor ranch on our way back home. Neither of them is in an interesting condition but knowing these men, it won't be long. They're a pretty virile group are our men around here." Abby laughed as if in a private joke.

The Macgregor ranch was even a larger two-story house than the Greggs' with a wrap-around porch on two sides, as well. There were flowers and plants around the foundation of the house with the green front door off set to one side. Large windows looked out toward the drive coming into the ranch and several buildings were to the left. Rebecca was impressed with the sizes of these ranches and the obvious prosperity in the area. It would be very satisfying helping these ranchers continue another generation.

Abby stopped the buggy in front of the steps and tied the reins on the break before getting down from the seat. Rebecca did the same, holding onto her medical bag as usual.

James Macgregor came out in his stocking feet calling out, "Abby, so glad you came by. Showing Mrs. Johansen the area? Hello, Mrs. Johansen, welcome to our home." And he led the women into the house.

"Honey, Emily, looks who's here. I told you it wouldn't be long before you met the new midwife," called James to the back of the house.

A very stunning young women dressed in the height of fashion with her brunette hair up with an abundance of curls coming down the back of her head was followed out by a very pretty women dressed more sedately, a neat brown bun at the base of her head, drying her hands on the spotless apron she was wearing.

Both ladies had bright welcoming smiles and went directly to Abby to give her hugs and kisses. They studied Rebecca and seemed pleased with what they saw. "I'm Emily Macgregor, my husband is Mac." And she extended her hand.

Rebecca shook it as the other woman added, "I'm Mavis Macgregor and I'm married to Jamie. We're so glad you've decided to move to Sweetwater. There aren't very many young women close enough to visit and we keep Abby so busy she usually can't get away from her sewing machine."

"We were paying a call on Julia and Seth brought Callie there so Rebecca has been introduced to most of the young wives in the area," Abby explained.

"Would you like some tea, coffee or something to eat?" offered Emily.

"No. I simply wanted to introduce Rebecca and I highly recommend you to visit with her and let her explain everything to you. It's never too soon to be prepared," Abby said sagely.

Rebecca said, "It's not really necessary. I'm there, though, whenever you feel you need me."

"Well, we may get together socially at least. We get into town and then visit with Abby, mostly spending our husbands' money." And the two wives laughed as James looked on indulgently.

Abby teased, "And the men encourage them to. I can't believe how spoiled these two are. Mac is as bad as Jamie and they both want what they want yesterday. Men have no idea what it takes to design and sew a dress. They'll come in twice a day to see if I finished it yet." She shook her head at the impatience of the Macgregor men.

"They're like that for everything. I've gotten used to it, at least, but Jamie is a sweetheart and does dote on Mavis, as he should," Emily explained showing a strong affection for her sister-in-law.

Abby again suggested the four of them get together during the next week and the women parted ways with hugs and kisses for Abby and a friendly goodbye for Rebecca.

The blond, younger man who had been introduced as Jessie at the railroad station came down the stairs and walked directly to Rebecca. "Are you enjoying the scenery? I can maybe take you for a ride up to the lake if you want to see more than the side of the road." His amazing grin, with dimples, shone brightly.

Rebecca was proud of herself for not stammering. "That would be nice. Once I'm more familiar with the women in the area, I should have some free time."

As Abby and Rebecca rode out of the gates onto the main road, Abby said, "I know Julia and Callie really liked you and said they feel they're in good hands. I have to agree. I learned so much today I feel more comfortable for my friends, too."

"They sure grow their men big and handsome around here. There were four of them to greet me when I got off the train and I almost had heart palpitations," teased Rebecca more comfortable with the easy-going Abby after spending the afternoon with her.

"I know how you felt. They're so large they can't get ready-made shirts to fit them so I do a lot of their sewing when they can't get into the big cities to a tailor. I've had to measure an in-seam more than once to get it right." Both women laughed knowing Abby was exaggerating.

"So, you've known these men longer than you've known the wives?" asked Rebecca.

"Over four years now. I met them all within the first month or so of arriving in Sweetwater," Abby admitted.

"Am I missing something here or are these men blind? Why aren't you one of those husband's wife? You're beautiful and slim and smart. What were they looking for?" questioned Rebecca.

Abby stayed quiet a moment then said, "I knew each of them was interested. After all, there aren't very many women of marriageable age here but it wouldn't have worked out."

Rebecca's heart ached at the expression of pain crossing Abby's face. "I'm sorry. I shouldn't be asking such personal questions. My mother often said I cross the line with my inquisitiveness. This has no bearing on anything I should know."

"No, if anyone should know, it's you." Abby took a deep breath and continued, "When I was much younger, I had a miscarriage and the doctor told me I wouldn't be able to bear a child again. I, of course, knowing how important family is to a ranch's prosperity let the men who began to show an interest in me know. We usually end up good friends. I have a lot of good friends." Neither woman mentioned the tears in Abby's eyes. "I guess I'm just not the marrying kind."

"But there is a Matthew?" She knew she remembered that from the conversation earlier. "Doesn't he know, yet?" asked Rebecca, hoping she wasn't opening the wound even more.

Abby smiled merely thinking about Matthew and Rebecca was glad she had mentioned him. "I told Matthew but the first thing out of his mouth was that we would adopt. He thinks I was made to be a mother and he said every child should be wanted by loving parents. I had never thought of adoption. Most men want children from their own loins. Matthew said he wanted such a large family that no wife was going to be able to fulfill the need anyway. He says he loves me and I'm trying to decide if he will regret the marriage later and want children of his own."

"Matthew is Callie's brother so that means he was in the orphanage with her?" At Abby's agreement, Rebecca finished, "Then he knows about living without parents. I think if he says he would love an adopted child as much as he would love a biological child, then I would believe him. Who would know better?"

"I know you're right. I've been alone for so long now I don't know if I can live as a wife and mother. I thought it impossible and so made a completely different kind of life for myself. But if anyone could make me change my mind, it would be Matthew," Abby told her new friend.

"I look forward to meeting him then."

As they pulled up in front of Rebecca's home, Abby said, "I know you make remarks about your weight but you're not really heavy. You have good proportions but I think I may be able to help you see yourself as you could be."

"I'm open to any suggestions. I know when I look in the mirror, I'm not happy with anything I see so I'm sure I'm a disappointment to any man. I don't want to try to be eye-catching or anything but less dumpy might be good."

Abby laughed saying, "Less dumpy I can do. Bring that dress to me and I'll sew it into a dress that shows off your hour-glass figure."

"I'll do that and thank you for helping but I would be surprised if you can find an hour-glass figure in me. My sand has all shifted to the bottom, I'm afraid," Rebecca said getting out of the buggy.

Once back in her little white house, Rebecca went back over her notes and then thought about Jessie Macgregor. He seemed honestly interested in her and that was very flattering to a woman who always felt too fat, too portly to attract anyone's attention let alone a man as good-looking as Jessie. Now wasn't that interesting, Rebecca thought. I placed Jessie in a good-looking category and then look down on men that place me in a less complimentary category. I'm just as shallow, it seems. I have to remember beauty is as beauty does. Listen to my mother's warnings and I'll be all right.

The next few days seemed to be one visitor after another stopping by. First Doctor Winters came past to welcome her and to tell her to call on him if she ever had a need. Rebecca asked if there were any more women expecting and he responded that the last births he had attended were of a set of twins that lasted far too long but were born healthy.

The next visitor really surprised Rebecca as she answered the door to find an older, well-dressed lady standing at the door holding a basket of freshly baked cookies.

Rebecca took the offered goodies and invited the pleasant lady in to enjoy them with tea but that kind lady shook her head. "Oh, that wouldn't be right, I don't think. You don't want someone seeing me coming out. I simply wanted to let you know the town is glad you're here," she said backing away.

"You said your name was, Miss Lily? Don't you own a shop where you fix ladies' hair? The men who brought me to Sweetwater said you helped Abby get the house prepared for me. I wanted to thank you personally. Please, come in." Rebecca stood to the side so the older lady could enter.

Miss Lily glanced around quickly to make sure no one was about in this quiet end of town and stepped over the threshold of the first home she had ever been invited to enter in Sweetwater except her own.

"I loved helping Abby with getting this house ready. She has such beautiful linens and things to make a home special," said Miss Lily as Rebecca led her to the dining table and placed the cookies on it.

"The water's hot. I'll just start the tea and bring it in here. Do you take cream?" she asked going into the kitchen.

"Not for me, thank you. A little sugar if you have it, dear."

Rebecca brought a tray into the dining room and then sat down to get the real reason for Miss Lily's visit. "Have you been in Sweetwater very long? So many people I've been meeting are new to the area except the ranchers, of course."

"Lordy, I've been here since before you were born. I know these ranchers and their daddies," laughed Miss Lily.

Changing the subject and hoping for more information on the other women of the area, Rebecca said, "I'm very interested in the women of the town since I help with all female related illness along with infants. The old doctor of my hometown was extremely overworked since everyone was so spread out and he trained me to take some of the day to day cases of childhood diseases and birthing. My mother had been midwife for our area for over thirty years."

"You aren't from a big city or town?" Miss Lily seemed curious as to Rebecca's qualifications and where she came from.

"Not really, I think it was intended to grow but the train tracks didn't come anywhere near so it's a saloon and dry goods store and a couple of empty buildings. Ranches and farms spread out for miles around so it takes a while merely to see the patients. I've attended over fifty-six births and half of them I delivered on my own. I find it very rewarding to help bring all those little ones into the world," Rebecca said filling the teacups again.

"Did you ever lose one?" asked Miss Lily. "It must be hard to see a little one die."

"I have been with women who have miscarried but never a stillborn. At least, none with women under my care. Once I get involve, I think I mother-hen the women so much the baby simply sits it out and comes when I'm available." She smiled lost in memories of the many safe deliveries she had witnessed.

"I must confess I'm a little more than a hairdresser." Miss Lily gazed directly into Rebecca's eyes and continued, "I have a home where women can live and fill a need unmarried ranch hands have for female conversation…company, if you understand."

"I understand, completely. I don't provide aid in getting rid of an unwanted baby but if the ladies need any other help, please make them feel comfortable in coming to me," she urged Miss Lily. She could never bring herself to end a life but she would help a woman with anything else. And had in the past so wasn't offended that this kind woman was a type of women most others kept their distance from.

"I think we're knowledgeable enough not to get in the family way but I would certainly encourage them to keep the baby. It would be nice to have a child in the house, at least until they got a little older. But then, with so many unmarried ranch hands in the vicinity, the woman would probably accept a proposal and move away from me."

"Has that ever happened?" asked Rebecca.

"Over the years? Yes, many times thankfully. I get letters once in a while letting me know how they're doing. There are some who live less than an hour away and I see them in town once in a while. I'm happy they got on with their lives. My house may not be the best place to meet a future husband but many of my ladies have found happy homes. At least they see a lot of unmarried men. I dissuade married men from visiting." Sipping her tea, she continued, "Sometimes the ranch hands are merely lonely for a home and they come in and have cookies or coffee for a couple of hours. I don't serve alcohol there, either. I don't want to have to deal with a mean drunk. I try to protect my ladies, I guess, and make my place a house of refuge. As I said, sometimes the men simply miss female companionship."

"Don't the families of your ladies get upset when they come to live with you?" asked Rebecca because Miss Lily seemed open to any questions.

"No, these aren't local girls." Tipping her head in

thought, continued, "I've never been approached by a local girl, come to think of it. I probably would talk her out of staying and instead urge her to return home to patch up any riff." Taking another sip of tea, explained, "I get these ladies from the cities. Usually they're tired of the troubles that come with big city places. Right now, I only have Stella and Lacy. I don't know if those are their real names or not but they're the ones they told me. Nice young ladies but not too young. I don't go with wanting perverts hanging around my house," Miss Lily said firmly.

"I look forward to meeting them, Miss Lily. I'm glad you came to visit and I'm really glad you brought these cookies because they're wonderful." Smiling her thanks, Rebecca finished the sugary delight.

After two pots of tea and several of the cookies, Miss Lily said her goodbye and left saying how lucky Sweetwater was to have gotten a midwife of such wide knowledge.

The third and last visitor of the day was the most handsome, Reverend Walters. Tall, of course, well built without any extra weight on his long torso dressed in a dark suit, white shirt and cleric collar. His dark hair had a tendency to curl and fall over his wide forehead, dark brows emphasized the blue eyes fringed with dark lashes, almost too long for a man but looking anything but feminine on him. He stayed on the porch of the little white house, hat in hand and introduced himself.

"I'm Reverend Daniel Walters and I wanted to make you welcome here in Sweetwater. I'm extending an invitation to visit our little church across the street on Sunday. There's a Bible study group on Wednesday evenings and we have socials every once in a while. It's a good place to meet people from the outlying farms and ranches." He finished with a wide smile showing even, white teeth.

"Well, thank you, Reverend Walters. I'm Rebecca Johansen and I was planning on going to services unless I'm called out to attend a birth. My time is not always my own but right now I don't seem to have anyone except Mrs. Greggs requiring my attention," she told the man who appeared to be several years older than she was.

"I look forward to seeing you there, then." He smiled that devastating smile again and Rebecca would have sworn her knees weakened. The Reverend turned and walked across the dusty road toward the church. Rebecca watched him move. She liked the masculine movement of his hips with each stride, his hands down to his sides, head erect. Oh, yes, she wouldn't miss a Sunday morning watching him if she could help it.

Rebecca was pleased with her reception so far. Sweetwater seemed to be a very friendly place. She was sure she would be happy here forever.

The next morning, Rebecca, wearing a white shirtwaist with fitted sleeves that buttoned tight against her wrists and a grey skirt that emphasized her comparatively narrow waist, was out on her porch trying to decide the best place to hang her name plaque. Her father had carved it after learning that his daughter was leaving home and starting up her own practice in Sweetwater. Rebecca was reading it again for about the hundredth time. *Rebecca Johansen* and under that the word *Midwife* when she heard a wagon stopping.

She looked up and her face formed a wide smile of welcome for Jessie, dressed in tan trousers, plaid shirt, wide leather belt and boots, instead of the city suit she had always seen him wearing. He took off his Stetson saying, "Good morning, Mrs. Johansen. Fine day to be outdoors, isn't it?"

"Yes, it is. But, please, call me Rebecca. I don't stand on formality. I was just trying to figure out the best place to hang this but I'm not sure if it can be seen from the road."

"I think it may need to hang out from the post." He approached her carrying a wooden crate and set it on the edge of the porch to consider the placement of the sign with her. "Do you have any tools?"

"No, not even a hammer," she confessed in feminine truthfulness.

"I'll come by in a couple of days with the right tools and hang it for you if you can wait that long."

"That will be fine. I think I've met all the women who have need of my services already." Explaining why the sign could wait.

"Well, I was sent to deliver this box of provisions. Fresh milk and eggs, stuff to tide you over Emily said. She said to stop and invite you to dinner, whenever you can. Someone from the ranch comes by a couple of days a week this time of year so you can hitch a ride. Let the owners of the mercantile know and they'll pass on the message to the driver." He turned to leave then stopped and asked, "Do you like to fish?"

Rebecca didn't need to think too long on that question. "Oh, I used to fish with my father when I was younger. I spent many a happy, sunny day fishing in the nearby streams and lakes. But maybe because I was fishing, I always thought the days were happy and sunny."

"When I come back to hang your plaque, if you're not busy delivering babies, we could go out to the stream and try for some trout. I'll bring the gear," he said flashing that Macgregor wolfish grin she had seen on James MacGregor, as well.

"That sounds wonderful. I'm looking forward to doing just that," Rebecca said with an answering smile.

Rebecca watched Jessie continue into town and pull up in front of the mercantile. She couldn't believe her luck. She had just been asked out by a man. Perhaps fishing wasn't really someone's idea of a romantic date but Rebecca thought it couldn't have been any better. She bent down retrieving the box Jessie had left and was delighted to see another of those meat pies tucked inside. She was going to weigh a ton if people didn't stop feeding her like a heifer going to market. That thought didn't slow her down as she put away the provisions Emily had sent, though.

CHAPTER 3

Later in the week, Rebecca heard the little bell chime as she opened the door to Abby's shop. She called out and Abby, all smiles, came out through the curtained doorway saying, "I'm so excited to see this gown on you. I think you'll be surprised at what a little boost to the morale a good fitting dress can be. Now come back in here and strip. I have a little secret we woman of fashion know about."

"I'm not sure I know what you're talking about but I'm willing. How much worse can I appear?" asked Rebecca poking fun at herself.

Abby chided, "We discussed that kind of talk. Women who feel good about themselves have more confidence, less reticence in meeting new people, and by that, I mean, men."

"You're right. Keep a positive spirit. I'll do that," Rebecca told her new friend.

Abby took out a box and pulled a lacy, frilly, beribboned bit of nonsense out of it as if she were a magician pulling a rabbit out of a hat. "Voile! Every women's best friend - or it should be. I ordered it especially for you, for your frame."

"Oh, Abby, its beautiful. It should be worn on the outside of the dress it's so pretty. No one will ever see it. What a waste," Rebecca said feeling the lovely silk ribbons slide through her fingers.

"Well, I'm hoping someone besides us gets to see it. Like some man," teased Abby.

"I won't go as far as that but it is lovely, none the

less." Rebecca fingered the pretty corset.

"Let's get this on and then we can see the whole outfit put together." Abby eagerly helped Rebecca into the inventive creation and showed her how to cinch in the waist. Telling Rebecca, she didn't need to wear it tight all the time, maybe only for evening dresses. Abby left the laces looser for daytime wear.

Rebecca was admiring her new svelte figure when Abby brought in a lovely purple dress with black lace trim and buttons down the front of the fitted bodice. "Oh, that's the loveliest dress I've ever had but, Abby, I can't afford a new dress."

"This one you can. It's your own dress dyed. A lady of certain proportions should not wear plaid and the rusts and yellow greens of that plaid were all wrong for your skin tone," Abby explained as she pulled the dress over Rebecca's head and proceeded to button up the front. She turned Rebecca around to face the full-length mirror asking, "How do you like it?"

Rebecca took a minute to realize the stately, fashionable woman in the mirror was herself. "Oh, Abby, I can't believe this is the same dress. I look taller and slimmer and well, womanlier." She turned to see herself from as many angles as possible.

"You should never wear double breasted anything. You have a lovely neck and shouldn't wear wide collars. They will merely make your body look wide. A high collar tight to the neck like this one with only a trim of lace and ribbon would be best for daytime," Abby explained as she tweaked and patted to get everything just right. "I put some tucks under the breasts to accent the female form and then slimmed down the sides by pulling the extra fabric into the bustle in back making the curve of your back stand out. It's difficult to see where the bustle stops and you start. It's a very flirty look from the back, I assure you."

"I can't believe you did all this out of the dress I gave you. I find it amazing but isn't it cheating?" she asked worriedly. "I mean it's like I'm advertising something I'm not."

"Heavens, women have been doing that for centuries. Corsets, wigs, hair dyes and even face paint have been used for hundreds of years. We try to get the male's attention and then the male finds out how wonderful we are and the world continues to go around."

Accepting the truths of life, Rebecca smiled. "I don't know how to thank you." Rebecca continued to preen in the mirror amazed at how much nicer the dress looked now.

"Simply allow me to alter a few of your other things and…oh, I almost forgot, you should wear these combinations," She held up a one-piece lace trimmed item. "It's a new piece of clothing incorporating drawers and camisole together. It will give you less items under your dress, plus they're cooler to wear in the summer."

"I really appreciate everything you did for me. I can't wait to have a reason to wear this beautiful dress. I'll pay you, of course, for all your time."

"Don't worry about that. I give a special rate for friends plus this was a chance for me to try new things. I don't get to sew many nice dresses except for Julia and Callie at this time of year. And then only because they were increasing."

A couple of days later, Jessie, true to his word, stopped by with the wagon and some wood and tools and hung the plaque where it could be seen by passersby going either direction. Then he asked, "Are you ready to go fishing today? I let the Greggs' know you would be with me if they needed you and Emily packed a picnic for us. I don't plan on eating all that food by myself so don't send me away alone. We won't stay out late but Emily did say she'd fry me up whatever I caught."

"Let me change into boots and I'll be right with you." In less than a minute Rebecca returned with a wide brimmed straw hat and wearing a serviceable pair of boots.

"Good, a woman who knows the value of time when fish are waiting. Let me help you up into the wagon and we'll be sitting on the grassy edge of a clear cool stream in no time at all."

Again, true to his word, Jessie had pulled the team to the side of the road and unloaded the wagon, giving Rebecca a couple of poles and a small box while he took a large picnic basket. He led the way through the green growing grass toward some small trees and bushes. The stream was just behind the brush-line and soon Jessie had their lines in the water and a refreshing lemonade in their hands.

"I thought maybe you cast fished when you talked about trout," Rebecca said, watching the bobbers float gently with the current.

"I do but I'm feeling more social today. Casting is a solitary kind of sport, you know. Just you and the fish. Good when you want to contemplate. You can't really hold a conversation while standing in the water without scaring off all the fish. Do you normally cast?"

"Oh, we did all sorts of fishing. Depends on the fish, time of day, time of year. I even can catch these catfish that live in the banks of one river back home. They would wiggle themselves in and then you have to reach in and drag them out, trying to keep from touching the fins wrong and getting hurt. Difficult way to catch supper but sometimes we had to resort to it to keep food on the table," she admitted knowing Jessie wouldn't think less of her for eking out a subsistence living.

"Heck if I'd like my dinner to bite back but it sounds kind of interesting to wrangle a fish for supper," he replied leaning back on his elbows while still able to see the bobber.

"It was a fun way to spend a morning. Of course, you have to be prepared to get soaked and muddy up to your elbows and knees and that's only if you don't slip and fall in. When that happens be prepared to go home in a very unpleasant condition." She laughed remembering more than once showing up a soggy mess but with fish.

"Do you think there are any of those kinds of fish around here?"

"Not if we're lucky," she responded.

The picnic was delicious and intriguing since Emily had sent a wide variety of items. A salad of spring greens with a sweet dressing and another of those meat pies, split between them. A mixed fruit compote' over a flan that melted in Rebecca's mouth finished the repast.

"I wouldn't miss a meal if Emily cooked like this all the time for me." Then looking embarrassed she finished laughing at herself, "I know I don't look like I've missed a meal as it is."

Appearing serious, Jessie said, "I don't think you need worry about that. I think you're the perfect size. I don't know why women base so much on weight. A skinny woman doesn't have anything to see her through when she gets sick, nothing to fall back on. I kind of like to have a little something to hold on to." Then it was his turn to look embarrassed as he realized how personal his conversation had gotten.

Rebecca exclaimed, "Oh, did the bobber just go under?"

Jessie jumped up to grab the pole that was propped into the soft bank. When he came back the conversation returned to the friendly talk that had been between them previously.

Standing in front of the window over the sink, Daniel stopped to watch the midwife descend from the buckboard driven by Jessie MacGregor.

"Now what does that young pup think he's up to?" came out in a whisper but Daniel thought he knew exactly what that 'pup' saw in the pretty midwife. It's what he and half the bachelors saw in her but, other than himself, the others had a better chance of getting her than a college boy still in classes.

Daniel had removed himself from the list of men seeking the midwife's attention right after meeting her. He was lost in her sherry colored eyes and restful smile and all the reasons it wouldn't work between them rose to the surface. The memories of why he was doing what he was doing and where he was doing it.

Nothing could cleanse him of his sin. The worse sin man can make and becoming a minister to a small town without one was one way he felt he could atone for a thoughtless youth. A youth wasted on self-indulgence that ended in tragedy. It had taken him years to be where he was now and his future didn't include a loving wife or family. He didn't deserve such a blessing when others would never see theirs.

He watched as Jessie waved and the young woman so much on his mind went up the steps and into her home. He waited but there was no light in the parlor so she must have gone into the kitchen or bedroom. To change, perhaps?

Growling in disgust at his thoughts, he purposely forced himself away from the window. He would finish the dishes later when he could keep his mind from sinful thoughts. Thoughts of what a young healthy woman needs, what a woman used to having the comfort of a husband would miss most. He felt his body stir. Something he never allowed, never had to deal with. Here he thought he was the one in control of his body and its urges when, in fact, he was merely dormant due to never having been attracted to anyone here in Sweetwater. It was easy to be celibate when there were no women of marriageable age and another thing to remain celibate when an attractive young widow lived right across the street from you.

Going to the room where he wrote his sermons, a quiet place where he had always felt at peace and closest to God, he couldn't find the usual tranquility he had found years ago. Years of finding the right path to take for reparation of his transgressions. The right path to earn his blessing of a much longer life than some received. But that didn't mean his debt was paid. It could never be fully paid and he had dedicated his life to doing the best he could toward amending the sins of the past.

Taking down the Bible with its well-read pages, he fingered through searching for the book he needed to lessen his carnal thoughts and remind him of who and what he was now. A man who owed God and man too much to have a private life of his own.

Sunday arrived and Rebecca went to services wearing her newly altered dress and straw-hat sans the bouncy flowers. Abby had convinced Rebecca a simple dark ribbon around the brim was all that was needed to bring attention to her chestnut hair. Seeing Reverend Walters in the pulpit, looking so much the man of the cloth made Rebecca a little uncomfortable. She had looked at him as simply another man but now it seemed he was above her, above the worldly wants and needs of man or woman.

She saw Miss Lily sitting next to two other women dressed appropriately for church. Miss Lily gave a little shake of her head to indicate that Rebecca shouldn't acknowledge them and the three women left together without any one besides the Reverend speaking to them.

Rebecca left the church, after being greeted by several neighbors she hadn't met before, feeling a little off, something not quite balanced. She hoped she wasn't becoming ill. She had never been sick since early childhood and she had no idea what it felt like so this not-quite-right-feeling was the closest she had come to it.

Sitting on the porch in the shade, she watched as the minister walked from his home over to hers across the dusty road wearing the same suit as he had earlier that morning except for the dark hat. He tipped it, saying, "Mrs. Johansen, it was good to see you in church this morning. As you could see, we aren't a large congregation but hardy. I thought the hymns were well sung."

"Yes, it was very pleasant and I met several new people. None who appeared to need my services but from what I see here in Sweetwater, there seems to be several young families and newly married couples. I look forward to being of help when I am needed."

"A commendable ambition, I am sure. Like a doctor, you give help and keep families together. I find it very admirable of you. Someone so young taking an interest in others is to be encouraged."

Now why did she think he was still preaching from the pulpit? The man seemed to see himself as always being a minister, a pastor of a flock that couldn't move without his guidance. She felt awkward but saw no way of sending the man on his way. After all, he must have had some destination in mind when he left his house. Seeing her sitting here drew his attention but she wished he would leave her in peace. His intense gaze made her uncomfortable and his words didn't seem to match his thoughts as she felt him study her dress as well as her face and hair. She decided to take the bull by the horns as her father would say.

"Is there something about my person you are having a problem with, Reverend?"

That seemed to have brought him back to reality quickly, "What? Ah, no, not in the least. I must have lost my train of thought. Sorry." Glancing toward town he nodded, "I should be off. Again, it was nice to see a new face at service. Feel free to come for Bible study, as well, when you have time." He tipped his hat once again before leaving her.

The next couple of days went by quickly. Rebecca visited the mercantile and met the middle-aged husband and wife who owned it, Helen and Al Murray. And of course, a daily visit to Abby, often enjoying a meal or sewing together in the evening at one or the other's home. Abby lived above her shop so it was nice for her to visit Rebecca's house for a change. The estimable Matthew hadn't been back for quite a while and Abby was beginning to worry he might have lost interest.

Rebecca tried to boost her new friend's morale but she didn't know anything about Matthew, really, so she wasn't much comfort for Abby. It was one of these evenings that a buckboard pulled up and a man was calling for Mrs. Johansen. Both women went out to find a ranch hand from the Greggs saying Ben had sent him for the midwife and to return as soon as possible.

Abby asked, "Should I come with you? What can I help you get?"

"All I need is my medical bag but can you close up the house? You know, bank the fire and that kind of thing? If she's just gone into labor, she won't give birth for a few hours. Come out in the morning if you want and bring a change of clothes for me. Tonight is going to be preparing Julia for what's to come." Finishing the statement to Abby, Rebecca climbed onto the buckboard seat and held on tight as the almost frantic driver turned the wagon and headed back to the Greggs' ranch.

The entire house was lit up when they got to the Greggs and Rebecca was ushered into the bedroom to find Julia in a pretty nightgown sitting against a set of beautifully embroidered pillowslips.

Julia started apologizing right away. "I told Ben it was too soon. I'm not in any real pain, yet. I'm sorry to have dragged you out here so late at night."

"I would much rather be here too soon as the other way around. Now let's see what's going on, may I?" She closed the door blocking the men on the other side in the hall.

After a quick exam, Rebecca announced happily,

"You are in labor and probably by this time tomorrow, you'll be holding your son or daughter."

"Not both so I can get this over with once and for all?" teased Julia.

"I'm afraid I didn't feel another little head in there although sometimes I get a surprise bundle. But twins usually arrive early rather than late so I'll stand by my original pronouncement of only one at a time."

Julia got very quiet and the smile disappeared from her face. The experienced midwife knew her mother was worrying about what was to come. All the pain and possible outcomes for her little one.

Rebecca tried to instill confidence in the first-time mother as she went through a mild contraction. "Don't hold your breath during a contraction. Both you and the baby need air all through this, so keep breathing, no matter what's happening."

"I'll try, I'm sorry," said Julia contritely.

"You don't need to apologize. You'll be fine. I'll try to remind you of breathing but there's going to be a time, as we discussed, when you might want to tear apart everyone around you, especially your husband. That's the reason I keep the men out of the way until after the birth. As I explained, they want to be in here giving you comfort, holding your hand but then get frantic when they can't bring you relief. Then the mother can get a little touchy about them being around. I can take the verbal abuse and I want my mothers to have a marriage intact when I leave," she teased, but meant every word she said.

Abby drove up before breakfast and tried to get Ben to eat but settled for making more coffee and then tea for the others. Abby tapped quietly on the door and asked for entrance, which was granted. Julia appeared tired and sweaty, Rebecca had been wiping her forehead with a cool wet cloth and holding her hands through the contractions which were progressing to longer and longer lengths with shorter intervals between.

Julia gasped quickly, "Everything is as it should be. Rebecca says it shouldn't be too much longer. I'm more than half way there." A slight expression of panic entered her eyes.

"Remember we don't watch the clock," said Rebecca getting her 'mother's' mind off the time it was taking to give birth. "Babies come when they are ready, not by a clock. Do you want a little tea? Lemonade? I'm sure Abby can get you either."

Nodding, Abby asked Rebecca, "Do you need me to be here during the birth? I've been through it and I can hold her hands and wipe her forehead. Keep her focused on giving birth when she needs to be."

"That will help a lot. But you say you gave birth? The baby had gotten that far along?" Rebecca was surprised to learn this.

"Yes, he was perfect, a little boy but stillborn. I named him and then they took him away. The doctor wasn't very sympathetic saying what did I expect after getting in the family way without being married. He made it sound like it was my just punishment or something," Abby said sadly.

The two women had been talking quietly together and Rebecca said, "We'll need to speak of this again. I don't want to take my mind off Julia even for such an important conversation."

"I have finally gotten over it. It was a long time ago and I'm fine with it all now," said Abby as she went to the side of the bed telling Rebecca to go and have some food to keep up her strength.

A few hours later, after several minutes of intense pushing and encouraging words from both Abby and Rebecca, Julia gave birth to a baby girl. Julia was tired but elated already talking about the next time. Excited and wide-eyed even after being awake over twenty-four hours.

Ben was happy that both his wife and child were alive and in good health. The two women left the three of them as a family and went out to the porch to sit in the cooler air.

"I'm glad that's over," said Abby.

"I am, too. It all came out right so I'm glad of that," Rebecca said gratefully. "I'm going to stay here for a day or two. Her mother will be here by then. Ben sent a message by telegraph as soon as Julia began her confinement. I'll return to town when Mrs. Minor arrives."

"I packed you some things but if you need anything else, let me know. I have an unending supply of material to make anything you need."

"Well, hold off for now but remember Callie will be due in a month or so and we'll do this all over again." The two women groaned in sympathy and Abby got up to drive herself back to town.

CHAPTER 4

Three days later, Rebecca found herself back home secure in the knowledge that Julia was in good hands with her mother helping her. The woman seemed capable and clearly a good mother so she could pass on information as well as Rebecca could. She had been asleep for a few hours when there was pounding on the back door.

Rebecca, used to disturbed nights, got up and pulled on a wrapper, pushing her feet into the slippers waiting under the bed. The sounds of the pounding were now accompanied by male shouts of her name, well the name she used here anyways. Rebecca hurried to the door pulling it open as soon as she could unlock it.

Reverend Walters rushed in pulling a man carrying a young woman, pale and semi-conscious. Rebecca showed them onto the back room which was now outfitted for giving medical care. She helped lay the woman on the clean examination table.

The reverend stood back explaining quickly, "This man's wife went into labor on the train and they dropped them off at the station. I didn't know about it till just recently and we came right here. She's lost a lot of blood. I didn't know the human body had so much blood." He seemed considerably shaken by what he had witnessed.

"It might be amniotic fluid mixed in. Let me check her. I'll call you if I need help." Rebecca started to lift the woman's dress.

Both men turned and rushed from the room. Once in the kitchen, Daniel stirred the stove ashes into a flame and added wood. He put several large pots of water on to boil. He wasn't sure why but he remembered somehow women needing it when giving birth.

There were groans and then screams coming from the room where the men had left the expectant mother. Daniel glanced at the man and noted his paleness on an already thin, weathered face. He didn't think the man was as old as he looked but life had evidently been hard on both he and his wife the last few years.

"Do you want to pray?" he asked the man sitting at the table as if he wanted to bolt from the house and forget everything, he was hearing behind him. At the man's shake of his head, Daniel began a silent prayer for the woman, for her child and for God's benevolence to make sure everything turned out as it was meant to be.

There was silence coming from the back room in waves and then a gusty cry, which seemed to go on forever. Daniel waited expectantly for the midwife to return to the room to tell them the baby and mother were well and healthy. And that the little family could be on its way in a day or two.

Mrs. Johansen did finally emerge, wearing a bloody apron and carrying a small bundle, almost too small to be a real, live child saying quietly, "I have your daughter but I'm sorry to say, your wife lost too much blood and couldn't make it through the delivery. I'm so very sorry for your loss." There were tears of pain, of regret, of personal grief in the midwife's eyes.

The man looked from the Reverend to Rebecca and back again but didn't put out his arms to take his daughter from Rebecca as she was plainly trying to have him do.

The man said, still shaken, "I don't know what to do

for a baby. I, we, hadn't planned on a family, not yet at least. We had decided to move up north to get to the place where they're mining gold. Right out of the sand, no blastin' or anything. All you have to do is dig a little and then rinse off the sand. We thought, me and Melly, we could do that. Me diggin' and her washin' the sand off." He gazed hopefully from one to the other adults in the room. "We were gonna be rich." He let his voice die off as he realized that dream was no longer a possibility.

Rebecca began, "I can help you with the baby until you're more used to handling her. I have a bottle and..."

The man jumped to his feet and the Reverend moved closer to the door to keep him from bolting and abandoning his daughter.

Reverend Walters said calmly, "I know you've had a shock but you also have a healthy newborn that needs you to pull yourself together. I can get clothes and things donated to you and Rebecca said she will help care for her until you're ready to take it on by yourself."

"I ain't ever gonna be ready. I don't know how to take care of a baby or a kid, neither. I don't want it. I don't want the baby at all. I want to get back on the train and git to the goldfields." The scrawny man wailed emphatically, "I don't have time for no baby."

Rebecca appeared lost as Reverend Walters continued, "If you give up this child now, don't come back later saying you want to be her father." At the man's nod of agreement, the Reverend said, "Wait here, I want to get your signature stating that."

The Reverend asked if Rebecca had any writing paper and ink and she pointed to a drawer in the dining room. The Reverend returned, sat at the kitchen table and wrote out almost a full page before asking the man if he knew how to read and write.

"No, but I can make my mark," he said so the Reverend read the entire written document which covered giving up all parental rights of the baby girl. The man never hesitated but signed his mark on the bottom and the Reverend signed as a witness then had Rebecca sign the document as well.

The man jumped up as soon as he had made his mark and was going to leave when the Reverend asked, "What about your wife? Aren't you going to stay and see her buried?"

The man looked at him with wide, wild eyes saying, "I can't stop that long. Others are gonna get there ahead of me. I can't wait for no funeral. I gotta go!" He raced out the door without a backward glance.

Rebecca, still holding the now sleeping newborn looked as if she were crushed. The Reverend didn't hesitate to pull her into his arms as she let the tears flow down her face for all the loss she had just witnessed.

"I'll be all right. You don't need to stay with me," she choked out as she got herself under control.

"I believe that crying is something you should never do alone. It's something to be shared." He slowly rocked her in his arms until she could pull herself together and care for the sleeping infant she held.

Standing away from the large comforting shoulder, she wiped her eyes. "What will happen to the baby? I mean, now that her father has left her?"

"I need to contact the county and let them know we have an orphan. They will take her until she can find a permanent home. Usually infants get adopted easier than older children and we know who her parents are so that is a blessing, too. People aren't eager to adopt a baby

they have no knowledge about where they came from."
He cleared his throat before stepping back.

"I'll contact the undertaker. We'll probably have a simple ceremony for the mother this afternoon," he said, used to getting the practical things underway.

"Please let me know when. I think this little girl needs to be there. Something she can be told when she's grown that she saw her mother properly buried in a church yard."

"I see we agree on that. I'll let you know but I want you to get some rest. Sleep when the baby sleeps - isn't that the rule for new mothers?" he said smiling while making Rebecca sit in a chair at the table.

"If it isn't, it should be," said Rebecca securing the baby in her arms. "Could you tell Abby what's happened? She might have things I'll need for the baby."

"I'll do that. Go get cleaned up and take a nap. I'll see you later today." Then he left.

Taking the baby into her bedroom, Rebecca opened a drawer in the bureau. Pulling out all the clothing, she placed clean towels in the bottom and lay the sleeping baby into it.

Rebecca looked down at her bloody apron and wrapper and sighed. She had never lost a woman in childbirth before. It was a deflating feeling and one she never wanted to experience again.

She heard the men accompanied by Reverend Walters come for the body. They moved quietly, trying not to wake her thinking her sleeping but she had merely been resting, listening to the almost silent breathing of the tiny baby girl.

Thinking about the past few hours, Rebecca realized the stuffy minister hadn't been in her house last night.

Only a much more caring man who had worried over a newborn's future and her own feeling of grief and loss. He hadn't prophesized or sermonized anything. He hadn't condemned the father or made a saint of the mother. He was more human and she liked that man much more than the one in the pulpit or the one who visited her on her porch.

So, which was the real Daniel Walters? The strong man who thought quick enough to get the father's mark on a document allowing the baby to be adopted, to know the name of her birth parents if she ever wanted to check the documents or the straight-laced man who pontificated from the pulpit looking down on his 'flock' of followers?

Again, she knew which one she liked better and hoped that was the man she would see again. The human who held her while she cried and never berated her for doing so. The man who told her to rest since he knew taking care of this newborn was going to be tiring. The man who had been up all night as well and still had to see to a stranger's funeral. That man she would gladly talk to on her porch.

Later Abby came tapping on the back door. She leaned over the baby Rebecca had just fed and cooed little bird sounds. Rebecca had baby bottles in case a new mother couldn't lactate and had warmed cow's milk for the newborn. Abby was cooing and baby talking although the newborn wasn't paying any attention. Too young to focus on any one thing or recognize voices as individual people.

"May I hold her?" asked Abby.

"Please," said Rebecca holding out the baby to her. "I need to set up a bath for her and was wondering if you have any infant clothes? I have some diapers and small blankets but nothing else."

"I brought some of everything. They were meant for Callie but she won't mind and I'll make more before she's due."

Rebecca had placed a towel on the table and had a pan with cooled boiled water and a small soft cloth to wet and thoroughly cleanse the baby. She didn't want to submerge the infant, yet, since the umbilical cord was too fresh but she washed the baby and put on the clean diaper. Abby stood to the other side of the table, watching everything avidly, questioning anything she didn't understand.

Soon the baby girl was dressed in clothes that were too large for her at this time but within weeks will be too small. Abby put out her arms to take the small bundle while Rebecca cleaned and put everything away.

The door was still closed to the back and Rebecca said, "I hate to face that room. It was simply too late by the time they brought the mother to me. I thought I was going to lose the baby, too, but I just reached in, caught her around the neck, and pulled her out by the head. I was afraid she wouldn't be able to breathe. She's tiny and I thought, at first, she was premature but she's full term. Her mother was malnourished and that makes for a small baby."

"She's all right though," asked Abby worriedly as she pressed the baby closer to her as if trying to protect the infant from any more harm in its very short lifetime.

"She's perfect. Simply a little small. With good food she'll catch up with others her age and she'll be fine from then on. It won't take long," Rebecca assured her friend. "Watch her for me? I'm going to tackle that room and burn or wash everything. I want it back in a usable manner as soon as possible."

"I can stay. I put a note on the door that I'm closed today. No one has a dress emergency," she said, taking the baby into the parlor.

Rebecca had taken the final load of boiled linen out to the back lines to hang up to dry when she saw Reverend Walters cross the road and walk toward the house. She went to the front porch and learned there would be a funeral for the infant's mother in the churchyard as soon as the baby could be made ready.

Rebecca, with Abby carrying the baby, walked across to the churchyard where an open gravesite waited, the wooden casket already in the bottom. An unexpected guest appeared as Miss Lily, carrying flowers that she dropped down onto the casket, stood by the grave and listened as Reverend Walters said the encouraging passages that have helped people get through funerals for hundreds of years. Then, surprisingly, Miss Lily sang a beautiful rendition of *Amazing Grace*.

Rebecca felt better after the service, her heart a little lighter. She was going to write down everything that occurred and would send it with the little girl when she was taken by the state. Rebecca's heart constricted on the thought of giving up the baby she had cared for since her birth. She had felt a strong bond from the moment the infant took her first breath.

When they were back in Rebecca's home, Abby, holding the sleeping child asked, "What's going to be done with her now?"

"I'm not sure. Where I lived before, the state took such orphans and placed them in a home then tried to get them adopted. It wasn't located near my little town so I don't know anything about it. I never lost a mother before so I haven't really had any contact with it, either." Rebecca admitted. "The reverend made the father sign a paper and told me he had to contact the county board to let them know. He didn't seem to think an infant would take too long to find a home."

Abby, soft hearted said, "What did Reverend Walter's have the father sign?"

"I'm not sure, of that, either. I was there and I was listening but I don't think anything sank in. I was in shock that any father would abandon his only child. I still have difficulty understanding why going to a mining field was so much more important than seeing to burying your wife and taking care of your daughter. I know the reverend was angry but was controlling himself all the time he was writing that document."

"I think he plans on coming over tonight to see the baby. I'll ask him then," said Abby going into the parlor with the infant while Rebecca got them some supper and coffee. It may turn out to be another long night if this infant stays true to form after sleeping all day.

After dinner there was a light knock on the door. Reverend Walters was there and said, "I thought you both were here so I stopped in to see how the baby was doing. She's still, all right? No complications or anything?" He peeked into the blanketed bundle Abby was holding.

"Just fine. She's hungry all the time, which I'm thankful for. Strong sucking instinct and doesn't have any trouble digesting the milk. I plan on getting a goat since it has better milk for the baby. She'll put on weight right away and everything else is still normal for a full-term infant," explained Rebecca.

"Reverend, I need to know something," asked Abby. "Do you think I can adopt this baby? I can provide well for her and I already know I can love her. Do you think a single woman would be considered for an adoption?"

"I'm unsure, Abby. I had the father sign away his rights. Signed the baby over to Mrs. Johansen and myself as guardians but I don't know how legal it is for us to assign the baby to another." At Abby's look of total loss, he added, "Let me see what I can do. I already realized that a newborn would be difficult for Mrs. Johansen to care for if she gets called out on a birth. Taking the baby with her doesn't seem right and she can't leave it alone, of course. Being a widow makes it complicated. I'll check on her tomorrow but for now, you two can decide where the baby should reside."

Abby peered hopefully up at Rebecca. "I know you would take good care of her but as the minister says, you may get called out to Callie any day now. I can move in here if that is better."

Rebecca said, "I don't have a doubt about your ability to care for this baby. What I don't want to happen is for you to get a broken heart if the authorities have other ideas about what to do with her. I think we should share the caregiving for the next couple of days until the Reverend can tell us something for sure about the legal aspects of this."

"You're right, of course. I never thought I could fall in love so quickly. I always thought a mother has feelings for her child because it came from her body but that's not true at all. The love blossoms like magic and I can't imagine a child born from my own body could be loved more than I love this child," Abbey said intensely.

"I know they get into your heart so easily. You take

first watch but she should be put into her bed until she wants to eat. She'll let us know when she's hungry again." She patted Abby on the shoulder as she passed.

Abby, on edge all the next day, kept glancing toward the street every time she heard a wagon or thought she heard one. She knew Reverend Walters would do as promised and check into the possibility of an adoption to an unmarried woman. Matthew flashed into her mind but she dismissed him as a possible husband. He didn't really want to get married or he would have asked her sooner instead of merely talking about a future marriage with children.

It was after supper when the anxiously awaited knock on the front door announced Reverend Walters. He came in looking tired and not at all like he had good news. Abby braced herself for the information as the reverend apologized, "I don't really have anything to tell you. They have very few adoptions in the district plus Abby being unmarried really had them searching for answers. I finally was told to go home and they would contact me. They didn't have any ideas as to what to do with the baby. I can't believe they aren't prepared for this but each township takes care of this in its own way. Since the baby's parents weren't actually from this area, merely passing through, they don't have a precedent. This must be a first for them."

"I don't know how to feel. I was preparing myself for disappointment. I was also preparing to run with the baby if the answer was 'no'," admitted Abby.

Both of the others gazed at Abby in understanding but they also knew it was too late to keep their friend from being hurt if she wasn't going to be allowed to keep this baby. They peered sadly at one another knowing that pain and heartache might be the very real outcome of this whole experience.

The next morning Jessie showed up on his way out of town and picked up Rebecca to take her out to the Harrison Ranch. They talked about the baby, who everyone knew of, about helping Abby secure the baby as her own, and how precious life was. Jessie even indicated he would adopt children when he married saying there were too many children growing up without parents and possible parents not knowing there were so many children waiting. Rebecca was impressed with his mature thinking considering Jessie seemed so young, although she knew he was a couple of years older than her.

The Harrison ranch was another large two-story house with wraparound porch surrounded by a neat yard with flowering bushes and plants framing the house. Callie came out to greet them and Rebecca noted the pronounced waddle along with Callie's usual limp. Callie smiled and greeted them both warmly.

"Thank you, Jessie, for picking up Rebecca. Do you want to stop in for some coffee or anything?" she offered.

"I don't want to put you to any trouble, Mrs. Harrison. I'll just pull over to the cookhouse and see if they've got some on the stove." He tipped his Stetson and pulled away.

Rebecca climbed the steps to the porch with her medical bag in her hand. "I know everyone asks this, but how are you feeling? And I really need to know about any twinges, bloating, swelling, the whole thing." Rebecca smiled in commiseration knowing all the changes a woman's body goes through and how trying many of them are.

"Do we need a bed this time? Can we sit out here?" Callie asked pointing to the shaded porch.

"We can meet out here if you're comfortable." Rebecca followed Callie to the side porch away from any eyes in the compound.

Rebecca listened to Callie's heart and looked into her eyes before bending and pressing the slightly swollen ankles gently with her fingertips. "Hmmm. You should cut down on salt. Just don't add salt to anything you eat at the table. Canned food already has salt in it so you have to consider that when you're cooking. And try to keep your feet up when you're sitting and sit more often if your ankles are swelling. Everything else going as we discussed? No back pain or anything like that?"

"No, I sit and rest and any pain, really just aches, disappear. Seth is also good at giving massages now." Callie shot bright red at what she had almost disclosed.

Rebecca thought she understood perfectly. "It's all right to continue marital relations as long as it's done gently. Though during this last month, you may want to try those other positions we discussed. And there are other ways of being intimate married couples can provide one another." This is where Rebecca flushed red.

The two women became quiet, trying not to think too much on the subject being discussed. The two young women glanced at each other and a laugh escaped Callie and Rebecca followed suit.

"I can't believe I'm talking about such things let alone understanding what we're saying. I have come a long way in the past year," Callie confided still smiling.

Just then Seth, in all his six-foot-six magnificence, came around the corner and Rebecca heard Callie express a long sigh. He glanced worriedly at his wife and then turned to Rebecca asking, "Everything all right?" At Rebecca's nod, he continued, "I saw Jessie at the stables and came right over. I didn't know you were coming out today." He was watching Rebecca as if trying to decipher a conspiracy between the two women to keep him in the dark.

"That's why I didn't let you know. You have to let me handle this my own way," explained Callie to her still annoyed husband.

Seth's frown disappeared immediately and he smiled, touching his wife's shoulder. "I know, Darlin' but I just worry. You're so small. I need to know you'll be all right."

Rebecca, seeing the love between these two people, wanted to ease the worry that may become contentious between them. "I know your wife is small statured but she is more than capable of giving birth to a full-term baby safely. Her size doesn't affect this. She'll be fine even with a large baby. This one, being her first doesn't seem to be above average size, though.

"Mr. Harrison, there are always risks during a birth, but please don't focus on those. Enjoy one another and look forward to welcoming your son or daughter into the world. I would tell you if there were any indications that this was going to be anything besides a normal delivery," Rebecca said earnestly.

Seth looked down at his wife. "She's very precious to me. I'll try not to keep over-thinking this." But both women knew he wasn't going to be able to set aside his worries and enjoy the upcoming birthing process.

After he left them alone, the women relaxed. "I understand she's fallen in love with that baby. How do you think she'll do if they make her give it up to the state?" Callie asked but both women knew who they were discussing.

"I never saw a woman fall in love so quickly – even mothers with their own infants. She's strong and it will be difficult knowing that baby could have a loving mother right here in town. I don't know what happens in those orphanages run by the government."

Inhaling deeply, Callie explained, "I've heard horror stories but that's from older children, those who never had a chance at being adopted. The nuns who ran the foundling home I came from loved what they did so they did it well. In these state facilities, the people running them are sometimes only doing so for the money and that isn't all that much. The children are given the bare necessities and sometimes sent to work outside the home. I don't want to think of that little darling going someplace like that but I don't think I can take her. Not this close to my own child's birth but I know if worse comes to worse, I can convince Seth it's exactly as it should be."

Patting the other woman's shoulder, she stood to leave seeing Jessie driving the buckboard up from the cookhouse. Rebecca told her patient, "Nothing is decided, yet, so don't worry about that baby. For now, she's being well tended and you need to concentrate on yourself and your child."

"I'll pray on it. Give Abby my love when you see her."

Rebecca waved until she could no longer see Callie then turned her attention to Jessie for the drive home.

CHAPTER 5

Two weeks later Rebecca was called out to the Harrison ranch when Callie began labor. The water broke just as Rebecca got there and she scrubbed up and sat by the bed next to Callie while Seth washed telling her he was wearing all clean clothes and planned on staying with his wife, no matter what.

Going to the foot of the bed, Rebecca made sure the extra dry sheets and towels were in place and then checked Callie to see how close she was to giving birth. It was going to be a few hours and Rebecca let the anxious couple know.

Seth held Callie's hand or rather Callie gripped his. He allowed her to tighten her grasp as every contraction ebbed and flowed through her body. He kept Callie focused on him, reminding her to breath as Rebecca had told him to do.

As the last contraction faded and another began to torment the now exhausted Callie, Seth leaned down to his wife's ear and kept up a chant, a prayer, "Never again, never again. Just make it through this and I swear, never again."

Callie panted, "I'm fine. Don't say that. I want more children. It's all right. I can take it." Seth wiped her brow with a cold cloth keeping his own counsel.

Rebecca gazed into Seth's worried eyes saying quietly, "I think the cord is around the baby's neck. These contractions should have done the job and we should be holding your child. I see the crown and then it disappears again."

Seth asked panicked, "It's not breach? You're sure the head is there? What about cutting her and taking the baby that way? I read about that. Is that safer?"

At Rebecca's nod, she said, "I can cut the baby out if this other fails but blood loss and trauma should be avoided. I can try to push the baby back and get my hand in there to unwrap the cord, which is tricky if the cord is wrapped around more than once. Or I can pull the infant with the next contraction, hopefully get the baby out far enough for you to cut the cord."

Seth, worry lines creasing his forehead, said, "The last one. I think we should go for the last one."

"Cut where I place my right hand, cut and then get out of the way," Rebecca instructed her anxious helper.

Seth kissed Callie, now almost crazed with the never relenting pains. He stood by Rebecca as she pulled on clean white cotton day-gloves spreading a white jell on the back of her gloved hands.

"What the hell…." began Seth with worried eyes, sweat forming on his forehead.

"This is slippery work and I want the first time I get hold of the baby to succeed. Got the knife? Now cut from the inside out." Both of them focused on Callie with bated breath. "Here comes the next contraction. Hold on, Callie, we almost have your baby in your arms. Keep breathing, and here it goes…." Rebecca instructed as she slid her small hands into the womb finding the infant's head and shoulders before the contraction ebbed.

Getting her hands on each side of the baby, she pulled as the next contraction tried to spit the child from the womb. There was resistance on the baby, something refusing to let this child be born. Rebecca found the cord and pulled it out from the back of the baby's neck while

Seth cut as he had been told.

Rebecca placed the baby on a waiting towel and held on to the end of the cord, telling Seth to tie it off as he knew to do. The baby laying so still brought a pang of regret to Seth's chest. A son, they had lost a son. Callie would be so broken hearted and Seth never wanted to put her through this again.

Picking up the baby, Rebecca turned it over and put one cloth-covered finger into the mouth wiping from back to front. Then covering the tiny blue mouth with her own, she did several quick breaths. On the last one, the baby startled and a strident yowl erupted.

Yelling loudly and shaking with the trauma of birth the infant met his parents. Rebecca held Callie's son up and wrapped him in a waiting blanket, handing him to his grateful mother.

Callie was crying profusely at this point. "Why is he so blue? I thought he would be all pink and rosy."

"He was short of air, oxygen, every time you had a contraction and he was being pushed out. It's not uncommon for a baby to roll and get the cord wrapped but it causes for some scary moments during the birthing process. I'm going to finish here and clean you up but you and Seth spend some time getting to know your new son. It's over now and you need to rest. Let the baby cry like that for a few minutes until he is nicely flushed. Then you should try to feed him, the sooner the better."

Seth leaned over, kissed his wife then kept gazing at his son, so small, so perfect, and so loud. Tears formed in his eyes but he tried and failed to keep them there. Callie pulled his hand over to kiss it saying quietly, "You were there for me and our son. You can't imagine how proud I am of you."

"And I'm proud of you, Darlin'. I never thought I could be happier than the day we married but this comes darn close."

Callie's eyes drooped closed and she gave one last contented sigh as she rested from her ordeal. The baby had settled from his crying and was yawning as his eyes dropped closed for a little nap of his own. Seth sat next to his wife and child looking somewhat amazed at the turn of events this day had taken.

Rebecca took the pail and bloody sheets from the room to give the new family the time to get to know one another better. She would be staying for the next few days to make sure Callie was well and that the feeding process for both baby and mother was proceeding properly.

Marie, Callie's Mexican housekeeper, took the discarded items from Rebecca saying in her accented English, "I am glad is *el nino*. Now Mister Seth will start to eat and sleep again. If little one lets him sleep. I am glad Miss Callie is strong woman. It took long time. That isn't always good thing." Then she smiled brightly saying, "There is food in the kitchen. Help yourself to anything you want."

Rebecca went into the kitchen wearily to find Jessie there.

"I'm to carry the news around to the various ranches. Everything all right?" he asked worriedly.

"Yes, I'm just tired but not as tired as Callie. She did wonderfully well and Seth was great, too." She thought about her mother's insistence that fathers remain out of the birthing room. "I don't know why husbands aren't in the birthing rooms to help more often. I mean they were there at the conception, all the fun part but then desert their wives when the going gets tough." She froze when she realized to whom she was speaking.

Jessie sat there with a wide grin on his face. "I don't suppose those men want to see the reality of it all. After all, I grew up around cattle having calves out in the fields and I can't think it's much different for humans."

"Yes, but at least we don't have to do so standing up, although there are societies where the women squat over a bucket." Then looking appalled, said, "I can't believe I'm having this conversation with you. It just shows how tired I am. Have you been here the whole time, since you dropped me off?"

"Yep. I slept down at the bunkhouse and ate with the hands. They have great food here by the way, even better than Emily's, but don't tell her I said so," he replied with a grin as he stuffed the last piece of buttered biscuit in his mouth.

"Well, you can be on your way, Paul Revere, and let everyone know the Harrison family now includes a healthy son, unnamed at this time, and mother and father are doing fine."

"Will do. And seriously, I'm glad you're here for my friends and their families. Mavis has been looking a little green around the gills every morning. I have a feeling there's going to be an announcement fairly soon." He grabbed an apple out of the bowl on the table and left whistling.

Another baby. How nice. Rebecca made a cup of tea and thought about the ecstatic couple upstairs and then about Abby and her wanting a baby so badly now.

Seth came down saying happily, "I think Callie needs you to help, um…she wants to feed our son." The pride in his voice on that last word melted Rebecca's heart completely.

"Seth, I want you to know what happened today with the cord and the baby isn't that common and it doesn't mean it will ever happen again to Callie." Rebecca tried to comfort the new father, knowing how much the man fretted about his wife.

"I know. It was just at the time, I was so afraid of losing her, of losing them both. Actually, I now feel if we can get through a tough birth like this one, then we can slide right through a normal one." He appeared more relaxed than he had all day.

"I wouldn't put it quite like that to Callie, just yet. One baby at a time but I'm glad you realize you can't live in fear of a difficult birth." She offered hesitantly, "There are methods to prevent more births if you want me to get you information?"

"I'll leave that up to Callie. She's the one who has to do all the work. Even after all this today, she's talking about a daughter next and after that she said she didn't care which we have." Shaking his head, he smiled at the resilience of his little wife.

"I'll go up then to help get her started nursing."

"I'm getting her some tea but she says she's hungry. Anything she shouldn't have?"

"I know Maria's going to be upset but I would keep anything too spicy away from her. Sometimes newborns are sensitive to the flavors as it passes through the mother," warned Rebecca.

Seth nodded his head slowly, taking in the advice. "Kind of like getting wild garlic in the milk cow's hay. It can taint the milk for days. It makes sense, I guess, thinking about it."

Rebecca climbed the stairs once more to help the

new, young mother conquer one more challenge to motherhood.

By morning, Mary Elizabeth, who usually cooked for the ranch hands, was in the kitchen making breakfast. She was young, friendly and chattered excitedly about helping take care of the baby. It evidently was something she had helped with at the foundling home. At least for the short while infants stayed at St. Michaels.

Seth said, "I'll be taking Callie's meals up to her and staying with her most of the day. I'll sleep when she does, if that won't be harmful for the baby."

"No, but, let the baby sleep in the cradle or you might roll onto him in your sleep. I also think it keeps the baby knowing when it's time to sleep and when it's time to play. It usually takes a day or two and I think Callie already has a good sense for a first-time mother," Rebecca reassured him.

"She's been around infants at the home the same as me so she's taken care of dozens. Each seemed to have their own schedule and personality right from the beginning," Mary Elizabeth explained as she cleaned out the pans and sunk them into the hot sudsy water. "Many were newborns dropped off at the gate. We had a special outside door that spun the baby into the room inside the home and a bell would sound. Then the nun on duty would retrieve the infant and bring it to the nursery. Some nights we got more than one."

Rebecca rose from the table to go upstairs. "When you're ready, come up and I'll introduce you to the baby and Callie can let you know how much she wants you to do for her. I have a feeling it won't be much. She seems to be the kind of mother who wants to do it all herself."

"I know but at least I'll get to see the baby before

most of the others. Callie will be a good mother since she already mothers all of us here. Young Jamie adores her and he's only known her for a year."

Mary Elizabeth came up to the room and watched Rebecca care for the umbilical cord and then diaper the infant letting Callie have her meal with Seth. After watching the young girl handle the baby, Rebecca had no hesitation in leaving Callie and the baby in her care. She would stay for a few more days giving Abby more time with the baby girl before returning home.

CHAPTER 6

Jessie dropped off Rebecca and her bags and headed into town for a pick-up from the dry goods store. Rebecca opened the door to find Abby there feeding the baby in a rocking chair that was new to the parlor.

Abby's face lit up as she said, "Behold the conquering hero. I am amazed at how easy you make it all seem. Even Doc was impressed with your work when he heard about it."

"What are you talking about? Callie did all the work. I simply catch, remember." Rebecca laughed at her own joke.

"Not from what I heard. They're saying you saved both Callie and the baby. That they were both half-dead and then you pulled out the baby and breathed life back into him. It's like a miracle," enthused Abby.

"It wasn't that dramatic but I did what had to be done. I've done it only once before and I was scared to death. This time I knew it could work so I was more confident. I can't say I would want another birthing to go like that but Seth and Callie did great and their son, Warren, by the way named after Seth's father, is going great guns. I swear he grew before my eyes. And speaking of growing, how's this little one doing?"

"Eats and sleeps. Has quite a life going for herself," laughed Abby, but there was a softness about her now. A glow of love Rebecca had recognized immediately.

Rebecca went over to peer at the baby wrapped in a soft yellow blanket and smiled down as her little cupid lips mouthed hungrily for the feeding bottle Abby had withdrawn so she could put the baby up to her shoulder to burp.

There was a rapid tapping on the door and Rebecca turned to open it thinking Jessie had returned from his shopping. Instead, standing there wearing a city man's suit with a double bowed tie and polished boots was a drop-dead gorgeous man with curling dark hair, the bluest eyes she had ever seen and a wide generous mouth. He needed a shave but other than that he was perfect.

"May I help you?" Rebecca asked, pleased her voice sounded normal to her ears.

Just behind her Abby said in surprise, "Matthew, how did you know where to find me?"

Matthew appeared as surprised to see Abby. "I didn't know you were here. I came to see if the midwife would come with me to see a girl at Miss Lily's." He turned to Rebecca, "You don't mind going to Miss Lily's, do you? I don't want to move her any more than needed and she's completely worn out." He was pleading with his eyes if not with his words but Rebecca was already grabbing her bag.

"I'll be back later, Abby," Rebecca said, turning. "I'll go with Matthew and he can tell me what's happening."

Matthew gave a longing look at Abby and complied with Rebecca's request.

As they walked briskly down the road and turned onto the street where Rebecca knew Miss Lily's house was, Matthew was trying to explain about the girl he was taking Rebecca to see.

"She's been beat up but I don't think that's the worst of it. She worked in a brothel and the guy that ran it isn't known to take care of his girls, and I do mean girls. Lucy looks about fifteen, if that. I got her out of there and was bringing her to Callie but I don't think she can wait that long." He looked worriedly at her saying, "I think she's bleeding. I think she needs you."

Rebecca straightened her back, nodding in understanding. She'd had to handle difficult situations before but always with her mother at her side. There had been times when a husband kept getting drunk and beating up his pregnant wife or the time when the young woman was impregnated by either the father or her brother, they never had found out which. Either case caused severe deformities in the baby but Rebecca's mother got the girl out of the house with a lot of threats and the use of Rebecca's father's shotgun.

Mathew took the steps up to the front of the neat two-story house and opened the door without knocking. Miss Lily met them in the parlor, which thankfully was empty of any patrons and led Rebecca up the stairs. Matthew held back as they entered a bedroom. There was a small body curled up in the middle of the single person bed. Rebecca shooed Miss Lily out while closing the door.

Moving to the side of the bed where she could face the girl, Rebecca crooned softly, "There, there. You're safe now. No one will be able to hurt you here. We have Matthew and Miss Lily and Stella and Lacy and me, I'm Rebecca. None of us will let anyone else anywhere near you. Do you understand? Do you believe me?"

A very blue eye peaked out from the blanket covering Lucy. Rebecca smiled. "I'm here to help you. Matthew said you were hurt, hit, and kicked even? Let me see. I can help"

71

And then Lucy opened up, both by taking the blanket off and straightening so that Rebecca could see the damage done to her abused body and also verbally, saying in a rush, "I thought he was going to kill me and Melvin was going to let him. They told me to stop screaming but I couldn't. I couldn't stop myself even though they hit me and then when I couldn't stand up anymore, they kicked me. I don't know how many times." Her voice died off as she relived some of her nightmare.

"Anything else, did he do anything more? I know what you were paid to do but that doesn't matter. I need to know if there is a possibility that you're hurt inside," Rebecca said quietly.

As Lucy admitted to the possibility, she broke down and began sobbing. Rebecca calmly told Lucy what she needed her to do and Lucy complied. Her entire body seemed to be a large bruise, one starting where another ended. Oddly, the only mark on Lucy's face was a bruise over one eye while the rest of her was going to be unnatural colors for weeks.

Rebecca went to the door to ask for cool water and found Matthew standing there propped against the wall, a questioning expression on his face as she leaned out.

"I think most of the damage is repairable. I need to suture but I want to clean off the blood to make sure the bruising is just that. She needs rest mostly but could you ask Miss Lily if she has anything to make a light soup or broth from? And a nightgown?"

Mathew pushed himself away from the wall. "I'll make sure she has something or I'll get something for her myself."

Rebecca returned to the girl and began the process

of her healing.

After a light meal, clean nightgown and with Rebecca sitting guard, Lucy felt secure enough finally to sleep. Rebecca had made Matthew aware she would be staying the night and asked if he would inform Abby of what she was doing.

He looked wearily at her but agreed and left Miss Lily's to go to talk with Abby even though it was late. He knew he had to explain his actions and his reason for being away for so long without any word from him. This was the part of his life he didn't want to touch any other. This was the dark side of being on the streets so long he could see someone in need better than anyone else. And he couldn't turn away. Hell, he didn't want to be the kind of man to turn away. It wasn't pleasant but then he could think back and know he helped save lives. He helped people get back the lives they lost. He helped those who could no longer help themselves. He understood why he did what he did but he found it difficult for others to do so. People unused to the backstreets of big cities.

It was after dark when Abby heard Matthew's footsteps on the porch. She went to the door before he could knock.

"My God, Abby. I missed you." He put his arms around her and held her to him.

Abby didn't reciprocate but stood there, neither accepting nor dismissing his hugs. Her passivity sunk into Matthew's consciousness and he let her go. "I never meant to be away longer than usual. I was on my way home to you, you've got to believe me, when things kept getting out of hand. Things I had to take care of," he tried to explain.

"Things like the young woman you needed Rebecca

to help?" asked Abby mutinously.

"Yes, I guess so. It's something I never wanted to touch you, the dirty underbelly of city life. I don't want to soil your life with what I do when I'm away from you," he said trying to pull her into his arms again.

"And just what is it that you do when you're away from me, Matthew?" she asked frostily.

"The hotels where I stay know that I always ask about houses, about brothels, and they let me know where they are and where I could get a woman to do things for me, for money."

As he was saying these words out loud an expression of understanding came across his face and then quickly corrected what he was sure Abby was thinking. "No, not that way. I mean not for me, not for anybody. Geeze, Callie knows." He stepped away but kept hold of her hands. "I go there, to these places, and I look around to make sure the women are there because they want to be, you know, of their own choice. Too many times I've found woman, girls actually, kidnapped and then held to pay back some little amount of money the pimp had loaned them or even for their own food. I either pay off their debt and walk out with them, get them set up somewhere safe or I steal them and hide them until I can get them out of town."

"So, the woman today? She had been coerced into being a prostitute?" Abby asked confused with learning of Matthew's activities that before now she hadn't had a hint about.

"She's just a girl, too young to know what they were going to do with her. I got there just after they left her beaten, attacked. They were two full-grown men but I didn't go after them. I practically carried Lucy out of the place and took her directly to the train station. If the conductor and I weren't well known to one another, I think he would have called the authorities and had me arrested right then and there. Lucy was basically unconscious but I was trying to bring her here to you or Callie."

"Callie just had her baby, a son they named, Warren. Six days ago, now. Rebecca returned home here this afternoon right before you came to get her. I've been living here taking care of the baby while she was out with Callie," she explained and then closed up again when reminded of the baby she wanted so badly. Would Matthew think she wanted to marry him now simply to ensure she could keep the baby?

"So how long have you been doing this? Saving women? Is that why you've been so attentive to me, because you think I'm a fallen woman and are trying to save me?" she asked, trying to keep the hurt and anger out of her voice, but failing.

His gaze met hers through narrowed lids. "All right, why are you trying to start a fight? I'm not going to be driven away, not after it took me so long to get back to you. Be honest. Your honesty was the first thing that drew me to you. Well, maybe not the first." He peered appreciatively at her breasts. "But one of the first." He tried nuzzling her neck not past using his sexuality to convince her they were right for one another.

"Honesty? You want honesty?" At his mumbled agreement into her neck, Abby said recklessly, "I want this baby and I need you to get her for me. I don't want to know you won't help me because I want this baby." And with that announcement started sobbing into Matthew's suit jacket.

75

Mathew was flummoxed, the breath knocked out of him. What in the world could he do to get the midwife's baby for Abby? Did she expect him to kidnap the little thing? His heart went out to the woman he loved, knowing the loss she had sustained when she was barely a woman. "I want to help you, really I do, but you just got too attached to this one. I'll take you to the nearest big city with an orphanage and we'll get a baby, maybe two. Really, Abby, you're breaking my heart here.

"Come on, please stop crying and we'll start making plans tonight. We'll get married and then get on the train and find us some babies. Doesn't that sound good?" he asked unable to calm Abby, the usually calm, take charge Abby, who was now crying even harder than when she first told him about wanting this baby.

Finally, Abby got herself under control and said petulantly, "I don't want you to marry me simply so I can get a baby. I don't want your pity. I want this baby." Before she could start sobbing again, Matthew caught the gist of what she had said. "Abby, Abby, listen to me. I'm not marrying you so you can get a baby. I love you. I was planning on asking you on this trip back home."

Trying to get his hand into his pocket, he said, "Look, I bought this ring for you. I was going to get us a bottle of wine and a good meal and then I was going to ask you to marry me. I'm just letting you know if you want to spend our honeymoon finding a baby to adopt, I'm fine with that. Anything as long as we're together." He held Abby as close as they could get wearing clothes. "I may as well confess I had plans on bedding you right after I asked you to marry me so as long as Rebecca isn't going to be home tonight...." He raised his eyebrows in a question.

Rebecca took a handkerchief out of her pocket and slapped him on his arm saying, "Mind yourself. There's a baby sleeping in that room."

"She won't mind and I don't mind. That just leaves you to make a decision. Will you marry me? I need you so much, I couldn't concentrate on anything this last trip. Please Abby, say you will." This time he was the one pleading.

"Yes, yes, I will. Can we apply to adopt this baby? It isn't Rebecca's. The mother died in childbirth and the father wanted to abandon her. I saw her and it was instant love. I don't think I could go on without her," she confessed.

"Hmm, so I owe it all to this baby if you marry me?"

"I love you, Matthew. You know I do but the baby pushed me into admitting that I'm a marrying kind of woman. I thought loving a child not from my body would be difficult. I didn't think you would settle for only adopted children and worried I was denying you a child of your own by marrying you. But now I understand how easy it is to love a child – any child. It doesn't need to be carried around inside you for months. I can't believe how much I love this baby and I have known her less than two weeks."

"You simply got broody having this baby to care for." He nuzzled her neck again kissing the tender spot just below her ear.

"Matthew? Did you just compare me to a hen?"

"Ah-h, no?"

She seemed to be in good spirits with him because she focused on other things immediately. "I'm glad you were so persistent in pursuing me. I have to thank Callie for coming to Sweetwater and bringing you to me." She raised her face up to accept the kisses Matthew had been holding back.

"I've already thanked her for the same thing. Now where is that bed?" he asked and Abby pointed the way.

The two quietly undressed each other, this was not their first time together as lovers but it seemed that way to both of them. She undid his buttons while he undid hers. Then he paused and kissed her lips and throat before lifting the dress off over her head, chuckling quietly as the yards of fabric seemed to go on forever. Abby made quick work of removing her corset and combination leaving her as God made her and Matthew admiring every inch.

He had dispensed with his clothing and now had his full attention on Abby. They lay down on the opened bed and Matthew renewed his knowledge of every contour and plane on her person. He was working his way down her body when he murmured, "I didn't think I was gone that long, but I swear you're more than the usual handful." He kissed the tips of each aching breast.

She arched into his mouth, yearning for his touch everywhere at once. "Does that mean you think I'm getting fat?"

"Hmmmm, no. I never said nor implied that." And he kept the kisses moving over her heated flesh, Matthew enjoying his mapping of her body with his lips.

"Good thinking to deny it now. I'll bring it up again tomorrow morning and you can beg me for forgiveness," she said enjoying his hand that was now working its way between her legs.

"I could ask for forgiveness right now. My odds are better now than they will be in the morning."

"Are you sure? You could be ready to beg a lot

sooner than that if my memory serves me." She smiled as he slid down to her stomach and she felt the warmth of his tongue as he licked and kissed his way lower.

Stopping him, she asked him to lay back which he did. That devilish grin emphasized by the dimples on both sides of his mouth caused muscles to undulate through her lower body. Pushing her fingers through his chest hair, she luxuriated in the softness covering the firmness of his muscles beneath. She allowed her hands to slide downward to the apex where the strong, firm erection grew from his body.

She loved the feel of his male perfection, the soft velvety crown, the smooth skin all covering a rigidity that was so gentle yet so strong. She went down and kissed the downy base and then up the firm shaft to the peak.

"It's been a long time, Abby, don't let me get carried away. I want to be in you, feeling you clamp around me, enjoying me as I enjoy you." He flipped her unto her back and proceeded to enter her ready and warm body. The two spent several minutes with the mutually satisfying friction of smooth skin against smooth skin until they both stiffened, thrusting through to their mutual ecstasy.

Matthew rolled to the side but kept Abby cocooned beneath his arm, up against his body and pulled the covers over them. Inhaling deeply for the first time in days, he felt that all would be right from now on. He had Abby, evidently a daughter and a new nephew. He was one very happy man.

CHAPTER 7

Rebecca came in from the front porch dropping her bag at the door, something she rarely did. Pulling the hairpins that weren't holding her hair in place anyway, she put them in her pocket shaking out her long tresses as she went. She didn't call out afraid she'd wake the baby and since it seemed that Abby was still sleeping, thought the two possibly had had a long night. Sometimes babies had a little trouble settling especially if Abby held her so much the baby wasn't used to sleeping by herself.

Tiptoeing to the bedroom, she thought to check inside when the door opened and she came face to face with a nearly undressed Matthew. He had pulled on his trousers and slid the suspenders over his naked shoulders but that was all and Abby really wasn't used to seeing that much bare male that close.

"Oh," she said quietly, still thinking about the baby. "I'm sorry. I didn't know you stayed the night. Umm, everything go, all right?" She felt herself blush scarlet. "I mean, you and Abby work everything out?"

Turning quickly, Rebecca entered the kitchen thinking retreat was the better part of valor. Matthew followed her explaining he had gotten up to use the facilities and Rebecca pointed him out the backdoor. Just as he went to open it, Reverend Walters stepped onto the doorstep poised to knock.

His shocked gaze took in a disheveled Rebecca and the half-dressed man and started to stammer an apology, "I'm, ah, I'm sorry to arrive so early but I have to leave soon and I, ah, I thought Abby would be here."

Neither of the other two wanted to get Abby involved in this situation so said nothing and that left it to the reverend to stammer more before saying in confusion, "Aren't you Callie Harrison's brother? Mark? No, Matt, er, Matthew."

Mathew looked at the reverend suspiciously as to why he was looking for Abby so early in the morning and coming in by way of the back door. "Yep," he answered the minister's questions but not all the minister's questions.

"I'll try to come back later or try her shop when I get back. I'll, um, see you later, too," he said glancing at Rebecca and quickly left the doorway.

Mathew dropped his head to his chest and said, "Damn, I wanted him to perform the wedding ceremony and instead it looks like I'm going to have to beat him up first."

He peeked at Rebecca and they both started to laugh. Rebecca caught her breath first saying, "I'm going to have to move to another town. I spend all night in a bawdy house and then get found by the reverend with a near naked man in my kitchen at six in the morning." She wiped the tears of mirth from her eyes.

"I'm sorry. Rebecca, is it? I'll explain to him that I was simply staying here for the night when I ask him to perform the wedding ceremony for Abby and me. Is he a reasonable sort of man? I only met him once but I was there to take photographs and didn't have much to do with him."

"I thought he was a reasonable man but I've learned men can be unpredictable. Except you of course. I knew you were going to be trouble the first time I laid eyes on you." She turned to get the stove ambers stirred to heat her bath water.

A short time later an unrepentant, smiling Abby said, "Matthew and I and the baby are going back to my house so you can get some sleep. I'm really sorry about this morning and I'll let the reverend know I was the one with Matthew and that you had just returned home."

Rebecca finished her tea. "Don't forget to tell him where I was all night so that you could sin in peace with Matthew. Knowing I was in one of the up-stair rooms at Miss Lily's will probably be an interesting topic for a church sermon if ever there was one."

Abby laughed hugging her friend. "Thank you, for everything. I'll get back with you later. Get some sleep, you're needed here in Sweetwater more than any of us thought."

And in a small whirlwind, the three of them were gone and the house stood in silence. Rebecca was going to miss Abby being so close. Now it seemed Abby was going to have a husband as well as a baby to care for, so there wouldn't be those evenings of dining and embroidering together. Maybe Miss Lily can embroider. Rebecca would have to ask her sometime. Possibly later when she went back to check on Lucy.

She laughed when she had seen Abby had changed the bed into new linen. What in the world had they done to the bed that it needed all new linen? Perhaps Rebecca shouldn't think too long on it. Climbing in, she pulled the covers over herself. It felt good to be home and able to sleep as long as she wanted. After almost a week with Callie and then last night, she was ready to sleep and sleep and sleep.

Rebecca had slept like the dead and woke up late in

the evening, hungry as usual. She got up and dressed, skipping the corset and pulling on one of her simplest dresses and a clean white apron. Winding her hair up, she pinned it on top of her head declining the need for a hat. Miss Lily's was one of the closest houses besides the rectory at that end of town and she felt secure in walking the short way to check on her patient.

Miss Lily opened the door for her wearing a pretty day dress and ushered Rebecca in and up the stairs. Again, the parlor was empty of patrons, thankfully, since Rebecca didn't know how to face any gentlemen later if she had met them there. Lucy seemed much stronger, sitting up in bed trying to read by the lamp light. She put down the book and smiled when she saw Rebecca come in.

Rebecca thought, oh, to be so young and resilient. She greeted Lucy, "You look much more the thing today. I hear you ate well and felt like more than soup and toast."

"I'm feeling much, much better. I can't thank you and Matthew enough. I really got myself into a mess. I don't know what I was thinkin' but everyone was so nice to begin with, you know? Like I was really liked and wanted." Then tears started down her face.

Rebecca sat on the side of the bed and pulled the young girl into her arms. "Someone very wise once told me tears are for sharing and you should never cry alone."

Lucy wiped the tears with a handkerchief indicating to Rebecca that tears had been an on and off thing all day. The young girl tried a smile. "I shouldn't be crying. I've been given another chance and I should be happy I got out while I could."

"Don't worry about the future. Matthew has plans to

get you situated with friends and a job that won't endanger you. Please don't fret. You have friends here and Miss Lily will give you a home." At the expression of alarm on Lucy's face continued, "No, not like that. Without having to work for her. She'll give you a home for the next few days until you're well enough to travel."

"I don't know how to thank you all." She mopped at her eyes still trying to forget the awful events that brought her there.

"Don't worry about that, either. We all do what we can. At some point in your life you may have the chance to help someone and then you'll know what it was all for." Rebecca became the caregiver again asking, "No pains, no problems anywhere?" Lucy shook her head unable to voice any words. "Good. I'll check in again tomorrow. Perhaps Miss Lily will show you how to knit." The older woman had confided that she spent her free time knitting and donating items to the church where they were sent to those in need throughout the county.

"I'd like that. I could make some socks or a scarf," Lucy said her eyes still shiny from the tears.

"Neck-scarves are the best to make. You just have to know when to stop." Rebecca rose from the bed and said goodbye to Miss Lily on her way through the still empty parlor.

As she walked back to her home, she saw a shadow on her porch that turned into the Reverend Walters. "I would like to speak with you if I may, Mrs. Johansen."

"Of course, you do. Come in Reverend, I'm not going to stay out here to be dinner for the mosquitoes." She entered her parlor with the reverend right on her heels.

Turning, she offered him a seat but he chose to stand

and hold his hat turning it around and around by the brim. Rebecca chose to sit on the small sofa and watch him until he got his nerve up to tell her whatever it was, he had to say and then she could go to bed again. She found she was still tired and wasn't in any frame of mind to placate any man, lumping all men into the category that had harmed Lucy - except Matthew, of course.

"I just came back from seeing Abby and, of course, Matthew. I'm not sure what was going on this morning." He paused and looked inquisitively at Rebecca.

Rebecca was in no mood to kowtow to his curiosity. Let him stew in his own low thoughts, she was thinking.

Then, not getting any further information, he continued, "But needless to say you probably know they are engaged and wish to be married as soon as possible. First, to be able to file adoption papers for the baby and second, to take a trip for a few weeks together. A honeymoon, I guess." Here he stopped again, evidently searching for the truth behind what Abby had told him and what he had seen that morning.

Again, Rebecca tried not to yawn but found it difficult.

The man of the cloth finally blurted out, "Rebecca, what is going on? I thought we were getting along so well. I was beginning to like you and I thought you felt the same way."

"I thought so, too, for a while but I am having trouble seeing you as a man and not only a minister. I don't think I can live up to your standards. You are too good of a man," said Rebecca seriously, finding his fussiness less attractive now she was tired. He needed someone who was as good as he was and Rebecca knew she would come up short in many ways. She accepted people and their flaws as readily as she accepted the minister. "You readily jumped to conclusions about me this morning. I find your assumptions that I was in the wrong or doing something wrong less than appealing. In my line of work, I run across all kinds of people and I must stay to my task. That of helping women give birth to healthy children. I do not judge or place blame. I don't think I am qualified to do that nor should I. I will give my patients all the help I am able but then I back out of their lives. I don't think you can do that and that judgement extends to everyone around you. I don't think we would suit given our basic differences."

"But I'm not a good man," he confessed truthfully. "I killed a man. A friend who would be alive today except back then I drank and gambled and ran around town all night long sometimes. We made a bet that whoever jumped off the Ferrysburg Bridge would get a pint bought for him by the other." He hesitated then continued, "I passed out and by the time I woke up the whole town was searching the river for Donny. I had spent time and money on liquor and tobacco and women. I'm not proud of it but after Donny's death, I promised not to be that man any longer. I found the calling and I have tried to be a good minister to my congregation."

"I'm sorry you still have such raw feelings about the past but you're right. I think you're a good minister and I think you are truly repentant for the past. That's all you would ask of your parishioners. Why should you be asked to do more?"

"I don't know, but I do. It has been over twelve years since I touched a woman in that way. Actually, twelve years since I wanted to. I don't know what is happening to me but I feel as if I'm losing control around you. I want to chuck the whole thing and be with you, know you. But I have to set a higher standard. I'm looked up to for guidance when someone is about to sin. I have to help them keep to the right path," he explained emotionally.

"I appreciate your confidences but I don't see how I'm involved. I don't judge you or your conduct. In fact, I can find nothing to condemn you for in any sense," Rebecca admitted but wanting to distance herself.

"But I do. I want you so very much I can't think long enough to put together a sermon. I was so jealous this morning I wanted to plaster my fist into Matthew's face and glory in the blood and the sound of a nose being broken." He looked at Rebecca as if she had instigated his reaction, his fall from grace. "You see, I became that man again. The old me, the one who reacts with his fists and anger before thinking anything through."

"Daniel." He startled at her use of his first name. Rebecca realized then that he probably hadn't heard anyone use his first name in years but continued, "Daniel, come sit by me. Just because you had those feelings that reminded you of another time and place, doesn't mean you've slipped back to that time. You did not 'plaster his face or break his nose' so that shows me you have evolved from the old Daniel to the Daniel I see here, now." She touched his lapel to forge a bond, to let him know she understood his dilemma of conscience.

Daniel took her hand in his and leaned toward her, searching for her lips, her warm mouth to give him succor. Rebecca leaned forward to meet his seeking mouth and to enjoy his very experienced kisses. Rebecca thought this is one part of his past that she couldn't disapprove of. Where ever he learned to kiss like this,

Daniel was all the better for it.

Rebecca leaned back or Daniel urged her back against the armrest, but either way they found themselves reclined on the sofa with Daniel enjoying the advantage of being above her. Covering her mouth, he sucked gently on her bottom lip, rubbing his tongue on the seam until she opened her lips to grant him access. His tongue gained entrance and he rhythmically entered and withdrew his tongue, setting a growing flame deep in Rebecca's womb, she was so sure of it she was surprised it wasn't obvious. She responded instinctively.

She felt Daniel's hands on her breast, his open palm circling an ever-increasing nipple, leaving the other peak aching with need. He undid the top few buttons to find his way to the now sensitive buds and continued to feel their hardness and then the weight of her breast in his hand.

Nothing was said, nothing was discussed. Everything was available to be tasted by his mouth and he did. Rebecca knew Daniel was beyond being talked down, that she hadn't put up any resistance and he was getting past reasoning after his long period of abstinence. She wanted to help him, wanted to give him comfort and release. That's when she realized she had the power to comfort him, to calm him. She had advocated just such behavior when women felt they needed a break between births. She taught them the method of counting days after their menses and then explained other ways to give their husbands pleasure and release when the timing wasn't safe. It kept the marriage on a good footing and many wives were glad of the freedom it gave them.

Rebecca didn't have actual experience but she knew the wives had used their hands, their breasts and even their mouths to stimulate and pleasure their spouses.

"Daniel, are you able to stop, are you able to leave me, now?" Daniel failed to answer so immersed in fondling her breasts he didn't hear or didn't comprehend what she was asking. She could understand the man's inability to freely stop himself. Rebecca felt overwhelmed herself with sensations she had no experience of and that felt so right making her want to do things to Daniel, things she shouldn't want to do.

But Daniel seemed to be in pain and she wanted to ease him, give him relief from his demons of the past.

She was able to unbutton Daniel's trousers. He moved to allow her access and then was kissing her again. Desire and passion were definitely in charge of his every move. She felt his erection spring into her hand, a surprisingly satiny feeling skin covering a rigid muscle, eager to be held, to be coaxed to a release.

Daniel was rocking, stroking her breast and kissing her deeply, his tongue imitating the thrusting of his hips. He hadn't said anything for so long Rebecca feared he may not be aware of anything that he, that they, were doing. Finally reaching his culmination, spasms racked his body. Rebecca had used her apron to catch his seed and let Daniel lay on her until his breathing returned to normal.

He sat up, breathing heavily and covering his face with his hands. They had never lit a lamp and the only illumination was from the moonlight coming through the front windows.

"I'm sorry, I'm sorry. I don't know what came over me. I think I must be going mad," he apologized, unable to meet her gaze, even in the near darkness.

"Daniel, don't do this to yourself. You're a man,

with a man's needs. We won't speak of this again. Go home and rest. I think you've been missing your sleep. Please, don't berate yourself over this. I simply wanted to help you. I thought you needed something to make you feel better," she said quietly, hoping he knew she didn't think badly of him.

"I must go." Without even tucking in his shirt, Daniel stood then hurried from the house without another word.

CHAPTER 8

The next day, Matthew and Abby were married and Rebecca found herself standing next to Daniel as he read the words that began every wedding in the little white church. Abby looked lovely in a dress she had designed herself and she walked down the aisle carrying the baby wearing a wreath of flowers on her almost bald head.

Abby handed the child to Rebecca during the ceremony and then Abby took the infant back after Matthew kissed the bride and they left the church as a family. Not many were able to attend the ceremony with such a short notice although Miss Lily was there and a few local couples who had heard of the wedding from other townsfolk.

Matthew and Abby, along with the baby and Lucy were set to leave on the train later that day. Daniel disappeared immediately after the ceremony through the church's rear entry door so Rebecca had no chance to speak with him. To inform him she didn't want the other night to change anything between them. That it was a friend helping another friend, not meant to be anything more.

On Sunday, Rebecca, dressed in her best dress and a new bonnet that gave her some much needed height, walked to the church and joined the other townspeople on the long white pews. They nodded to one another and then settled turning politely to listen to the Reverend Walters' sermon. Usually the sermons were about helping others, keeping a Christian home, giving the benefit of forgiveness to others and the love of God for his children.

But not this Sunday. Today he was the wrath of God himself. Preaching hell and damnation for those sinners who drank, who gambled, who fornicated. From the original sin caused by Eve disobeying God to Delilah and Bathsheba, every woman that was evil in the Bible was raked over the coals of the reverend's wrath. A condemnation and warning for those unable to resist female temptation.

He didn't look directly at Rebecca but she knew he was speaking directly to her. She knew her face was flushed but she was hoping others would think it was due to the warm church on a summer Sunday.

As soon as the minister was finished, there was a stunned quiet from the congregation. Rebecca excused herself to get out of the pew as quickly as possible and left before anyone could gather themselves and leave. She didn't want to have to act pleasantly to Daniel as he stood at the church door saying private farewells to the parishioners.

Shaking by the time she got home, she couldn't sit but was pacing the small parlor and chewing a nail, saying all kinds of rude truths in her mind to Daniel high-and-mighty Walters. She was furiously calling him every name she could think of under her breath when there was a knock on the front door. If Walters thought he was going to say anything more to her she was going to slap his face till his ears rang.

Whipping the door open, she faced a startled Jessie. Honest to a fault, he asked, "What bee got in your bonnet? You look mad as a wet hen. Spoiling for a fight, are you?"

"No, come in. I was merely letting my temper get

away with me." She stood back to let him enter then left the door open hoping it would catch a breeze. A small hope.

He looked behind him to the people still standing around the churchyard saying, "I just came to see if you wanted to go fishing. Emily packed us a lunch." He smiled broadly as she took the bait.

"I'll have to change but I won't be more than a couple of minutes," she promised.

"I'll wait in plain sight in the wagon. Just bring a hat and we're ready to go." He replaced his Stetson, turned and descended the steps.

Rebecca hurried into her room and carefully removed her hat and dress, putting on a soft pink shirtwaist and brown skirt. Grabbing a sunbonnet, she took a quick look in the mirror satisfied with herself. Her color was back to normal and she decided to leave her displeasure with the minister where it belonged – at his own front door.

As she climbed up onto the wagon seat, she slid closer to Jessie and actually slid her arm through his. He smiled down at her and taking one hand patted hers. A little farther down the road Rebecca slid over to her usual spot letting out a sigh.

Glancing over to his companion, Jessie asked, "Rough day? Can I help?"

"I don't think anyone can help. I'll be okay. Let's just catch some fish." She smiled as they neared their favorite fishing spot at the turn in the river.

After the poles were baited and set in the side of the river, the two friends sat on the blanket and watched the river slide past. The hot sun beat down on their hats while the light breeze crossing the water cooled their skin making the day down right pleasant.

Not looking at Jessie, Rebecca said, "I did something stupid."

Jessie, taking a piece of grass out of his mouth and tossing it said, "Yeah, me too."

"I don't think I can make mine better. I don't think I'll get the chance," she admitted.

"Yeah, me too," he agreed.

"Why can't we take back a day or an hour, like being able to wake-up and start the same day over again only being able to change the things we did wrong?" she asked.

"How come you can have plain old good days, over and over till you're so bored you'd like to scream but one bad day can wipe out all the others? I'd like to get one of those bad days back, like you said, and do it all over again. Of course, with my luck I'd open my big mouth and say or do the same thing that got me in trouble in the first place." He seemed to chuckle at a memory.

"What are we going to do? I almost feel like I should move on but I owe so much to all the fathers-to-be. And, everyone has been so good to me here. Why should I let one person drive me away? He should be the one to leave," she said now with tears in her eyes.

"Is there someone you want me to beat-up for you? I had three older brothers who didn't hold back anything when in a temper. I'm pretty good in a fight," he offered seriously.

"No, it would be more satisfying if I did it myself." She smiled. Her anger was really more hurt feelings than anything else. She wasn't sure her emotions, like love, had ever been involved. Rebecca had been trying to make Daniel feel better but if he wanted to turn it into the sin of the flesh, then let him.

"I was so happy this morning and then I got a big letdown from someone I thought highly of," she confessed.

"Yeah, me too," Jessie agreed.

They stayed longer than they usually did, almost till dark. Rebecca worried that Jessie wouldn't be able to see well enough to make the trip home safely.

"I'll stay at Miss Lily's." At Rebecca's shocked expression he smiled explaining, "She lets me rent a room upstairs. It isn't used for the men. Just if I've stayed too long at the saloon some evening. I found the breakfasts more than adequate, plus she'll feed me cookies when I get there tonight."

"I can believe everything you say. I don't know how she keeps open. I've never run into any, er, patrons when I've been there."

"So, you've been visiting, Miss Lily? Did she dress your hair? I know Abby thinks she's great," he said. "But leave it to you to visit a place other women run from."

"I simply like her. She's actually very nice and has a beautiful singing voice."

"Yeah, she used to be on stage singing and acting." As they approached her house, he asked, "Can I leave the buckboard to the side of your house? I'll take the horses to the stable for the night but there's not enough space for the wagon over there. I'll pick it up in the morning if that's all right with you."

"That's fine. Have a good night. Tomorrow has to be better, right?" she said smiling letting herself into her front door.

"I hope so. Good night, Rebecca."

Jessie didn't come by until noon and Rebecca felt

the need to tease him, "Quite a night, Jessie. Are you sure you slept in that single bed?"

"How do you know I slept in a single bed? You been talking to Miss Lily?" he asked smiling in return.

"No, just a guess. Are you heading home to face the music?" she asked seriously.

"I am. It's not my home where I'm getting into trouble. I'll think it out and either it works or it won't. It's getting time for me to settle down and get busy with my chosen profession. I'm a licensed attorney and I should be setting up an office in a big city but I wanted one last summer at the ranch, like I always did between terms. Guess everything changes."

"I kind of felt the same thing when I decided to finally leave my parents' home and come here."

"Did your husband live with your parents, too?" he asked innocently.

Dreading his possible response, she explained, "I've never been married. My mother thought I should take her maiden name and say I'm a widow or people wouldn't take me seriously as a midwife. I never meant to lie. I didn't know I would get so close with so many of my patients and their families. Forgive me?"

"There's nothing to forgive. If that's the worse you can come up with, you're pretty much an angel compared to most of the rest of us."

Leaning over, he gave Rebecca a kiss on the cheek. "This is for luck. Seth always kisses the cook which, of course, is his wife but I give a kiss for luck." Then he winked and got up onto the wagon bench.

Rebecca noticed movement in the graveyard across the road and saw Daniel taking the short cut to the rectory. Lifting her nose, she sniffed then turning, entered her home.

That evening, there was a knocking on Rebecca's back door. She just knew it was the minister. Well, he could stand out there till the cows came home. Rebecca was in her bedroom already with the curtains pulled. She'd stay there till she was sure he was gone. It would be dark soon and then he'd go away.

At least she was hoping he would go away. She didn't have the energy to argue with him and that was going to be the outcome of any confrontation right now. She was still angry at him and that anger would be the first thing to show itself. Daniel wasn't the man she thought he was and she didn't want the man he was. Eventually she thought she heard him leave but didn't dare take the chance of looking out the front window.

Changing into her nightgown in the dark, she went to bed. Disturbing dreams of her and Jessie on the riverbank doing everything but fishing filled her night's sleep. She woke up unsettled and unfulfilled. Her and Jessie together felt wrong and she knew she could never feel for him what she had felt for Daniel.

But as Jessie said, you can't redo a day and if you did you would probably do it the same way the second time. She hadn't gone against her basic instincts or morals with Daniel. Her natural wish to help someone, especially someone in pain, will always win out. She had too much empathy to ignore someone in need if she could lessen their hurting in any way.

She didn't think what she did with Daniel was a sin. Merely assist a bodily function to help him over whatever he was going through. It's not as if she had coitus with him. She never even considered doing so although by his reaction one would think she had done that and more. Charged him for it. The man wasn't worth her time and energy – or her thoughts. From now on, she would act as if he weren't right across the road from her home.

Daniel dropped his head at the silence meeting his rapping on Rebecca's back door. What had he really expected, after all? A warm welcome? Not after he had assaulted her from the pulpit. Not after he had misused his position as a minister to deliver an undeserved reprimand. And the disappointed expression in her eyes would haunt him for a long time – something he deserved.

He had also seriously let down his congregation. Having been so wrought up in his own misery and guilt, he hadn't even considered what such a sermon could be misconstrued as meaning. Miss Lily and the two women who always attended church with her smiled and shook his hand when they left as usual but he could see the pain in the older woman's eyes. He had done more than send a message to Rebecca that they had to stay away from one another, he had hurt a woman he had no right to offend.

In fact, the silence at the end of his sermon was more telling than any words could have been as the members left. No one offered any words toward his message as some would usually have done. How it pertained to them or how they could take a piece of his advice and put it to use in their own lives. The reason he turned to pastoring in the first place. The atonement he was searching for that his life touched others in a positive manner.

Now he was here to ask, no beg, forgiveness of the one person who had deserved his angry tirade the least. A woman who has dedicated her life to help others, to bring into this world another generation. How had he become so lost again? And why did he think he had the right to judge others when he was so flawed?

This woman who he had driven from his church hadn't deserved his angry words or thoughts. She was behaving true to her nature and he was the one at fault for not remaining true to his. Or perhaps that was the problem? His nature had never changed. He was still that sinner who needed to atone for his sins. He wasn't such a youth that he hadn't understood the repercussions of his actions then or now.

Praying hadn't been enough. He needed someone to guide him back to the path he wanted to take. The path God wanted him to take. He needed to find a man of God who could minister to him and help him understand himself. Keep him on the path of the Lord.

The next afternoon, Rebecca went to Miss Lily's with a satchel and as always, her medical bag. Miss Lily had invited Rebecca to use the big copper bathtub located in the room off the kitchen. The cowhands sometimes paid Miss Lily for a bath, sometime supervised and sometimes not, depending on the need. But Rebecca wasn't going to look a gift-horse in the mouth as they say. She hadn't had a real bath since she left Callie's and she was going to enjoy herself with a long, long soak.

Rapping lightly on the front door, Miss Lily opened it for her. The older lady was dressed as neatly as ever as was both Lacy and Stella. They had been having tea and invited Rebecca to have some with cookies, which she accepted. After several cookies and two cups of tea the women decided to get out their tatting and embroidery and Rebecca headed to the back of the house where the water had been heating.

After filling the tub and adding bath salts, Rebecca submerged herself into the luxurious scented bubbles laying against the slanted back of the tub. She closed her eyes and lay there till she almost fell asleep. Opening her eyes, she blinked trying to wake herself when she saw movement above her.

Rebecca laughed out loud when she saw herself, open-mouthed, pink from the hot water and naked. A mirror suspended over the tub on the ceiling made Rebecca think all sorts of erotic and interesting thoughts. No wonder the men paid to bathe here. Rebecca herself made a definitely sensual picture and she was far from sexy.

After the bath, Rebecca let the water out of the tub and cleaned everything to leave it in as pristine a condition as when she found it. It could not be said that Miss Lily didn't run a clean establishment. Miss Lily was in the parlor and Rebecca offered to pay for the bath but Miss Lily told her friends were always welcome to use the facilities. Rebecca was charmed to be thought of as a friend by this kind lady.

As Rebecca walked home, she saw Daniel come out of the rectory. She was hoping he was going to the church because he wasn't wearing his hat but he seemed to be making his way to intersect her before she could gain access and safety in her home. Rebecca sped up but so did Daniel. Other than turning around and heading back to Miss Lily's, she would have to stand and fight.

Rebecca made it to her door and pushed it open just as Daniel stepped in behind her. She turned and confronted the interloper. "Don't you think someone will see you in my house unchaperoned?"

"I'll take my chances." His response was almost a growl.

"My reputation doesn't matter, then? Why is it always about you?" she asked insultingly.

Daniel's nonplussed expression told Rebecca he had never even considered anything other than from his prospective. "Sorry, but I needed to speak with you, Mrs. Johansen."

"I think you can call me Rebecca seeing as you've had your tongue down my throat and I've had my hand down your pants," she snapped irritably, still angry at his hypocritical ways.

Daniel flushed scarlet, his ears almost steaming and his mouth tight with embarrassment, not understanding Rebecca's attack. He always thought of her as shy and submissive. He wasn't sure whom he was confronting at this point.

"I wanted to speak with you, Rebecca, about the other night. I want to apologize for my part in the situation that got out of hand. I'm willing to try again to be friends and I'm hoping you will think likewise." He looked her straight in the eyes to show his sincerity.

Rebecca counted to ten, but it didn't work, it never worked, and said with a wide smile, "Daniel, you are a stuffed shirt. You think way too highly of yourself, of your place in the world and, obviously, of your place in my life. When you can admit you are simply a man, with a man's needs, with a man's failings, I will reconsider my thoughts about you. I will not be used as part of your self-flagellation, your own private punishment for being a foolish young man. It could just as well have been you lost to the river. Would you want Donny living his life in a self-made purgatory because of it? Are you so self-centered?" she scolded him, her hands on her hips. "Quit blaming me for your lust. Until you stop thinking of me as Eve and my vagina as the apple, I refuse to have any contact with you what so ever. Are we clear?"

Daniel stood there, completely flummoxed. Rebecca's verbal attack and use of a word he hadn't heard since he was much younger had him thinking about how she saw him, how he appeared to others.

Then Jessie appeared at the still open door saying, "Becca, I need you to come with me. There's a woman having a baby and she needs someone."

Rebecca headed toward the door, bending and picking up her bag as she did so. She pushed past Daniel without saying anything more to him and followed Jessie to the buckboard. He turned it in the street and headed out of town toward the ranches.

Jessie tried to fill in as much as he knew about the woman. "She's a squaw, married to one of our men but they live in a cabin back of the range. Dave brought her in to the house but neither Emily nor Mavis has any experience and they're scared for her. They think something's wrong. I don't know…Dave is about to lose his mind she's in so much pain."

"Do you know how old she is? Does she have other children?" Rebecca asked, trying to get as much information about the mother as possible.

"She looks young, maybe a little younger than you. It's hard to tell, she was in pain and I didn't stay long. They said to go get you and I did. Dave is about forty but they've been together about a year and a half. They stay to themselves pretty much. I've seen Dave every couple of months but she never came with him. I'm not sure she speaks English but her English name is Mary."

"I've been in this position before but it makes things more difficult. Like riding a horse blindfolded, you know you're heading somewhere but you're not sure where."

Jessie pulled the lathered horses up in front of the porch of the Macgregor ranch house. Emily was there to help Rebecca in and led the way upstairs to one of the neat bedrooms. The bed had been made ready with extra towels and sheets nearby. Mavis was at the woman's head, bathing her forehead with cool water and there was more water waiting by the washstand.

The woman was young and pretty and her dark eyes were wide open. She was wearing a white nightgown which Rebecca thought belonged to one of the Macgregor wives and her long ebony hair was braided to the side of her head. Someone had given her a thick piece of rawhide to bite down on when a contraction hit which seemed to be at the same time Rebecca entered the room. Rebecca finished tying the clean apron around her waist, washed her hands and went to the foot of the bed to examine the young woman with the next contraction.

"Hello, Mary, I'm Rebecca and I'm a midwife. I have helped deliver many healthy babies and I'm going to help you deliver this one. Now I'm going to lift the sheet and see what's happening. Will that be all right?" The young woman didn't respond other than appear frightened.

Turning to Emily, Rebecca asked, "Does she know any English at all?"

Both Macgregor women shook their heads. "Is her husband the type to help, would he be able to come in and help her. I know most men don't want anything to do with this part of life."

"Mac has been holding him back on the side porch.

I'll go and ask Dave. I think he was going to do the whole thing alone but became frightened when the time came. He was worried he didn't have enough knowledge and she is completely innocent according to him," Emily said as she stood.

"Go get him. I need him to explain what is happening to her. If he can't then at least his being here may calm her," said Rebecca pulling what she needed from her bag.

Mavis smiled saying, "Here's your warning. Mac will definitely be in the room when his child is born, no matter what anyone says to the contrary. And this was before Seth had talked about his son's birth. I never saw a happier father than Seth. I hope Jamie responds as well."

"So, you are expecting? Do you know when?" Rebecca asked while waiting for the father-to-be.

"It will have to be a guess. Jamie and I anticipated our wedding by a couple of weeks and I've never been regular, so it's going to be a surprise," Mavis said calmly while wetting the cloth again and wiping the young woman's forehead.

"Let me know when you want my services but we should get together soon and then we may be able to get a better idea. The closer it gets to the birth the closer we can set the probable date."

A tall, lean man came through the door and hesitated slightly before going to the head of the bed opposite Mavis. His hair was long enough to brush his broad shoulders and serious brown eyes took in everything in the room before settling on his wife's face, already showing weariness.

Bending, he whispered words unrecognizable to

Rebecca and the young woman responded by tilting her head toward him, turning slightly in the bed as if to take refuge in him. Rebecca was reassured she had done the right thing to bring the husband into the birthing room.

"Can you tell her I'm going to have to check her physically during the next contraction, the next pain?" Rebecca instructed the worried husband.

He nodded, and said, "I can do that. Is this all normal? I didn't know she would be in so much pain. I can't lose her. It took me so long to find her." He whispered more words to his wife that had no meaning to Rebecca.

The young woman grabbed hold of her husband's hand and started to squeeze. Rebecca told the husband not to squeeze back or he could break his wife's fingers. Men, this man at least, was so much larger and stronger than his wife, his squeezing would be too powerful.

He nodded in understanding and allowed his wife to squeeze his hand as the pain built and Rebecca checked the progress of the contraction, which was good, probably a few more hours though.

"She's doing fine. The baby is in position and the contractions are doing their job. She can have sips of water. We don't want her dehydrated and she's been sweating out her fluids with this labor. Is this her first child?" she asked getting some basics down before the birth.

"Yes, this is her first and maybe her last," he said seriously.

"Everyone thinks that during this part of the process but don't make up your minds, yet. She looks healthy and strong and so far, there isn't any reason to think she won't deliver this child safely."

Mavis said, "I'll leave you, unless you need me? Can I get anyone anything, tea or coffee?"

"I will need a large pot of water, boiled for five minutes and then cooled. I'll take it later if that's all right?" she asked Mavis as she left.

"Dave, if you'll feel more comfortable out of the room, I think I will be able to handle things from here," Rebecca offered.

"No, I wanted to be up here all along. I'll stay out of the way but Mary's frightened and I'm the only one she knows. She's here because of me and I need to know what's going on. It was driving me mad down there not knowing how she was doing." He brushed back his wife's hair sticking to her damp brow, his concern evident, his love more so.

"I'm afraid it's going to take a while. Tell your wife what you think she can handle knowing but it will be maybe four to five more hours of this with the contractions getting closer and closer together. When they are almost constant then I'll have her help by pushing and resting between contractions. The baby's presenting properly so now it's up to Mother Nature. Keep reminding her to breath, the first thing women do is hold their breath when in pain. That's not good during a birth so you need to remind her."

Dave nodded, another man not fond of talking and murmured softly to his wife. Mary didn't seem afraid any longer and Rebecca was glad to know the couple had a loving relationship with one another. That wasn't always the case with these kinds of marriages. Mostly the man simply wanted an outlet for his male needs and in an area where white women were scarce, took an Indian squaw, most of the time not formalizing the union. Rebecca noticed that Mary wore a wedding band.

Mary had fallen asleep and Rebecca let her rest. Dave was still by her side and Rebecca needed to know more about these two people. "Have you chosen a name for the baby?"

Dave looked up surprised to realize she was still in the room. "No. It is custom to wait until the baby is born and then the name will come to you when you see the child and raise it to the sky."

"That's a lovely custom," said Rebecca.

"Mary's real name is Snow Bird because she was born on a day that had one of the fiercest snowstorms, and everything was covered with several feet of snow." He looked lovingly upon his sleeping wife. "She wanted an English name, a Christian name to put in the register when we got married. She remembered a priest coming through her village and telling them about Mary and Jesus. She decided that was the name she wanted, too. It had a reason behind it, not just some random name given to her like they do at the missions."

Rebecca tried not to think about Daniel, but asked, "Were you married in Sweetwater, then?"

"No, most churches don't want to be associated with a marriage like ours. I didn't even ask. I knew of an old Catholic priest who had worked with the tribes for years and he was happy to perform the ceremony. Said more men should stand up and marry the squaws they were living with. I made sure he realized it was different with me and Mary. We were a couple, destined to be together, and I cherish every day I get to be beside her," he told Rebecca earnestly.

Rebecca was touched by his openness knowing this was not a normal conversation for him. He was worried and gave his emotions free rein while he waited for his wife to go through more pain. A contraction woke Mary out of her sound sleep and she looked with wide eyes at her husband who talked her through it, reminding her to breathe, reminding her that it would be over and then they would have a healthy child.

Rebecca didn't need to understand the words to understand their meaning. When Mary was back resting, Rebecca told Dave he should take a break now because it was going into the last couple of hours and things were going to get busy.

Dave whispered something into his wife's ear and kissed her on her forehead before standing and leaving the room. He was back in less than half an hour, hair combed back and looking refreshed. He sat in the chair next to his wife's head and took her hand in his.

As Rebecca had thought, the final hour seemed like one long contraction. Mary bore her pain with a modicum of sound, biting down on the rawhide when the contraction was at its maximum. Dave was by her side urging her to breathe, soothing her as the contraction released its hold on her.

Finally, Rebecca could tell Mary to push and then there was a newborn crying, a boy, cradled between his mother's legs as Rebecca cut the cord. She wrapped the baby in a small blanket and laid the blanketed baby into Mary's arms. Mary immediately offered her breast to her child, no unneeded modesty, no shy glances at her husband. Dave continued to gaze on both his wife and child with a wide smile and the softest expression in his eyes Rebecca had ever witnessed.

The infant nuzzled then opened his mouth before latching onto the nipple that had been presented to him, suckling lustily. Rebecca smiled at how nature reminds us we were not always humans living with all these written rules of what is and what isn't proper behavior, who can and cannot marry, who can and cannot live free. Rebecca returned to her duties and began the clean-up before bathing the baby and caring for the mother.

CHAPTER 9

Rebecca found herself in the midst of a family dinner, Mac and Emily, Jamie and Mavis and, of course, Jessie. Dave had chosen to eat up-stairs with his new family. The food was marvelous as she knew it would be with Emily cooking and the dessert was divine furnished by the fine hands of Mavis. This was also the night Mavis told the family she would be a mother within the next seven months. Jessie caught Rebecca's gaze and winked as she covered her laugh with her napkin.

Rebecca caught a look pass between Mac and Emily but they didn't say anything except to act excited and congratulate the new parents-to-be. Maybe they were counting the months since their wedding and figuring out things or maybe they, like Jessie, had already figured out that Mavis was pregnant. Either way, it became a much happier dinner and they sat out on the porch late into the evening talking.

The next morning, after a very good breakfast of eggs Benedict, sausage, and biscuits with honey, Rebecca went over everything with Dave about what to look for and what to expect again. He wanted to take his new family back to their cabin as soon as possible but promised to bring Mary and his son into town in six weeks or so for a check-up. Rebecca made sure he would let someone know if there were problems and Mary couldn't be brought into town. Rebecca would come to them if need be.

As Jessie drove her back home, she asked, "Did you ever get the stupid thing you did fixed?"

"I think so. Beth, you know, Mary Elizabeth out at the Harrison ranch, is making my life hell. I was just sort of flirting with both of the Marys to begin with. You know me, I wasn't serious or trying anything. Callie or Seth would take me apart if I touched either one of the Marys. Anyway, I found I really like Beth but she has sided with Mary Margaret. Now neither of them will talk to me. Even Callie has been cool to me and I'm not sure how to go back and make it right," he admitted to his lone female friend.

"I would say you need to tell the truth. What you just told me. If I were you, I'd start with Callie. If you can't convince her, you're never going to get the Marys to agree to talk with you," Rebecca told him remembering the two orphans Callie had brought from New York to begin a new life in Kansas. They both were sweet girls who had been through a lot and had helped Callie with the baby after Warren was born.

"Callie, huh? I think Seth would be easier, being a man, he'd understand better," Jessie told her.

"No, it has to be Callie. Even Seth will follow Callie's lead in this. She's the law when it comes to the Marys. I saw that while I was there after her baby's birth."

"I know you're right. I was just trying to make this easy," he said on a deep sigh.

"It's never easy." And neither Jessie nor Rebecca was sure what she was referring to.

Rebecca was thankful when she saw her own little house again. It seemed like so long since she had spent a night in her own bed. She didn't want to remember the confrontation between Daniel and her in the parlor. Perhaps she could start another page in her life and simply be the midwife, living on the fringe of town, the fringe of people's lives. There when she's needed, but never a real part of anything. Rebecca went inside while Jessie turned the wagon in the street and drove away, lost in his own thoughts.

Spending a little time getting settled, she really wished she had Abby to talk with. Abby always seemed to see things as they were. Rebecca was too emotional, too angry at Daniel for failing to be what she wanted him to be - but was that fair? Daniel never meant to mislead her. He simply wasn't knight-in-shining-armor material. But then again, she wasn't a lonely princess locked up in a tower. Or perhaps that's exactly what she was.

Rebecca woke up as dusk was falling. She never fell asleep sitting up but there she was, still sitting on the sofa and the day gone. She hadn't slept much the night before. All these late nights and worry were beginning to take their toll. She looked over at the church and rectory but there were no lights on so either Daniel wasn't home or he had already retired for the evening. Rebecca told herself she didn't care either way.

Well, it was too late to visit Miss Lily. If the ladies had patrons, they would be there at this time of night and wouldn't expect to run into the midwife. It might affect business poorly.

Rebecca tried to embroidery but the light seemed too weak tonight so she switched to knitting but she was too fidgety for that. Reading bits of *Moby Dick* and then *Frankenstein* were both dismal failures at keeping her attention for more than a few minutes. She looked over at the rectory to find the house still dark. This was going to be a long night so she decided to bake cookies.

In the morning after another short nap, Rebecca sat

in her kitchen eating cookies and drinking tea. A short rap on her door and a female voice called out. Abby, looking radiant and splendid in a very stylish outfit and new hat Rebecca was sure Abby hadn't created, came in carrying a baby dressed just as splendidly. She wasn't sure how her friend always looked so stunning and noted the larger than usual bustle and ornate waterfall effect of the material along the sides. She also realized that spending time with Abby had made her more aware of materials and how they drape and hang. She laughed at her own conceit at knowing this information when two months ago she had no idea of what was fashionable versus merely affordable.

"Oh, Abby, you're back. I'm so glad to see you and just look at the baby, she's grown so much, I swear," Rebecca said getting up to greet her friend with a hug and kiss on a cheek.

"Rebecca, meet your niece, Grace St. Michaels. Grace, this is your Aunt Rebecca," said Abby joyfully.

"Oh, you finally named her. I think it's perfect," enthused Rebecca.

"I wanted to wait until she was really mine, well, ours. Matthew is part of the family, too, of course. I'm so fortunate. I can't believe all this has happened so quickly." Her lovely friend smiled broadly evidently unable to keep the show of happiness off her face. "I never dared believe I would ever have a family."

Rebecca was happy merely watching her friend's animated face as she related their trip to make Grace part of their family and then setting up Lucy with a safe haven. The young girl had seemed very grateful to both Abby and Matthew and pledged to stay in contact with them.

The newly married couple stopped by to see the friend with the dress shop in St. Louis where Abby used to work. The woman who helped Abby make a new start after she lost her baby and was denounced by her parents. And, of course, she showed off Grace to everyone and anyone who came within a yard of her, Abby unabashedly disclosed.

Rebecca's head was reeling trying to keep up with Abby's regaling of the past few days. She offered tea and cookies when Abby had finally stopped to take a breath.

"No, tea tastes off to me, real bitter so I stopped drinking it. Coffee is worse," Abby said smiling down on the baby laying face up on her knees. She made cooing noises trying to coax more smiles from her daughter.

"Cookies then?" She held out the plate offering the tasty looking confections.

Abby peered at the delicate crisp cookies wrinkling her nose saying, "No thanks. Matthew thinks I'm getting fat so I'll skip them this time."

"Did Matthew really say you were fat?" Rebecca was about to get hold of Matthew and give him a piece of her mind for making her friend self-conscious of her weight which hadn't seemed an ounce more than when Rebecca had first met her.

"Not really. When he first came back, he said my, umm, my breasts were larger. And he told me to stop cinching my corset so tight, it was leaving marks, but I don't fit into some of my dresses if I don't cinch it tighter."

She again cooed down at the infant trying to get Grace to smile, just a little smile. "Matthew can get this baby to smile but she doesn't for me. Simply stares and stares into my eyes as if she sees something there, I don't see. I don't know what he does differently," Abby complained.

Rebecca asked boldly. "Abby, when was your last menses?"

Abby stopped playing with the baby and drew her brows together in thought, "Well, before Grace was born, I know that. No, it was before Matthew went away. I thought how perfectly timed when he came to visit, I was free to be with him." She blushed but then smiled remembering that last visit before they were married.

"Abby, do you think you could be with child?" asked Rebecca.

"No, oh, no. I was so sick with my son. I couldn't even look at certain foods and they started tasting funny, like an iron fry pan or something." An expression that went from fear to awe appeared on her friend's face. "Oh, Rebecca, could I be expecting Matthew's child? But I was told I could never have another baby. A doctor told me," Abby said with conviction.

"Well, I've delivered many babies that weren't supposed to have been conceived and yet there they were. I can check and we'll know now, or we can wait and time will tell," offered Rebecca.

"Where can I lay Grace down? I want to know right now," Abby said quickly.

After a brief time, Abby was redressing and said, "How am I to explain this to Matthew?"

"I would think he knows how it happened so what else is there to explain?" teased Rebecca.

"I mean, I practically forced him into marrying me so we could adopt Grace and now I'm going to saddle him with another? What will people think when they see me with Grace and waddling down the street ready to burst?" asked Abby sounding worried about the future.

"Matthew will swing you up into his arms and kiss you thoroughly or he isn't the romantic I think he is. Remember he said he wanted so many children one woman wouldn't be able to have them all. And don't worry about what other people think. They call them Irish twins where I come from." At Abby's confused expression went on to explain, "You know, babies born less than a year apart. Matthew's Catholic, he understands about these things."

"Oh, Rebecca, you are going to have to come home with me and help me tell him," Abby groaned.

"I won't do that but I'll take Grace for the night and you can tell him in your own way," Rebecca offered, eager to take care of the infant. Hoping her friend was going to let her have Grace overnight.

Picking Grace up, Abby held her close. "No thanks. This may be easier holding Grace and appearing Madonna-like. I can't believe it. You don't think I'll lose this baby, too, do you?" she asked worriedly, dark memories haunting her eyes.

"There is no reason to suppose you won't carry to full term. You're healthy, you're not spotting as you said you did with the first and you're not a worried, stressed unmarried girl. Don't worry about what might happen. Enjoy the moment now and we'll deal with any complications if they come."

"I know. It's all so new to me. Being a mother and now becoming a mother. I really couldn't be happier." She hugged Rebecca goodbye as she left blushing with excitement.

"I couldn't be happier for you."

Looking out the window, Rebecca saw a buggy in front of the church. She didn't recognize it as belonging to one of the usual parishioners. As she stood there, Daniel and a priest in dark robes came out of the building, shook hands, and then the priest climbed into the buggy and drove away from town.

Rebecca stepped back. She didn't think Daniel could see her in the dark house but didn't want to get caught staring just in case. She was starting to see her new life take shape and she was content being Grace's aunt and soon aunt to another of Abby's babies. She would visit Abby and Miss Lily and there will be others. She was becoming friends with the Macgregor's and knew Julia and Callie well enough to feel comfortable going to their homes for dinner or visits.

Sweetwater was really becoming much more than she had thought it would. A husband would be nice but there was time. She was barely twenty-one, plenty of time to find a husband and start a family. She had to be in less of a hurry. Live for the moment as she had advised Abby to do.

The next afternoon, Rebecca was sitting in the swing in the back yard under the leafy tree. She had begun to bring her embroidery outside in the cooler shade where there was some chance of a breeze. She felt him there before he said anything and stiffened when she heard his voice.

"I had a talk with Father Manuel. He came by to ask to use the church for the Harrison baby's Christening next weekend. He said I was being foolish, trying to set myself above the people I serve, the God I serve. He reminded me I was a 'man of the cloth' and that the word 'man' came first for a reason."

Rebecca wasn't sure she wanted to hear this but was curious what more he had to say. "He told me he has to think about his commitment to the Church daily because he is tempted daily to break his vow of celibacy. He said men have these urges, these needs to ensure that the human race continues and I've been trying to make those needs a sin although they're not. Not for me and not for you. 'God's purpose was for man and woman to be united, to become one flesh.' I was denying His purpose by denying my feelings for you." Daniel's words were like a prayer.

"I had hubris, thinking I could dictate my feelings or blame you for them. Not taking responsibility for my own decisions. God gave man the ability to make choices, God gave man free will. And Father Manuel reminded me of the passage, 'Heal me O Lord and I shall be healed, save me, and I shall be saved'. I'm sorry, Rebecca. You were right about me taking myself too seriously. I am just a man, with all the failings and mistakes that man makes."

Now she was glad she had stayed. Not that what he said made her feel better but she felt vindicated hearing Daniel admit he thought her correct in her estimation of him.

"I don't expect you to forgive me for hurting you when you deserved none of my wrath and I am praying for His forgiveness for using the pulpit to punish you when it was I who I meant to punish. If there is a punishment due, it is up to God. I'm only his messenger and not meant to be more."

Rebecca had stopped her embroidering but had not looked up, still tense, trying to keep from running into the house and locking the doors. She didn't want Daniel to know he still had an effect on her, that his speaking with her was painful.

He continued, "I'm asking you to give me a chance to show you how I feel. I have true emotions for you and I would like to court you if you could see me in that way."

She would need to reflect upon her feelings about this admission and answered softly, "I will have to think on it."

"How will I know when you make a decision?" He hesitated a moment, then finished, "Will you put a lighted lantern on your porch to let me know I'm welcome? I don't want to keep bothering you if you decide you can't accept my apology or if you can't think of me as a husband."

Rebecca nodded silently, not trusting her voice not to break. She could feel the tightening in her throat.

"Thank you, Rebecca, that is all I can hope for." He walked quietly away, back to the rectory.

Another disturbed night of sleep. Rebecca tossed and turned trying to find a cool place on the sheets to lay. There wasn't a bit of breeze and the night insects kept up a constant buzz. The worry over Daniel didn't help her find any comfort on her once soothing sheets, either.

CHAPTER 10

Rebecca made her way to Abby's shop hoping to catch her alone but both Grace and Matthew were there, as well. Matthew hugged her in welcome and explained he had taken a buggy out to Callie's the day before to see his new nephew.

"They're doing fine, by the way, and Callie's trying to talk Seth into bringing them to town to meet Grace. He's still very protective of them both. I just came down to get Grace and take her upstairs for her nap so Abby can rest." He bent to take his daughter from his wife.

"You're taking her up there to play on the floor with her. I can sometimes hear you laughing you're having so much fun while I'm left down here working." Then his wife waved him off. "Just go upstairs. Rebecca and I will spend some time gossiping."

Once Matthew was out of the room, Abby said, "Out with it. You were holding something back yesterday but you threw me so much with my pregnancy, I was distracted from your problems. Has it to do with the handsome and highly attractive Reverend Walters?"

"In a way." Now the time to share her worries had arrived, she felt shy of how it would all sound. "Well, I guess he's at the center of everything. He has been very attentive and one evening we, I, no, we got carried away and went past polite chit-chat." With Abby's raised eyebrows, Rebecca hurried on, "No, not that carried away but there was passion and hands and well, he left and I thought everything was going to be all right between us."

At Abby's encouraging nod Rebecca went on, quieter now that she had to say the words out loud. "During church service, he started saying all sorts of hurtful, dreadful things and I thought everyone there knew they were about me."

As Abby's brows lowered in anger, Rebecca continued, "He was talking about all the women in the Bible who had caused men of God to leave their righteous path. That women brought the downfall of man, that women were the devil's handmaidens. I have never heard him preach that way. Hell, and damnation to sinners and fornicators." Shaking her head, she finished, "It was simply awful."

"Oh, Rebecca, I wished I had been there to support you and to hit the good reverend over his head with the biggest Bible I could get hold of. How dare he say those things no matter what happened between you. I hate hypocrites, he is always so holier than thou, when in fact he's just a pri...."

"Don't say it, Abby or I will not be able to stop myself thinking it and I'll end up saying it out loud when I should not." Rebecca said, thankful she had such a good friend to come to her defense without hesitation. "Anyway, he has apologized, said he was wrong and what he feels for me is real."

"And what did he say he feels for you?" asked Abby suspiciously.

"I don't know for sure. He mentioned he was willing to be my husband and that basically he lusted after me. The priest, Father Manuel, told him it was all right, to lust that is, after anyone. I don't know what I think. I thought the reverend and I were friends and we liked each other but nothing beyond that until that one night,"

Susan Payne

Rebecca said sadly.

"I say, give him a wide berth. I plan on completely ignoring him if we run across one another. I don't like men who don't realize what a jewel they have right in front of them. And he hurt you. I'll never forgive him for that, Rebecca," Abby said fiercely.

"I don't think he deserves your scorn. He seemed sincere in his apology but I hesitate to find myself in any position where he can get near me. I don't want to go to church or even see him in the street. I wanted you to know and have you listen to my problems before I did something stupid."

"Oh, Rebecca, being in love is never stupid. We can't help who we love but we are the only ones to know what we can do or do without. Life is a lot more fun with someone you love beside you and only you know if the reverend is that 'one'." Abby got up and hugged Rebecca.

"I'm so glad you are back." A tear rolled down Rebecca's face.

Rebecca returned home with a lighter heart. Abby had been a good friend, listening and then defending Rebecca and condemning Daniel. It helped Rebecca make a decision to ignore Daniel's request. She didn't need a man who was so unsure of himself and his emotions. There were plenty of men in the territory and she hadn't met very many of them. There was time yet to find a husband.

The Reverend Walters was standing next to the sign in the churchyard and raised his hand in greeting when Rebecca got to her home but she pretended not to see him. Turning, she went up the front steps to her porch entering through the front door. She peeked to see if he was coming across the road but he had turned away and was going into the church. Good, Rebecca thought, he got my message! Then she went into her room and fell sobbing onto the bed.

The next morning, Jessie stopped by to drive her out to see Mavis for a medical check-up and have luncheon. Emily and Mavis welcomed her warmly and spent a little time passing information along from Callie and Julia and their two healthy growing offspring.

Rebecca filled her notepad with the information she always gathered on her new mothers and then enjoyed a very extensive meal. Mac, in his stocking feet, and Jessie wearing shoes, joined the ladies adding to the affable conversation. Well, at least Jessie did.

Mac smiled at some of the remarks but added little to the actual conversation. He then got up, kissed his wife and thanked the ladies for a fine meal before disappearing back into an office by the front door.

Jessie offered to take Rebecca back to town and she decided it was time to leave the two married women. The buckboard was brought around and Rebecca made her goodbyes. She was still smiling as she got into the seat next to Jessie as he said, "I'm glad to see you a little happier. I was missing you."

"I'm sorry. I didn't know I was letting it show," Rebecca told her friend.

"Well, at least you're not trying to pretend everything is fine. You admit you're not happy and face up to it," he said evidently speaking of another person who was not being open with her feelings.

"You're still having problems, too, I take it?" Leading him away from thinking too closely on her problems and who may be causing them.

"Yep. I'm still being yanked from one end of the emotional line to another. I'm getting to the point I may have to move on, move back to the city and try to forget Beth," he confessed.

"Do you think you can do that? Move on, I mean, knowing she's right there at Callie's?"

"I'm not sure. That's why I'm still here, I guess," he admitted with a smile.

"Me, too." And she smiled in commiseration.

Once Jessie dropped Rebecca off at home, she got tired of looking over at the rectory and church every few minutes. Instead, she decided to walk to Abby's to see and talk with her good friend. They didn't have as much time together but Rebecca liked Matthew immensely and, of course, always had time to play with baby Grace. She was glad to be accepted as Aunt Rebecca and besides, she wanted to keep tabs on Abby's pregnancy.

She opened the door to the friendly little chiming bell and called out to Abby. Abby came through the curtained doorway, smiling and holding a grinning Grace. Rebecca took the baby immediately, saying, "I just got back from visiting with Emily and Mavis. They send you their best and will be in for new dresses to cover a growing condition. Mavis says she has given up the corset and her newer dresses aren't very forgiving."

"Speaking of dress sizes, I've noticed yours are getting loser around the waist. Are you cinching your corset tighter?" Abby asked her friend.

"No, I'm not wearing the full corset since I was on a medical visit and it makes it difficult to do a check-up if I am unable to bend at the waist." Rebecca explained. "I'm not about to try to deliver a baby wearing anything that prohibits full movement."

"Come over here." Abby grabbed her cloth tape measure and then proclaimed, "You are a full three inches smaller. I can always tell! I'm one of the first to tell a woman she's expecting but I missed it when it came to my own waist." Abby laughed at her own ignorance.

"You had other things on your mind." And then Rebecca was thinking for a moment. "I'm eating the same amounts, maybe even more since everyone tries to feed me but I am walking more. There was no town or neighbors within walking distance where I lived before. I stayed at home or delivered babies - not too many ways to exercise. I guess this is merely a side effect of being in an active town."

"Well, I don't think it is going to work for me for a while. Matthew won't let me do anything and he's watching me like a hawk since he knows about my first child," Abby told her friend.

"I'm glad he's being conscientious. He cares for you so much. I think it's beautiful. You are truly blessed but I think you know that."

Rebecca and Abby talked for a few more minutes and then Grace and Abby started yawning. "You both need your nap. I'll come and visit again in a day or two. I need to get in my walks it seems." Rebecca left the sleepy couple to their rest.

Still hesitant to return home, Rebecca thought she would stop in to Miss Lily's on her way. It was early enough the men wouldn't be in from the ranches, yet. As she was about to turn down the street, Rebecca saw a man on Miss Lily's porch. It took Rebecca another glance to realize the man was Daniel. She quickly changed direction and made her way home, frantically trying to think what Daniel was doing at Miss Lily's.

Pacing her parlor, Rebecca finally came to the conclusion Daniel was visiting Miss Lily for the same thing other men visited the house and it wasn't for the freshly baked cookies. Rebecca was trying to decide what that meant. Was he finally admitting he was a man with a man's needs? Or would he berate Miss Lily and Stella and Lacy in the sermon next Sunday? He wouldn't be that unkind, would he?

Miss Lily and the two ladies were not evil or corruptors. Should she go and speak with Miss Lily? Warn her just in case so she could decide whether to attend services or not. Rebecca saw Daniel on the street in front of his rectory and made her decision.

Miss Lily was surprised to see Rebecca at her door but welcomed her warmly. "Come in, dear. This is a pleasant surprise. You appear worried. Is there something I can help you with?"

"I'm not sure how to say this. I saw the Reverend leaving earlier," she confessed.

Miss Lily smiled and said, "He was simply visiting, having tea and cookies." At Rebecca's dubious expression, continued, "No, really dear. He came to say the church was getting an organ and he knows I can play. He wanted to ask me to be the church organist during services and at weddings and funerals if the folks want. He thought it would be nice if I did a solo hymn each Sunday. You know, to get the congregation in the singing mood. I agreed, of course." She smiled a little shyly.

"I'm, ah, I'm glad. I was afraid he came to preach at you or something," Rebecca confessed relieved to know Daniel hadn't hurt the older woman's feelings.

"No, he was as pleasant and mannerly as always."

Miss Lily stopped and thought before continuing, "I know you were affronted for me when the reverend went on his sermon of sin and retribution but I assure you I didn't take it personally. I've heard much worse in my time and that was the first occasion the reverend has ever given that kind of sermon. Something, or someone, must have had him riled up about sinning. He's been as considerate as always toward me and my ladies since then."

"I'm glad, as I said. I thought the sermon was uncalled for," admitted Rebecca.

"I've noticed you've been absent from the pews since that Sunday. Don't let worry over my feelings keep you from attending church service, dear."

"If I've been missing services it certainly has nothing to do with you, Miss Lily," Rebecca said truthfully.

"I would offer you tea but it is getting late. You usually visit earlier. There may be other visitors at any time. I wouldn't want anyone to get a poor impression simply because you have befriended me," she said trying not to appear rude or unhospitable.

"I understand, Miss Lily. I'll be on my way. I may come to a Sunday service simply to enjoy your beautiful voice." She hugged the surprised lady and then left, not meeting anyone on the way home.

Rebecca was standing on her porch, an unlit lantern in her hand, indecisive. She wasn't sure she could trust Daniel, but she hadn't spoken to him in days and what he was doing for Miss Lily was very kind. Accepting her for who she was, accepting that she had something to offer the congregation, accepting that the differences of people's lives did not preclude their similarity.

"Do you need a light?" offered a deep voice that had Rebecca gazing down shyly. "I've been watching you waver as to whether or not to light that lantern and I couldn't stay away any longer. Do you want me to leave?" Daniel asked, hope for her to answer in the negative bright in his eyes.

"No, I don't think so. It's difficult for me to accept that you have changed your opinions. You have held them for so long."

"I never meant to hold on to those old feelings and demons. I actually thought I had grown up, grown into a more mature person who didn't judge anyone. Instead, I find I was the most judgmental of men. It took me much meditation and talking to Father Manuel for me to understand who I am now," he told her earnestly.

"I'm glad for you. You sound as if you found peace with yourself. That isn't always easy."

"I found I was denying myself a life for no reason. I can minister to the congregation as well as love my wife and family." He looked at Rebecca, pleading with his eyes for her understanding.

"I'm glad for you, as I said."

"Rebecca, I love you. I think I always have. What I confused with lust was my physical attraction to you because I love you. It's not dirty or wrong or sinful. I became confused by my strong desire for you to be mine, to become my wife. Jealousy got in my way, as well. I wanted to lash out at you, drive you away so I didn't need to think too much about my emotions but it was wrong of me." He seemed to search for the words he wanted. "I also hated seeing you with any other man. It didn't matter who or when. I blamed those feelings on you when it was due to my inability to admit I was like any other man. I wasn't above the rest and that fear of failing, of finding myself as I used to be frightened me."

"I don't know, Daniel. I have conflicting feelings myself. I don't have these feelings with other men, I really don't. I don't know what they mean."

"Are they like what you had with your husband?" Daniel asked.

Rebecca's stomach sunk. She had never told Daniel the truth. "I have a confession. I've never been married. My mother, well both my parents, thought it would be best if someone as young as me were thought of as having been married. I mean who's going to listen to an unmarried woman? Consult with them about marital relations? I didn't think it would matter. Several people know the truth now that I've gotten established but by then everyone else thought of me as a widow and it really didn't seem to change things."

"So, you don't know if you have feelings that someday may grow into love for me?" he asked slowly.

"You don't care that I lied? That I've let people think I'm a widow?"

"It wasn't meant to hurt anyone. You did what you thought you had to do to help the women of Sweetwater. I think we can ignore a white lie."

Amazed at the change in Daniel, Rebecca smiled at him for the first time and then something snapped between them. Daniel took the two steps up to stand in front of Rebecca, to pull her gently into his arms, giving her the chance to back away if she wanted. She did not want.

"Oh, Rebecca, I am just a man and I need you so very, very much. I am so afraid you will leave Sweetwater, leave me. Every time I heard of a new expectant mother, I thanked God because I knew you wouldn't leave someone in need. Each new mother allowed me another chance, more time to get you to forgive me, love me and marry me." He kissed Rebecca's head, hoping she wouldn't bolt.

"I think I could do that, Daniel." She smiled up at him, knowing what she felt for this man now. She loved him. A man who made mistakes, searched for help and found that help to become a better man. She loved that about him. He would never fail her again. He would take responsibility upon his own shoulders, search deeply inside himself for any needed change.

Daniel led her into the darkened parlor saying, "I think we may have scandalized the neighbors enough. I want a little privacy while I show you how much I desire you."

In a teasing tone Rebecca asked, "Don't you mean lust after me?"

"That, too. It's all part of my love for you. I will always cherish you, our love for each other, and our life together," he told her earnestly. "Are you sure enough of me, of yourself, that I can ask Father Manuel to perform the wedding service for us? I don't want to rush you but I want our first joining to be as a married couple. Is that all right or am I being a prude?"

"No, I don't think that makes you a prude, merely staying loyal to your beliefs. I want to be a married woman when I commit to you physically, also," she whispered.

Daniel kissed his bride-to-be with the desire and passion that a man shows toward his beloved. He spent as long as he thought he could and went as far as he thought he should to show her what their life together could be like. She would not worry they were incompatible, not after he had to pull himself away and leave her to her chaste bed.

The ceremony was held the next afternoon. There were plenty of flowers and ferns decorating the pulpit of the church. Candles added to the glow of happiness on the bride and groom's faces. Word travelled quickly and the pews were well filled, everyone amazed at the quick turn of events. No one knew there had been a budding romance between the couple although every one could see they were in love.

The bride wore the altered plaid travelling dress she arrived in Sweetwater wearing. The new style and purple color much more complimentary to her new slender form. The groom wore his best Sunday suit without the cleric's collar.

Miss Lily played the new organ while Rebecca made her way down the aisle to her impatient groom. Then Miss Lilly sang a lovely song of love found and love cherished. A song requested by the groom. Father Manuel performed the non-Catholic wedding service and then proudly told the groom he could kiss the bride.

Abby, Matthew and Grace attended as well as Miss Lily, Lacy and Stella. Jessie had heard about the wedding and brought the two Marys, as well as Emily and Mac. Jamie stayed home with Mavis who was still fighting morning sickness.

After standing at the front door and accepting everyone's good wishes and a chaste kiss from each man, Rebecca exhaled a deep breath. Her first realization that she was truly a married woman and wife, well not completely but she would be soon, she was sure of it.

They all went to the rectory where a wedding cake

sent by Callie waited decorated with roses and vines. There was Champaign furnished by Matthew and cookies and tea brought by Miss Lily and her ladies. It was a festive celebration and Rebecca realized how fortunate she was to have made such good friends in so short a time. She had secretly hoped to find a husband but she was specially blessed to have found so many friends as well.

Everyone had left. The dishes were washed and put away by an ever-helpful Miss Lily and her ladies and the last of the Champaign filled two glasses in front of the couple sitting on the long sofa.

"Now that we are together and we are married, I don't know how to go on from here. Any suggestions?" Daniel asked with humility. "I worship you. I want everything for you but I have no experience with that. I was young and immature and I only knew the one part of sexual joining. I never made love."

"I'm not sure either. I love you. I want to be with you, joined with you but I don't know how. I think going to the bedroom, undressing and getting into the bed are probably the best ways to begin," Rebecca offered her thoughts on the matter.

"That sounds like a good idea, Beloved. Let me help you. That I can do right, I think," he said kissing his bride until she leaned limpet-like against him. Then he stood, lifting her to carry her into his once bachelor bedroom.

Pulling the cover down, he exposed the embroidered sheets and Daniel smiled admitting Abby had brought them over that morning as a wedding gift. Rebecca smiled, too, knowing Abby did so merely to embarrass Daniel. Her best friend really was going to torment him for making Rebecca feel badly.

Daniel began unbuttoning Rebecca's dress, gazing into her eyes, trying to judge if his movements were acceptable and relaxed when Rebecca began unbuttoning his shirt after removing his string tie. Smiling, he exposed more of her undergarments. The lacy corset with ribbons evidently pleased him because there was a hitch in his breath when he first saw it. He helped Rebecca take the dress off over her head and then watched fascinated as she removed the corset, watching to make sure he would know what to do next time. She had removed her shoes so she now stood in front of him wearing only her lacy combination and silk stockings.

Watching her avidly, he made short work of removing his clothing, everything but his trousers and drawers but wanting to see all of Rebecca. Daniel figured out how the combination untied and laid Rebecca on the bed to remove her stockings and then the combination leaving her naked and open for his viewing. Daniel unbuttoned his trousers and pushed everything down at one time, kneeing next to Rebecca devouring her with his eyes and then stroking the entire length of her body and back up again.

He kissed her waiting lips. Sucking her bottom lip into his mouth, he found the opening to pursue a closer joining of their bodies, his tongue instinctively imitating the thrusting and retreating of lovemaking.

"Father Manuel said what I feel for you is natural, what I want to do to you is natural, what I want you to do to me is natural," said Daniel whispering in her ear, kissing the soft skin and sucking the lobe into his warm mouth.

"What do you want me to do to you?" she asked breathlessly, wanting to please him too.

"I don't dare tell you. I'll embarrass you and myself. I spent hours thinking of us together in all ways, joined together and made as one. Please let me love you, Rebecca," he pleaded. "I think of you, your, um, apple. I really think a lot about your apple."

"And I think my apple thinks of you," she teased as she accepted his caresses there.

"After all, I'm only a man." He kissed the peak of one smooth round orb.

"Now you are using that as an excuse?"

"It's not an excuse, it's a fact. I really want to love you, to make you fully mine but I understand if you need to wait. I don't want to hurt you but I don't know what else to do besides to stop before we get to that point." He continued to attend to the eager peaks of her breasts.

"I will be fine. I trust you. We are doing this together. We will be fine together. What feels right to you?"

"I want to kiss you all over. I want you to touch me like you did before and I'm frantic to bury myself in you and send my seed into your womb." He pressed his body full length against hers, kissing her open lips once more.

"That sounds good to me," she whispered as she found his erect shaft nestled between them and felt Daniel shiver as she stroked him, explored its satiny feel, the velvety crown.

Daniel buried his face between her ample breasts and let himself feel Rebecca's every movement. "I think you better stop that, although I find it very nice, maybe too nice right now," he warned.

"I want you to join with me, become one flesh, now," said Rebecca making room for Daniel to nest between her thighs.

"I love you but if you need me to stop, I'll stop," he offered knowing this was an important step between them.

"I won't want you to stop." Then Rebecca urged Daniel to take his position as her husband, to enter her and become one with each other, forming the bond that will bind them together forever.

There was no tearing pain, just a mild sting and then Daniel was reacting by instinct and Rebecca was following his lead. She felt something deep inside, something growing and urging her to meet every push of her husband.

Daniel timed his thrusts to her little moans, made low in her throat. They nearly drove him over the edge knowing she was enjoying him. She was driving him mad knowing he was giving her such extreme pleasure as it built inside each of them. They both exploded to Rebecca's chant of "Yes, yes, yes...."

Daniel held his wife locked in his arms as they tried to steady their breathing and enjoy the aftermath together. "I don't remember anything that good. It does make a difference. Your partner, I mean. I love you and I'm rewarded for loving you. Are you all right?"

"I'm more than all right. It was more than I ever thought it would be. I even felt your seed enter me, warm me. I feel so blessed."

"No, I'm blessed. I have my Beloved and I'll never have to doubt what my fate is on this earth. I am living it now with you and with any children we bring forth," he said reverently.

Rebecca nestled into her husband's chest, saying sleepily, "I can't wait till we're able to do that again."

Her husband turned to her and began kissing her

swollen lips, coaxing her to join him in the lovemaking as he said softly, "I don't think you're going to need to wait very long."

And she didn't.

A New Face in Town

CHAPTER 1

The grandfatherly conductor helped Victoria down from the high train car. "You don't have someone meeting you, Miss? Do you know anyone in town?" He looked worriedly at the girl, hardly old enough to be called a woman, holding a flour sack containing her belongings. He continued, "I know a real nice couple here in town. Abby owns the dress shop right on the main street. Stop in and introduce yourself. She may know of a job you could get."

The young woman's sun streaked hair was pulled back from her face like a schoolgirl's and almost completely covered with the cloth poke bonnet. With expressive grey eyes and generous mouth framed by dimples, she replied, "I'm obliged for the information. I didn't intend to come this far west but 'the Good Lord will provide' my mamma always said. And so, He has." Then she smiled, those dimples deepened and her straight white teeth gleamed.

The conductor was taken back for a moment at the change it made. This girl went from plain to extraordinarily pretty with merely the change of a smile. The conductor couldn't help but smile in return and then tipped his hat and climbed back up the steps waving for the train to continue on its way.

Victoria shifted her bag from her right hand to her left, walked through the brick station's rear door and right out the front which led to the main street of

Sweetwater. Vicky had chosen this town because of its name and that it was as far as her ticket money would stretch. The name made her think of pretty lakes and streams and trees. There weren't many trees so she hoped somewhere there was a lake or at least a river named after it.

The main street was lined on both sides with painted two-story buildings, mostly having signs boasting their names and wares. There was a covered boardwalk along both sides in front of the commercial buildings. A few horses and wagons were standing in the street as the owners finished their business in town. It was clean, neat, and welcoming. She hadn't made another bad choice and she thankfully felt she could start over here.

Shifting the weight of her bag again, she set out to find the ladies' clothing shop the kind conductor had told her about. Halfway down, she saw it on the other side of the street, the window full of beautiful hats and lacy shawls. As she crossed the dusty street, she thought about what kind of work she could apply for. Growing up in rural Tennessee didn't give a young girl a lot of experience and she had no skill she could think of except hanging tobacco leaves faster than any of the others at the drying sheds.

After that, she pretty much was done with skills worth paying for. But she wasn't going to listen to the fears hiding in the recesses of her mind. Looking at the window display, she thought how plain her home-sewn dress would appear to a woman who made and sold these kinds of beautiful items.

Taking a deep breath, Victoria entered the door as a little bell chimed to announce her arrival. A beautiful woman dressed more elegantly than Victoria had ever seen close up emerged from behind a curtain, smiling. "I'm Abby, the proprietress, how may I be of service?"

"I'm Victoria Watkins and the conductor on the train suggested I should stop by and introduce myself." Then she smiled, really smiled because she felt a calm seep over her simply being in the presence of this lovely woman.

Abby hesitated. She was reevaluating this young woman, and then asked, "Did Matthew also send you? A tall good-looking man with beautiful blue eyes?"

Chuckling, she shook her head shyly. "No, ma'am, I would of remembered somebody like that."

Abby looked the girl over from head to foot and finally arriving at a conclusion, asked, "Would you like some tea? I always think better after a good cup of tea."

Just as Abby returned from the kitchen area, a baby called out from behind the curtain and Abby responded immediately, crooning to the small child. She returned with a gorgeous baby with dark brown hair and deep blue eyes. Abby introduced the baby, "This is Grace, my daughter. She is one reason I am so tired lately."

Abby laid the baby down on her back in the middle of a folded quilt but she quickly flipped onto her stomach and tried kicking her feet to make herself move forward. The two women watched the baby's antics as her hands waved and feet tried to gain purchase to push herself along.

"I think she could scoot along a wood floor but I always make sure she's on something she can't slide on. She is bound and determined to be anywhere but where I last left her." Both women enjoyed watching the baby's activity while drinking the strong sweet tea.

"Do you like children, Victoria?" Abby asked

141

watching the younger woman interact with Grace.

"Yes, ma'am. I'm the oldest of eight and I had the raisin' of most of 'em. I've had a lot of time in washing diapers and dresses, too. It was an everyday thing with so many young'uns and so few changes of clothes," she confessed happily moving her fingers to draw Grace's attention away from sucking on the quilt.

"I can imagine." Abby thought of what she had to wash for Grace and then for the new baby that was due in only a few months.

Abby was getting more and more inquisitive about Victoria so asked, "Was there a specific reason you stopped off in Sweetwater? Have you family here?"

"That's about the same thing the conductor asked me. Doesn't anyone new ever come to Sweetwater just because they want to? I just loved the name. There is a lake or something isn't there nearby?"

"There is the Sweetwater River that goes west of town and then about an hour away is a lake of sorts on the Harrison ranch and everybody goes up there to picnic. Seth, the owner, never minds," answered Abby.

"Well, that'll have to do then," said Victoria inscrutably. "I liked what I seen of the town so I hope to find a position that pays enough to cover my keep."

"Do you have experience in anything special, a skill perhaps?" asked Abby, curious as to how she could help this young woman who appeared in need.

"No, ma'am, I'm a hard worker and don't need any time off or nothin'. I'm used to working for my living and hope someone may need a home help. Or if there was a restaurant in town I don't mind doing dishes and pans all day long or laundry," she suggested in a rush. Hearing her talents out-loud made even Victoria worry about finding anyone to pay her for doing such everyday things.

"Victoria, I'm at a loss to figure out why you are here, in Sweetwater, I mean. And how you found yourself on a train with no real destination…" Abby said honestly.

"You're gonna think me all sorts of a fool or worse, Miss Abby. I answered one of them adverts in the paper for a wife. You know how men place messages looking for a woman to come out here and start a family with?" Abby felt her head nod and a sense of alarm went through her body at the young girl's words.

"I wrote back and a gentleman, no that ain't true, he weren't a gentleman. A man name of Bob Hill sent me ticket money. I had to pay for my own food and I had plenty to do that with plus a little extra. I got to the town and Bob Hill showed up at the station drunk, stinking of liquor." Victoria wrinkled her nose merely remembering the tainted smell.

Abby could see Victoria was having difficulty going on but she had to know all of it so if her husband, Matthew, had to be called she could wire him today.

"Go on, Victoria, it will actually help to put words to it. It becomes less of a burden if you let someone else carry part of it for you," Abby said softly.

"I told him to please stop touching me and he laughed saying, 'we wuz as much as married so it would be alright for him and me to go to the hotel for the night and get married the next day'. I didn't like him or his friend's that were with him. I turned around right then and asked the ticket seller where I could go with the money I had. I picked out the name of Sweetwater from the list on the board and here I am."

"I think you did the right thing. You are terribly brave and terribly smart to leave a dangerous situation. Bob Hill sounds like one of those men who prey on vulnerable women wanting a life in the territories. My husband is going to love you. He spends much of his time helping women, women who didn't take the opportunity to run when they could have, and they get into so much pain and suffering before they escape," Abby told her, disclosing Matthew's secret cause. She felt this young woman would understand Matthew's need to save others.

"I don't know if I'm brave or smart but it seemed the safest thing to do. Now I have to find a way to support myself all over again."

"There's no one back home to go to for help?" Abby asked feeling she already knew the answer.

"No, my ma died and my pa married again. The new missus wanted the house to herself. I had been doin' so long for the younger children and Pa but I understand her need to have the house to herself. Well, she, Pa, and the five kids still at home. I'm older than my ma was when she had me so its past time I should be out of the nest," she stated plainly the logic she probably used when making her decision to come west.

"May I enquire how old you are, Victoria?"

"I'm nineteen. I'll turn twenty in a few months."

"Well that's not too young to be on your own but you certainly appear younger."

"That's what Bob Hill said but he said it kind of sneaky like and the others laughed, too. I just got a queer feeling about all them fellas." Victoria couldn't prevent a shiver from going through her.

"For now, why don't I have you sleep on the cot in

the room off the fitting area. You can help take care of Grace for me so I can get some work done. I'm in an interesting condition and I get tired quickly. I am so afraid Grace will get into mischief if I fall asleep it keeps me from resting easily even with her in her crib next to me. Matthew helps when he is home but he's a salesman and travels to sell the products he represents. It would help me out for now. If we find you a better position you can take that and I'll return to watching Grace myself," Abby explained the plan to Victoria.

"Oh, Miss Abby, I wouldn't leave you in the lurch. I'm very grateful to you for allowing me to help you. I would be honored to care for little Grace. This is the age I just love. You know, watching their little faces every time they discover something new. I don't know what to say I'm so overwhelmed." Victoria wiped a tear from her eye with her gloved hand.

"You may think differently if I'm ill with morning sickness and Grace is full of spit and vinegar," Abby teased.

"I'm used to handling two to three at a time, Miss Abby. Grace and I will be just fine and she can help me with the laundry. I'll do whatever else needs doin', too. You'll need your rest. A nap every afternoon, at least," Victoria advised.

"That sounds lovely." Abby looked longingly at the curtained door.

Victoria picked up Grace and asked, "Grace's things are through here? And my cot?" At Abby's nod, the younger woman carried Grace through the curtain and Abby could hear her talking to Grace all the way.

"Oh, look baby in the mirror. Is that Grace? Is it? Wave hi to Grace, wave hi." And she laughed, as Grace must have waved.

Abby smiled and thought aloud, "Ask and thou shall receive. I needed someone to help me take care of my family - mysterious ways, mysterious ways." She turned the closed sign on the door and went to lie down to take that afternoon nap she so desperately needed.

It was almost dinnertime when Abby woke up with a start peering around in fear. Then she remembered Victoria and listened. She didn't hear anything and quickly went down the stairs to find Victoria in the rocking chair and Grace being fed a bottle.

"I found the bottle and Grace was hungry. I hope I didn't disrupt her schedule," Victoria said quietly, not wanting to disturb the baby's feeding time.

"No, she seems to change her schedule every few days. Right now, it's wake-up about six have a bottle, nap at ten, up at noon have a bottle, nap at two, up at four have a bottle. My friend Rebecca says that's all normal and to go with whatever makes the baby happy. Trying to change the child's schedule is like hitting your head against a wall." Abby smiled as she watched her oldest give her a milky smile.

"I have to agree. By the time you get them trained on one thing they get too old for that and you start retraining them again. Getting them to sleep through the night is about all a body can hope for. After that, the baby is in charge. If you doubt it, try to do it differently. Too noisy for me," she said patting Grace's back as she held the baby up to her shoulder.

"Thank you for taking such good care of her. I must be more tired than I thought. Matthew has been gone for over a week and that leaves only me...not that I am complaining. I love being a mother and becoming a mother again but it takes a lot of energy. I don't know what I'm going to do when I have both of them to contend with." She laughed at her own predicament.

"Well, you have me. I'll help with the second baby, too, Miss Abby," Victoria told her seriously.

"Just call me, Abby. We're going to be like family for the time you're here. You are too pretty to remain single for very long. There are a lot, and I mean a lot, of good looking, good hearted men here in Sweetwater. I have a feeling as soon as they know you're here with me - they will come calling. One thing is true, there aren't very many women of marriageable age in this area and what there are don't stay single very long. There have been five weddings in less than a year and two births with another two on the way besides me. The population is growing by the week. As I said, you won't be alone for very long. But I appreciate whatever time you can give me." Abby told her new employee, or rather, her new extended family member.

"We'll see. I'm not looking for more adventure since the last one didn't work out too good for me." She sat Grace on her lap and made faces at her until Grace was giggling.

Abby excused herself telling Victoria she was going to warm a stew for their dinner and the two of them ate later that evening. Being well rested helped Abby's appetite, as well, it seemed. Usually she was too tired to even warm anything let alone eat it. As they ate, Abby held Grace on her lap and the two women discussed recipes for their favorite stews.

Taking Grace upstairs to her apartment, Abby left Victoria to settle in and unpack. The shop had the two rooms, one used as a display area and the other used for a fitting room. Victoria surveyed her domain. A narrow cot was located in an area opening off the fitting room.

There was a bassinet in the fitting area but Grace would be outgrowing that quickly. It wouldn't contain a child intent on pulling herself up or trying to walk. She would speak to Abby about that later. The baby probably had a sturdier bed upstairs.

The kitchen was against the rear wall with sink and hand pump as well as a stove with an oven which could be used for heat during the colder winter months. A cabinet set against the wall for dishes stood alongside a table and chairs. Abby had brought down the stew so Victoria surmised there was a kitchen in the upstairs apartment at the top of the stairs, as well. The upstairs' apartment used the same rear door and privy so they were open to one another.

Victoria wasn't very tired even after the disaster of the other day and spent some time looking out the big window facing the street. There weren't very many lights on in any of the upstairs rooms opposite her. She wondered if that meant no one lived in those rooms or that the residents weren't home yet. Across the dirt street there were lights on at the hotel and the saloon next door. Several horses and a buggy were tied up outside their doors.

Then there was the sheriff's office. That, too, was dark and the only single-story building on that side of the street. Victoria had noticed even the fire department was a two-story building but it was closer to the train station, made out of the same red brick trimmed with green.

She thought she could see a sign for the livery just past the sheriff's office but she couldn't be sure from this angle and she wasn't going to open the shop door without permission. The closed sign had been up all afternoon and she didn't want to disturb anything simply because she was nosy about her new home. She had plenty of time to learn more later.

Victoria wondered if Sweetwater had a library as her own small town did since she loved to read. She knew she had learned about more things than she would have otherwise. If it did, then she would get some books and read them to Grace even if the baby didn't understand them yet as she had done with her siblings. Stretching, she yawned and decided to get ready for bed and try to get some rest. Babies were notorious for waking up early when the people who cared for them were tired. Somehow, they always knew when you had a bad night.

Victoria and Abby set up a routine of care for Grace and to get the menial housekeeping chores done as well. The goat had to be milked, chickens fed and eggs collected daily. Shopping for fresh produce and meat almost daily, as well. Laundry - every other day except for Sundays and the cleaning and cooking fit in between.

Abby was able to catch up with the orders for dresses and hats that had been placed, plus make clothes for Grace's growing body. Also, for the new infants who kept making their appearance in the town's population even if their mothers could sew. There were still only so many hours in a day and sewing came in the list of to-dos after children, husbands and meals for most women.

Abby semi-complained as she sewed. "I've stopped wearing my corset and soon I'll need to make some alterations to my dresses. Possibly a couple of completely new ones to accommodate the size I'm afraid I'll get. Many of my close friends are going through the same thing. But they won't be done with their larger dresses before I'll need them so we won't be able to pass any on to one another.

"I am really worried that Rebecca, my friend the midwife, will become in an interesting condition and then I don't know what the rest of us will do. We have really begun to depend on her but she married the minister a few weeks ago. I'm not sure she will continue with her practice. It is very demanding work and pulls her from her home for days at a time."

"I helped with my mamma's births, well, the last five anyways. I know what to do if the birth is straightforward but mamma never had any trouble having babies. Just finally wore out I always thought. Wasted away and one morning didn't wake up. The doctor couldn't say why but I never thought he was much of a doctor, either. I think he would have tried harder if it were a man wasting away. Just my gut feeling, you know?" said Victoria as a matter of fact.

Abby kept her own counsel on what Victoria had disclosed but realized the girl had lived a hard life. That she knew more about living and dying than a much older person would have experienced. She wanted to talk with Matthew so badly about Victoria and she missed him as usual. Having him near always settled her so she was hoping he was on his way home to her.

CHAPTER 2

Abby was at Murray's Mercantile buying some basics when the sheriff, a tall man with light brown hair and only a year or so older than Abby, walked up and asked, "May I walk you home, Miss Abby?"

Abby had been Miss Abby to all the towns' people, especially the unmarried men, for so long she had given up reminding them she was a married lady now. They weren't being disrespectful. Simply thought of her more as a family member than anything else. Mason, the sheriff, took the bag Abby was carrying as they left the general store together.

The sheriff kept to a slower pace, matching his much longer strides to hers as they walked on the boardwalk. They would cross the street to the meat shop before heading home. Abby smiled to herself, thinking she knew what the sheriff wanted. It would be about the pretty, unmarried lady now taking care of Grace.

"How can I help you, Mason?" she asked the handsome man wearing his personal uniform of blue calvary shirt, a row of buttons around the shield in the front holding it in place and tan trousers tucked into snake skin boots. His Stetson was pulled low over his golden-brown eyes which she knew missed nothing going on around them. She had never seen him without his six-gun on the belt with the big silver buckle even when they had been seeing one another romantically.

His eyes peered into hers as he asked, "I hear you have a lady staying with you. Is she someone you know?"

"No, she's a single lady who came upon hard times and I hired her to help me at the shop and with Grace. She's very pretty, especially when she smiles and has a sweet disposition," Abby said trying to be helpful if Mason was interested in courting Victoria.

"Is she someone Matthew brought to you? I didn't think he was back, yet," Mason asked and answered.

"No, she found me on her own. Simply luck on both our parts. She is a jewel with Grace and I am able to sleep more as well as get my sewing done. I will miss her when she is gone," Abby confided.

Mason jumped on this tidbit of information as he asked quickly, "She's not staying permanently? She say when she's leaving?"

"I think she plans on staying in Sweetwater. I meant that I don't expect a sweet natured, pretty, young lady would stay working for me for long. Some lonely bachelor will be at my door with flowers in his hand by week's end." She glanced up to catch a strange expression pass over his face. So, she had been correct in thinking Mason was interested in her new friend. Her heart sunk realizing how limited the time with Victoria's help she would have.

"I wonder," he mused. "She say why she chose Sweetwater as a stop off town? I mean, she doesn't seem to have any link to Sweetwater. No one knows her by name anyway."

"Why Mason, have you been checking out my guest? Why didn't you simply come by and drop in to say hello? We don't bite. That way you can see her for yourself. Want to come for dinner?" Abby offered her one-time suiter now turned old friend.

"No, but I'll finish walking you home and you can

introduce me to her then," Mason said and helped Abby up to the boardwalk.

"You are that anxious to meet her? I'll be happy to introduce the two of you but remember if this works into a wedding, I get the credit," she teased her former admirer.

"You'll get the credit, Abby, and maybe cash reward," he told her deadpan.

"I'll hold you to that one, Mason. I'm tired of setting up these couples merely to be ignored when they make a match." Abby walked into the meat shop to place her order.

Mason waited on the boardwalk, thinking how to protect Abby if this woman is the one wanted for helping robbers going through the state attacking mail cars on the trains. He wished Matthew was back in town so they could watch the woman twenty-four hours a day. He didn't like having the woman, any stranger near Abby, especially with Matthew away. If the woman got spooked, she may turn nasty and he didn't want Abby and the baby within range if that happened.

Abby opened the door to the friendly welcoming tinkle and called, "Victoria, I brought home a guest. Come out and meet him."

Victoria came from behind the curtain carrying Grace on her hip, a wide smile on her lips, which died immediately upon seeing their guest. Her gaze went to the sheriff's badge pinned to Mason's shirt and the gun strapped to his thigh. Her gaze darted between Abby and Mason but didn't see any fear in Abby's face. Victoria relaxed a little but was stiff at the greeting.

After Abby made the introduction, she took Grace and the bag of purchases excusing herself. "I'll just go and put these things away. I won't be long."

Mason gave Victoria a hard look and said nonchalantly, "So, you find yourself passing through Sweetwater?"

"I, ah, I'm not sure. I thought I would visit for a while and if I like it, I'll set up something permanent," she answered cautiously.

"Have you got to see much of town?" Mason asked, as if he had no care as to her answer.

"Just the train station and here. Abby suggested I take a walk but I'm here to take care of Grace, to make it easier for Abby to do her work."

"You know anyone in nearby towns? Maybe someone you spoke with on the way here?" Mason asked cryptically.

Victoria felt her throat tighten up and her hands and forehead bead with perspiration. She tried to wipe her forehead without being noticed, turning away from the sheriff but he could see her reflection in the big bay window.

"It's getting a little warm this afternoon. I may take Grace out back so she can visit the chickens," she said trying to cover her nervousness with talk. She felt her under arms become damp as well and wished Abby would return and take care of her company.

"I didn't notice," Mason said. "So, if I need...if I want to talk with you again, I'll be able to find you here then?" Mason persisted in his questioning the young woman.

"I plan on being here till Abby don't need me any longer." And that was one statement Victoria had no difficulty saying.

"Tell Abby good-day for me. I'll be seeing you

around." He didn't tip his hat as most men would have done. "Good-day to you, Miss Watkins." He opened the door but the little bell sounded more like a death knell to Victoria.

Abby came in a little later and peered around. "Did he leave?" When she didn't see the big cowboy hulking anywhere in the room continued asking, "How did you like him? He's one of my favorite bachelors and one of the best looking left. Not that the others are scary but, really, he sets the bar fairly high."

"Yes, um, yes, he's very good-looking. Does he stop by often?" she asked innocently.

"If we want him to, he will," Abbey told her.

Matthew returned home that evening, picking up first Abby and swinging her off the ground, kissing her soundly even knowing Victoria was there. Then picking up Grace and nuzzling his face into her belly making growling noises, which set the baby to such giggles all of the adults laughed with her.

Victoria liked Matthew right away. A man not afraid to show his emotions, his love for his family. Anyone watching would know he was a family man, this family's man and Victoria felt a little needle of envy poke her. This is what she had come west for but maybe she should look at it as a hope that her dreams were a possibility. She just had to find a loving man like Matthew to marry. She wondered if he had a brother.

After having dinner alone upstairs with Matthew, Abby asked quietly, "Victoria, would you mind if Grace slept downstairs tonight so that, um, so that she won't be disturbed. It will give Matthew a chance to sleep late."

Victoria smiled and said, "No, that's not a problem at all. I'll make sure I have everything she'll need tomorrow and you sleep as long as you like." She took extra diapers and clean bottles. Then scooping Grace up from her father, took her downstairs for the night.

It was almost noon the next day when she heard Matthew leave by way of the back door. Abby appeared soon after, happy and more content then Victoria had ever seen her.

"Matthew has gone to visit his sister, Callie, and her family. She lives about an hour out of town and I would have gone with him but Matthew thinks it is too much shaking for the baby." She placed her hand protectively over her abdomen. "I am feeling energetic so I thought we could walk to Rebecca's and see if she is free. It will show you more of the town at least. You haven't met many people and I feel guilty for keeping you inside so much. Now that I've caught up, I feel we can visit with others. It is always slow here at the shop in the summer. No one is thinking of clothing this time of year. It's busier in the spring and fall. If anyone comes in to town, most people know where I would be anyway."

"I'm anxious to meet Rebecca. You've spoken about her so many times, it will be nice to put a face to the name. Are Grace's sun caps down here?" asked Victoria heading to her cubical to get her own cloth poke bonnet.

The two women walked side by side down the boardwalk and then on the dusty street to the little white church with the spire and white picket fence. They turned toward the graveyard behind the church and came to a large two-story house with wide covered, front porch usually in shade of the taller trees as it was now.

A statuesque type of woman stood and waved to them from that porch, smiling a welcome to them both.

She moved quickly down the steps and took Grace out of Abby's arms, cooing and asking, "How's my Goddaughter doing? Oh, you've gained more weight than I have these past few weeks Grace, I swear you have." Then she made blowing noises through her lips to entertain the baby as she climbed the steps to the chairs waiting there.

Rebecca wasn't at all as Victoria had pictured her. She had expected a much older woman with boney hands and maybe a slight mustache. This woman was lovely, young and very active, the energy flowed out and around her.

"I brought Victoria to meet you and to get the daily exercise you ordered. I'll have more time now Victoria is here to help," Abby explained her visit and her new friend.

"It's nice to meet you, Victoria. I'm glad you could stay with Abby so she can also get the rest I ordered." Her smile included both of the other women.

"I owe so much to Abby for giving me a place to stay and taking care of Grace seems a breeze to the five I'm used to caring for." At Rebecca's questioning gaze went on to explain, "I was taking care of younger sisters and brothers when my mother got sick and after she passed, I kept doing it 'til my pa remarried."

"Then it got a little crowded around the house?" asked Rebecca bluntly.

"Yeah, I guess it did at that," answered Victoria just as bluntly.

"I think you chose well. Sweetwater is a wonderful place and I can say that because the people here were so good to me when I first arrived. And the men, oh, Lordy, don't get me started on the men. They grow them big, handsome and loyal. I couldn't believe my good luck when I got here a spinster posing as a widow. I had to fan myself simply walking to the Mercantile I passed so many good-looking men along the way." She laughed with Abby at the true but irreverent comment. "Now I'm an old married lady with my own big, handsome and loyal man. I can only hope for the same for you," finished Rebecca offering her guests some ice tea.

"I'm not here for a husband, not even looking any more. I'll be happy taking care of Grace and helping Abby around the house," Victoria said earnestly. "Can I help you get the tea?"

The three women settled down to get to know more about each other and compliment Rebecca on the fine lunch they were having.

Abby and Victoria returned home and fed Grace. After the mid-afternoon luncheon they had eaten at Rebecca's, neither of them was hungry. Matthew wasn't expected back until right before dark so they began working on baby clothes. The two women sat quietly, Victoria placing her small neat stitches in a hem and Abby embroidering her own designs of elephants and ducks, although not together.

CHAPTER 3

There was a rap at the door and Mason entered, dressed as he always was, including the Stetson, nodding at Abby and saying, "Abby, I don't like doing this to a friend but I have orders to take Miss Watkins into custody."

Abby walked quickly to stand between Victoria and the sheriff demanding, "What do you mean, into custody? Are you arresting her?"

"Not yet, I just got to take her over to the jail and hold her until I get a wire back from Preston. It shouldn't be more than a day or two," he explained to his friend, ignoring the small woman trying to hide behind her.

"Why can't she simply stay here? Matthew and I will make sure she doesn't leave town," argued Abby.

"I can't do that, Abby. I've got orders." He looked over at Victoria who was now cowering behind Abby.

"Wait until Matthew gets home and we can work something out…," Abby began.

The back door opened and Abby ran to her husband, placing one hand in supplication on his chest. "Mason says he's here to take Victoria, says he has orders. Can't you stop him?" she pleaded.

Mason glanced over at his friend who had moved closer to Victoria, the young woman was pale and her eyes appeared sad and frightened. "What's going on, Mason? Is Abby confused or something?"

"I've been ordered to detain Miss Watkins until I get a wire to confirm she's a woman we've been following. I can't say more than that right now but it's not something we do lightly and if they weren't ninety percent sure, they'd never have me hold her. I'm sorry that both of you got caught up in this but, Matthew, you know not all guilty people look it. Some look and act like angels when they want."

Doubt clouded Matthew's eyes and Abby started to argue for Victoria when Victoria stepped forward saying, "It's alright, Abby. It's not Matthew's fault and tomorrow when the wire comes, he'll let me go. After I get free, if you want me to stay and help you then I will, and if not, I understand."

Abby turned her tear-streaked face into her husband's chest while Mason took hold of one of Victoria's arms and led her out through the door. No one heard the happy little chime as he did so.

Mason didn't let go of Victoria's arm until they entered the small building that stated it was the sheriff's office on a sign above the door. They hadn't spoken since leaving the dress shop and Victoria was starting to feel angry about the unfair treatment. This was happening because she was an unprotected female. Even Abby and Matthew were run over by this big oaf of a man without an ounce of common courtesy in his whole body.

Mason brought her to the open cell and began running his hands through her hair asking, "Do you have any weapons on you, a hat pin or maybe a derringer?" He took a step back to discern whether there was any place to hide such a weapon.

Victoria pulled her head back from his seeking fingers demanding, "Get your hands off me. If I did have a hat pin it would already be strategically planted in your person. How dare you question me or, for that matter, hold me against my will?"

Mason smiled ironically saying, "Oh, now the kitten has claws. I wonder why you kept them sheathed when we were with Matthew and Abby. Still hoping they can get you out before the rest of your gang can get here to help? Maybe I should make sure there are no weapons. I'd hate to be shot or stabbed in my sleep because I made the mistake of being a gentleman."

And with that he brushed his hands down Victoria's body from her armpits to her feet. Then he grabbed the hem of her skirt and shook it, feeling for any unusual weight sewed into the lining. When Victoria tried to slap him away, Mason grabbed both of her wrists in one of his large bear-like hands and held them against her chest as he finished his search. His hand skimmed up one leg than down and moved over to the other being extra sure nothing was strapped to her ankles or thighs.

Victoria had tears of anger and frustration and humiliation running down her face by the time Mason had completed his search to his satisfaction. He raised Victoria's arms over her head and then took each hand in one of his leaning in to come face to face with her.

"No weapons, well, no normal weapons but you sure make a man not worry about his own safety with all that wiggling you were doing. I don't understand women like you. Why don't you just settle down, get married and have a passel of kids? Why get messed up with a gang of men that are going to end up at the end of a rope, maybe with you dangling right beside them?"

All the time Mason had been talking, Victoria tried to get her tears under control, tried to make sense of what he was saying. She wanted to settle down and have children. What did a gang of criminals and her have in common?

Victoria made one last try at dislodging herself from Mason's grip, but that turned out to be a mistake. Her arching from the cell bars brought her into closer proximity to his hard body, one part harder than the others. Fear flooded Victoria. She knew enough to understand that she was in danger and Mason was in control and much stronger than she was.

Grouping as much strength as she could, she fought for her freedom while Mason grunted with the required amount of strength it took to keep Victoria under control and prevent her from hurting herself.

Without thinking about anything but keeping Victoria safe, Mason covered her mouth with his own. Taking what he had dreamed of since meeting her, even as he knew it would lead to problems down the road. He couldn't become involved with a criminal, even one who drove him to distraction. Allowing himself some enjoyment of the moment, he felt Victoria's breasts push against his chest, her mouth open under his and then the quietness of her acceptance.

Mason took his time letting go of Victoria's hands and placed his on each side of her, thumbs just cupping under each breast. Leaning in, he continued to kiss and stroke Victoria's tongue and the inside of her mouth with his thrusting and retreating, then doing it all over again.

Guilt and remorse kicked Mason in the gut all at once when he realized Victoria wasn't participating but merely submitting. Submitting because between fear and his brute strength she thought it was the safest way for her survival. Mason hung his head in shame and disgust at himself for the loss of control.

"I'm sorry, Miss Watkins." He almost laughed at the

incongruity of using the formal acknowledgment then said, "I'm sorry, Victoria. I don't know what came over me. I've never lost control before, not with a prisoner and never with a woman. I...you can press charges with my superiors in the morning. You won't have to worry about anything happening anymore tonight."

With that said, he opened the cell door wider and watched as Victoria, still in a state of shock over the quick reversal of their positions, walked in toward the cot. A jangling of metal sounded as Mason turned the key in the cell door.

"It's clean, you don't have to worry about that."

Victoria heard metal clatter at her feet and she looked down to find the keys lying there.

"I'll be right here if you need anything." Taking off his gun belt, he removed the gun to set it on the desk facing the door. Then he leaned his desk chair back against the wall, tipped his Stetson over his eyes and went to sleep.

Victoria finally felt Mason was going to remain at the desk and barely kept from collapsing on the hard cot where she tried to sleep. She didn't want to be awake and think any more, she didn't want to think about how easily she was in jail for something she knew nothing about and how easy it was for her to fall into Mason's arms. How right it felt to be there.

Matthew knocking then opening the door to the sheriff's office carrying a basket wakened both Victoria and Mason. Dressed all in black except for the pristine white shirt, Matthew looked first at Victoria with her hair tousled and not finding the sight to his liking, said gruffly, "Abby sent some tea and breakfast over for Victoria. Where are the keys?" He held his hand out to

Susan Payne

Mason for the ring of cell keys.

Mason flushed crimson but before he could say anything, Victoria volunteered, "They're over here on the wall." Indicating the keys now hanging on a hook outside the cell bars.

Looking skeptically at Mason, Matthew said, "Christ, Mason. I hope you don't leave them there when you have real criminals in the cell. Even Victoria could have reached them." He took the keys and opened the cell to place the basket inside with her.

"Um, could I use the facilities?" she asked, afraid to bring attention to herself but at the same time needful of a privy.

Mason rubbed his hands down his face saying, "Yeah, of course, but you better come back. I don't want to have to chase you down."

With that said, Victoria scurried past Matthew to the back door.

Matthew took a long look at Mason and asked quietly, "Okay, now what really occurred here last night?"

"Nothing I can't handle," responded Mason.

"That's not what I asked and you know it. Is Victoria safe with you or do I need to sit here with you both?" Matthew asked angrily.

"Victoria's safe enough." And Mason sighed. "Look, I know Abby's big heart has adopted Victoria and they've become great friends and all that but what if she isn't as she appears? What if Victoria does this kind of thing in different towns, befriending people and then conning them until her gang comes in to fleece them?"

"What are you saying? That you know Victoria has done this to other people?" questioned Matthew now worried about his family's safety with this virtual stranger.

"There's a gang with a female leader that hits towns along the railway, setting up scams and outright robberies. Sometimes it's a bank, a big ranch on payday, the mail. Never exactly the same but always getting away with a lot of gold and cash. Headquarters thinks the woman is the one that figures out the next heist while the men carry it out and then they move on. I can't let that happen here in Sweetwater, plus, I have an obligation to protect the mail, too."

Victoria came in at that moment and went directly into the cell, sitting on the cot looking like a lost kitten. Matthew fought his instincts to drag her home with him but if Mason was right, that would put Abby and Grace in harm's way. Victoria looked like so many others he'd come across and rescued. Young woman nearly at the end of their rope. He wished he had spent more time with her so he would have a better sense of who she was and why she was here in Sweetwater. The information he got from Abby wasn't very concise and his wife had been so upset it took him a while to stop her crying and calm her down.

Relocking the cell, Matthew dropped the keys onto the desk. "I'm coming back after noon and if you haven't received that wire, I expect Victoria to be set free. You can't keep her here indefinitely without charges." With that warning he left.

Mason stood up taking two steps to the stove and shook the coffee pot finding no responding sloshing. Placing it back where it had been, he stomped to the door saying, "I'm going for some coffee, you want anything?"

At Victoria's quiet, "No," he headed next door to the

hotel.

Victoria sat on the cot and drank the tea Abby had sent over for her but ignored the food unable to feel hunger over worry. She thought she saw Mason walk past the front window but he never came in. It seemed like forever sitting there. Too much time to think about last evening when Mason had shown so much anger toward her. She was trying not to antagonize him and having him away from the jail, from her, was a blessing over all.

Victoria regretted ever seeing or answering that advertisement for a wife. She would be home with her family. As uncomfortable as that had been at the time, she longed for its security now. She missed her younger siblings and their constant needs that had to be met. She missed working with her friends in the tobacco fields. The smell of the drying sheds and feel of dirt beneath her nails after pulling weeds between the rows. She even missed the rocky soil and the walks to and from town that always seemed to be uphill. What were all those people she once knew doing right now?

A shadow passing the front window and then opening the door showed Victoria that Matthew was true to his word. He picked up the keys from the desk and walked over to the cell, unlocking it, saying, "I've come to take you home, Victoria."

Mason was right behind him so that meant the sheriff had been sitting on the boardwalk all morning, keeping track of her, watching that she didn't try to escape. Tipping her chin up, she passed the sheriff and headed quickly towards the dress shop. She almost ran the last few yards but tried to keep herself under control. It's just that she would feel so much better once she was near Abby. She knew Abby didn't believe anything bad about her. She would have never let her near Grace if she had any doubts.

Victoria entered the shop even though the closed sign was out practically running into Abby's arms. Abby hugged her one armed because she had Grace on the other hip. Victoria tried not to cry but she was so relieved to be back with an ally she couldn't prevent the tears welling in her eyes. She knew she had a true friend when she realized Abby was crying, too.

"Here, take Grace, I want to speak with Mason a moment and then we'll go upstairs and rest," she said as she pushed the baby into Victoria's arms. Victoria cuddled the child and Grace pulled at Victoria's hair, now hanging down past her shoulders since all the hairpins had been removed the night before.

Matthew stopped both of the women from leaving when he said, "Mason has one last request before letting Victoria go."

Both sets of female eyes swiveled to where Mason, who had followed stood somewhat awkwardly, but he said in a clear voice, "The woman they're looking for has a birthmark on her hip. If you could look for me, us, Abby, then we can rule out Miss Watkins and I'll be on my way."

Abby took a deep breath, evidently deciding to forego any haranguing on her part if checking Victoria and then proving Mason wrong for accusing Victoria in the first place could accomplish more, she would do that. Abby turned to Victoria to usher her into the fitting room when she saw a look of total dismal gloom on the young woman's face.

"Don't bother, Abby. I have a birthmark but how

anyone would know that I couldn't guess." She went to hand Grace back to her mother and return to the jail with Mason.

Abby looked so sad now, too, that Matthew threw an angry glare at Mason saying roughly, "That doesn't prove anything. I can bring you ten women who have a birthmark on their hip. It doesn't prove anything, let alone guilt."

Abby looked at her husband, the tears still in her eyes, with both love and gratitude. They would laugh over this whole thing, especially his knowing ten women who had birthmarks on their hips after Victoria was out from under suspicion for being part of this gang.

The sheriff felt uncomfortable thinking about Victoria's bare hip, with or without a birthmark. He shifted his weight on his feet and thought about another night pretending to sleep while watching her in his cell, within reach if he didn't control his basest impulses.

Mason agreed to the point and finally said, "I'm leaving her with you but I'll be checking up on her. I may have more questions later." Then he looked straight into Victoria's eyes and said, "And I expect you to stay in town and not to speak with strangers. I'm taking a chance and I don't want these good people hurt. Understand?"

Victoria unconsciously pulled Grace tighter to her breast when Mason had talked about these good people being hurt. Would her being there bring harm to Grace and Abby or Matthew? But how? She knew no one who would hurt them so Mason was warning Victoria herself about hurting them. Since there was no way that would ever happen, she relaxed and turned away from the sheriff without making another comment to him.

CHAPTER 4

A few days passed and they hadn't seen Mason again. If Matthew was making daily reports he never admitted as much to his wife. The two women spent the days trying to stay cool and keeping Grace occupied. One afternoon, Abby asked if Victoria would mind checking for a package at the Mercantile that should have come in with the mail.

"The post office is in a corner of the store. Helen passes out the mail so ask if it's in yet," Abby explained.

"Anything else you need picked up?" At Abby's negative answer, Victoria went across the street to the general store. It didn't take long to retrieve the parcel and Victoria headed down the boardwalk, walking in the shade when three men jumped out from a walkway between two of the buildings. Startled, Victoria held the parcel to her chest and faced her demons.

"Wel-l-l, lookie here if it ain't my missus," drawled a not entirely sober Bob Hill. His two cronies laughed maliciously licking their lips as if they were looking over a table full of desserts.

"How did you find me?" she asked searching the street with her gaze, trying to find an escape from the grimy men while not leading them back to Abby and Grace.

"The ticket seller finally remembered where you bought that ticket to. Seems he has a soft spot for a broken-hearted man whose fiancée run off on her weddin' night," Bob Hill told her.

"Go away. I never married you and I never will. You

lied and tried to deceive me. Now leave or I'll tell my employer's husband you accosted me," Victoria said with more strength of conviction than she felt. She knew Matthew would help her but she didn't know where he was at the moment.

"Now the way I sees it, you owe me, missy. I paid out good hard cash to git you here and now I got no woman. That means you owe me," Hill said sounding more sober by the minute.

"I have a little money that I'll give you and then I can pay something each month till you're paid off," she offered bravely.

"I don't think that's gonna be 'nuff to please me, if'n you know what I mean," Hill told her looking her up and down. The dress she was wearing looked better than her original one after Abby applied a little sewing magic to it. She tried not to search the area around them and to keep her gaze firmly on the men so she could react to any further threat.

But before he could say more, a hulk of a man came up behind them and asked firmly, "You fellas got business in town?"

This time it was the three men's turn to be startled and they all jumped, turning to see a very big Mason, badge on his shirt and gun in its holster facing them down.

Bob Hill recovered first saying, "I was jus' havin' a little conversation with my wife-to-be, here."

Mason's gaze jumped to Victoria's and read the lie the man told him there. "That right? When did this take place?"

"I sent for her and she and me wuz suppos'ta get hitched in Preston but we, ah, kind of missed each other.

You know ships that pass in the night an' all." He glared at Victoria warning her not to discredit him.

"That right, Victoria?" asked Mason, ensuring the other men knew they had a closer than casual relationship.

Victoria took this opportunity to shed herself of the slime that once thought himself good enough for her. "No, Mr. Hill insists on claiming a relationship that does not exist. I want nothing to do with him."

"Now that ain't true. I paid for her and I got a right to what's mine," the still less than sober man stated missing the way Mason's hand went to his gun and the firming of the sheriff's lips in anger.

"How much?" At the dumb look on Hill's face, Mason repeated, "How much did you spend on her?"

"Them tickets wuz bout twenty dollars, cash," he said as if that sealed the deal and proved Victoria belonged to him.

Never taking his hand off his gun, Mason reached his other hand in his front pocket and pulled out a gold coin, which he flipped toward Hill, landing short as he intended and hitting the boardwalk.

Jumping at it, the greed glimmered in Hill's eyes, as Mason said, "Now you're paid back in full and I expect you boys to be on the next train out of Sweetwater."

Hill was beginning to realize he had been bested when he started to argue, "But I lost my investment. I wuz 'specting to be a respectable married man by now. I should be compensated or some such."

"I said you're paid in full. If I see you around Sweetwater again, I'll arrest you for vagrancy and forget where I locked you up," Mason told them in a firm warning.

The three men looked morosely at each other and finally headed toward the train station, arguing amongst themselves.

Mason took a moment to make sure the men intended to keep going and then turned to Victoria, eye's glittering with withheld anger and lips thin. "I need you to come with me. I think we need to talk." He held her arm as he had the night he arrested her.

Victoria tried not to flinch as he marched her down the boardwalk to the sheriff's office. She worried because he had warned her about talking with strangers and then there she was on the main street conversing with three of them. He was never going to believe anything she said now. How did all the evidence keep stacking against her? She couldn't prove she wasn't the woman he wanted. And now he knew she had been in Preston, too, which was another semi-lie she had told about getting on the train and coming here. Only Abby knew about the advertisement and her running away from Bob Hill.

They got to the office and Mason let go of Victoria like she was a hot coal. Victoria walked toward the cell rubbing her arm to get the blood flowing again.

Mason said, "Not in there, sit here." He pulled out a chair that sat in front of the desk.

Victoria sat as directed but didn't look up, afraid of his impatience, of his anger. She didn't know why Mason was always so angry with her but she was smart enough to know the less she antagonized him the better it was for her.

"Now I'll ask you one more time. Why did you come to Sweetwater and where are you from?" he asked quietly, evidently deciding that yelling wasn't going to work this time.

"I'm from Tennessee, like I told you. My pa remarried and I didn't fit in the family anymore. Where I come from most girls my age are already married for years and have children, families of their own. I was taking care of my brother and sisters so I kind of missed that boat back home. I read an article in the paper about the territories needing young marriageable women and answered an advertisement for a wife put there by Bob Hill. We each wrote two letters and then he sent me the tickets to get to Preston."

Victoria was worrying the ribbon hanging from her waist, unable to face Mason as she confessed to being so foolish as to meet a man, she had only two letters from.

Mason took her small work worn hands in his. "I can guess what happened but I need to hear it from you. I may be able to get Bob Hill on some charge if I hear it all."

Taking a deep breath, she continued, "I got off the train and Hill and his cronies were there, all liquored up. He said we should," another deep breath, "we should go to the hotel and, I think, celebrate. Then we would get married in the morning. I didn't like him or his friends so I turned right then and there and paid for a ticket to Sweetwater. It took about all the money I had."

"Is that all of it? You didn't leave anything out?" he questioned.

"He tried to get handy with me but we struggled and I stumbled trying to escape him. People were staring and his friends kept watching as if expecting some sort of show. I finally broke away and faced him holding a board like a hammer." She tried to remember the night she had pushed out of her mind not wanting to relive another second of it.

"Oh, Hill seemed happy that I looked younger than nineteen. They all seemed happy about that," ended Victoria and finally was able to look Mason in the eye now all secrets were out in the open between them.

"Christ," Mason bellowed as he dropped her hands and stalked across the room. He was there in two strides but he had to distance himself from Victoria to keep from shaking her or hugging her or both. "Do you realize how close you probably came to being forced into prostitution? These men take young innocent girls and lure them away from their families and friends. If you had gone to that hotel with them, they would have sold you or used you and then sold you. I suppose you told them you were a virgin?"

"I wrote that I was chaste. It was one of the questions he asked in his first letter. I mean it seems important for a potential husband to know." Victoria began to cry, almost sobbing, at her close call to danger, at the relief of not having to be afraid of Bob Hill finding her again and for finally having someone else know her story fully.

Mason stepped to where Victoria sat and pulled her up so he could hold her in his arms. He didn't care if it wasn't the smart move to make, he felt it was the only move to make. He kissed the top of her head and made the sounds adults have made through the ages to sooth and calm small children.

Victoria finally stopped crying. Little hiccups were the only sign of her outburst and, of course, the red rimmed eyes and red tip of her nose. Victoria knew she looked a mess but Mason never said a mean word about it.

"Okay, we have to get you home before Abby sends

out the troops. No hat, huh?" At Victoria's shake of her head Mason said, "Alright, stay on this side of me and I'll walk you back. We'll cross the street here because the other side is less busy. Ready?"

The couple crossed the street and walked down the boardwalk to Abby's shop. Mason held the door open to let Victoria in and said, "I want to check on some things so I'll leave you here." Then closed the door and headed toward the station.

Abby came out of the curtained room saying with relief, "Oh, there you are. I was about to wake Grace and go to look for you." Then she looked closely at her friend.

Before Abby could ask, Victoria confessed, "I ran into that Bob Hill and he was getting nasty but then Sheriff Mason saw us and took care of him. I'm lucky the sheriff was there."

"You've been crying. Are you sure Mason didn't do anything?" questioned Abby.

"No, he didn't do anything to make me cry. I do owe him twenty dollars, though." And she went into the kitchen to wash her face at the sink before Abby could question her further.

The next day Mason stopped by and before Abby could berate him, he put up his hands in surrender, saying, "I just need Victoria to look these posters over to see if she recognizes anyone." At the sound of Mason's voice, Victoria stepped into the room from behind the curtain.

"What have you got? Someone I should know?" she asked approaching Mason for the first time without being coerced.

Mason smiled, taking in Victoria's shy smile and

downcast gaze, then asked, "I just retrieved these from the train. They are drawings of men thought to be part of a robbery gang that's been working the area. Any of these men look familiar?"

Victoria studied each drawing and then shook her head, "Not really, the last one looks like a man that was at the train station in Preston but I was distracted and these are drawings. A man can change his beard shape or hair or shave. It must be difficult to catch anyone just using these." She handed them back to Mason.

"You'd be surprised at how often we do get our man. Of course, we run after a lot of dead ends but if we keep following them eventually, we run them to ground," explained Mason.

"But it must be dangerous. I mean you mark yourself with that big shiny badge that almost acts as a target and the criminals can hide behind barrels and take pot shots at you," Victoria said.

Mason laughed. "I'm sure glad I didn't talk with you before I chose to be a lawman. You make it sound downright treacherous."

Abby added, "Usually we are pretty quiet around here. Sometimes rustlers try to come in to the area but they learn that it isn't a place that strangers aren't found out. We are still pretty close knit. Not that strangers aren't welcome," she assured Victoria.

"I know I felt welcomed, Abby, and I'll never forget how comforting you were when I first arrived." Victoria reminded them both of their bond of womanhood.

"I might come by another time to see if Matthew has run into any of these fellas, if that's all right with you, Abby," said Mason.

"He'll be back this evening and I don't think he's

leaving me for a few more days, so whenever you get the time to come over...."

Tipping his Stetson, Mason left with the little bell chiming goodbye.

Mason came by the next day to show the posters to Matthew, who said he had seen all but one of the posters already but hadn't seen the men. He told Mason he always kept up with knowing who the bad guys are just like he knew all the good guys in a town. Preston, being one of the fastest growing cities, was being flooded with both at the moment. Matthew kept up with watching for anyone in the forced prostitution rings and was very interested to know Bob Hill's name and what his cronies looked like.

Matthew thought they sounded like procurers and worked getting women and girls for others. Wanting to be paid for a commodity and then not caring what happened to the women after that. Matthew said he found it interesting the three men were working at using the mail order bride type of advertisement. Matthew had hoped women were more watchful and asked for more information than they evidently did but he also knew these women were sometimes desperate and didn't have the time or money to investigate a future husband.

Mason went in search of Victoria, finding her sitting outside with Grace, watching the chickens. Grace rocked on Victoria's knee, both little arms flying in the wind trying to jump off her lap and catch a chicken.

"Victoria, is it possible for you to get a few hours off so I could show you the countryside, maybe go down to the river? It's cooler there and, after all, it is the town's name sake," he said smiling and holding his Stetson in his hand.

She declined graciously. "Well, thank you Sheriff Mason, but Abby needs me to watch Grace. Otherwise, it sounds lovely."

Abby poked her head out from the downstairs kitchen saying, "Matthew and I are going to take an afternoon for just us, meaning Grace and me, so you're free to do as you wish." Proving the woman had been listening all along.

Victoria smiled a tight smile and said, because Abby left her little else, "I can be ready anytime it seems, Sheriff."

"I'll get a buggy hitched up and be back in say, half an hour?" he asked smiling to have gotten his way. "And could you see your way to calling me, Mason?"

Ignoring his request, she merely said, "I'll get my bonnet."

After Mason left, Abby said, "Don't you dare wear that poke bonnet, either. You use it to hide from Mason. Wear the hat we made together for you, that little bird is charming and you look so elegant wearing it."

"I was going to wear my new hat, anyways. Besides church, I haven't found another place to wear it. And it will take his mind off my other clothes."

"I keep telling you to let me measure you and we can sew something more fashionable. Bustles are going to stay around for a while," Abby told her.

"Yes, and then there is the corset and ties and under dresses and jackets and buttons and bows. One thing leads to the next. A simple shirtwaist and skirt suit me fine but I thank you for the generous offer," Victoria told her new friend.

Matthew had come into the room for the last part of the conversation and Victoria turned a vivid red when she realized all of what he probably heard.

"Don't mind me. I'm a salesman representing half those items you were talking about. And although I hate the effort it takes to remove a corset, I do love the sight of a shapely woman in one." Then realizing his wife had to do without her corset because of the baby she was carrying, quickly added, "But a woman's natural form is as pleasing and one with child even more so."

Abby glared at her husband saying, "Nice bit of talk to save yourself, Matthew St. Michaels but it's going to cost you more than that to get back into my good graces."

"Anything, Love, you have but to command."

He reached for his wife as Victoria quickly said, "I'll wait outside for M-mason. It will be cooler there."

CHAPTER 5

As Mason and Victoria drove out of town, Victoria said her worries aloud to someone who evidently knew both people.

"I wonder if I'm in the way. I mean not having a home to go to, Matthew and Abby only get to be together as husband and wife when they escape upstairs and often, they take Grace with them. I'm not sure they feel completely spontaneous when I'm around." Victoria stated the same issues that drove her from her Tennessee home although she didn't think her pa loved her stepma in the same way.

"You think they'd be more, er, amorous without you there?" asked Mason bluntly figuring out the problem she was dealing with.

"I guess that's what I mean. Matthew is very attentive but I think there would be more contact, loving hugs and such if I weren't there. I can't be sure, of course, but it's a feeling I get. Like Matthew is holding back."

"Sounds like a normal man, especially a normal married man. I think Matthew is smart enough that if he wants his wife, um, closer he knows how to make that happen. Like he could take her on a buggy ride out into the country where no one could come upon them." Mason glanced over to see Victoria's reaction.

"Mason, you're not going to make me sorry I came out here with you, are you?" asked Victoria worriedly.

"I hope not. I mean I hope nothing I do will frighten you but I am interested in you that way," he stated baldly.

Victoria straightened her spine and seriously thought about jumping from the moving buggy. It wasn't travelling very fast but could she out-run Mason after that if she needed to?

"Now I've frightened you. Vicki you don't need to fear me. I'd never hurt you." Then he saw her hand go unconsciously to her upper arm, the arm he grabbed to haul her down to the jail after the confrontation with Bob Hill.

"Hell, I've already hurt you, haven't I? I didn't even know I'd grabbed your arm but I was so furious knowing that gang of no-goods almost had you again. I barely kept from breaking their damn necks but I was more concerned with you. I wanted to get you as far from them as I could. I was afraid you weren't going to come with me, that you'd fight me off, too. I didn't want them to know you were across the street in a lady's shop in case they didn't leave on the train. After I took you back to Abby's, I stayed with them at the station until I saw them all get on board."

"I bruise easily. It'll go away and no one gets to see it, not if I can stay out of Abby's reach. She wants to measure me for a new dress but I've been putting her off."

"You shouldn't have to do that. I just lose all sense of propriety around you." He glanced over to his passenger who was now hugged into her side of the buggy's soft upholstery.

"It's all right, really." Her voice sounded strained. "I'm getting a little tired. Can we head back now?"

"Please Vicki, give me a chance to explain then I'll take you back to the shop."

Victoria nodded her agreement and Mason nodded,

too. Then he put both reins in one hand placing a strong arm along the back of the seat asking, "Can you slide a little closer? It may make it easier for me to tell you. I'm not good with sharing my feelings. Hell, I would have said I was without feelings before I met you."

Sliding to the side of Mason, Victoria immediately felt a great calm come over her. She actually snuggled against the firmly muscled body that made her feel protected. Knowing she could depend on this man's strength always to be on her side.

Taking a deep breath, he began, "I had an older brother, Robert, a great brother and great friend, all around. He joined the Texas Rangers and that's one of the reasons I became a sheriff, so we still shared a bond even though we were hundreds of miles apart. After a couple of years, Rob was killed chasing a gang of bank robbers that would keep running across the Mexican border and then re-emerging when they ran low on funds. The Rangers took a lot of the gang members down with them but I've always felt if I had been with Rob he wouldn't have been killed. I would have had his back. After that, I didn't get close to many people."

"I don't think that's a realistic way of looking at this, Mason. Your brother was doing his job and you were doing yours. Did he ask you to join him?" At the shake of his head, Victoria continued, "Then you're trying to justify why you feel guilty at his death. I think you need to recognize you miss your brother. Not just the Texas Ranger he was but the brother he had always been. I understand being lonely while surrounded by others.

"I missed my ma although my life changed very little after her death. I hadn't even made future plans until I was pushed out of the nest like a cuckoo chick. I became my ma in many ways so the younger children didn't feel the pain I was going through. I'm not sure I did them any favors. They appreciated my work but they never seemed to miss ma like I did."

"It sounds as if you took on a lot of responsibility. I think you lessened their pain at your mother's death but you knew her the best, too. Some of them must have been quite young," Mason surmised correctly.

"They were and to many, for all purposes, I was their ma. My step-ma, I don't think of her as such but that's what she is, needed to be the only mother in the home. My father makes it hard for any woman in his life, he drinks up most of the money and what's left doesn't stretch to cover all the bills."

"I'm sorry you had such a rough life. I wish I had met you sooner."

"It made me what I am and I don't regret anything besides the early death of my ma. But you were going to tell me about yourself, not listen to me." She smiled encouragingly at him.

He glanced up to the sun before beginning again. "Our parents were already gone and losing my brother made me become, I guess, a kind of recluse. I have friends but mostly ranchers and I pretty much stay in town to keep close to any potential problems. I can't be an hour out of town if an emergency arises." Then he finished, "I just don't have much experience with women, I never wanted to."

"Not even at Miss Lily's?" she asked tentatively.

Mason tensed next to her before asking, "What do you know about Miss Lily's?"

"I know she's a nice lady. I met her at Abby's. She came in to shop but I think she was there to socialize more than anything and to meet me. Abby says she is extremely curious about everyone new in town and I was a new person to be curious about. But I found her charming and after she left, Abby explained, sort of, what she did. I thought that if I hadn't found Abby when I did, I might have ended up in a place like Miss Lily's."

His arm tightened around Victoria as he said, "I'm glad you found Abby first then, not that I think what Miss Lily and her girls do is wrong. It just seems to suck the life out of women. Miss Lily's is a rare exception to the rule for such houses. She keeps the roughnecks out and the men treat the girls like ladies or they aren't allowed back and it's a long ride to Preston."

At the sound of the name, Preston, Victoria shivered and tried not to remember the close call she had with Bob Hill. "I would have been close to death before I would sink to doing something like that."

"Then I am doubly glad you met Abby. She and Matthew have helped many young women escape from that kind of life. One they hadn't chosen for themselves. That's one reason I feel you're safe there. After I told Matthew about Bob Hill coming into town, he'll protect you as he does Abby and Grace."

"Does my being there endanger Abby and Grace? I won't stay if that's the case. I can move on to another town or something." Even the thought of bringing danger to Abby and the baby sent chills down her spine. She never wanted to repay their friendship with acts of violence or even threats.

"I don't think there's any danger since we know who Bob Hill is now and we don't think he'll chance coming after you again now that he's known. I'd take you and lock you up again if I thought you were in danger,"

Mason told her half-teasing.

Victoria couldn't stop herself from asking, "Would you throw in the keys again, too?"

"Probably should. I've been fantasizing about pressing you up against those bars or sharing that narrow cot every night since I brought you there the first time," he admitted quietly watching for her reaction. Hoping his honesty wasn't going to alarm her.

Mason must have noticed a change in Victoria and asked, "Have I frightened you again? Scared you of me? I wouldn't do those things. Not without your permission or acceptance, or...I'm making a mess of this." Expelling a deep breath, he asked, "Are you afraid of me, Vicki?"

Trying to be honest in return, Victoria admitted, "I don't know what I feel about you. When you talk like that, I get a sort of funny feeling in my stomach."

"Should I stop the buggy, are you getting sick? Want to, er, throw-up because of me?"

"It's not like that. More like fluttery little feelings rippling through my body. It happened in the jail that night, too. It isn't unpleasant, just makes me jittery, I think." Victoria said trying to explain the physical response she had to Mason. She didn't understand them but they were obvious to her whenever he was around.

Pulling Victoria closer, Mason seemed to relax. "I'm going to pull off up here and we can walk to the river. I think you'll feel better once were not bouncing around in this buggy."

Victoria agreed she wanted to see the river of Sweetwater, taste it to see if that's why the town was named what it was. The buggy went a few yards, following other tracks to the edge of some overgrowth and trees now fully in leaves and protecting the river from the sight of people on the road. Mason led Victoria through the undergrowth and then the clear, blue river flowed past them, inviting them closer. Welcoming them to sit on the green bank and watch the water ripple downstream.

Spreading out a blanket he had brought with them, Mason sat down, patting the place next to him for Victoria to join him. She hesitated and Mason smiled, saying, "Don't worry. I have myself under control and you have my permission to hit me in the head if I forget myself."

Returning the smile, she sat after tucking her skirt under her. Mason, now hatless, took off his gun belt and placed the revolver across the belt then unbuttoned his shirt sleeves and rolled them up to the elbow. Victoria watched intensely, licking her lips unconsciously as first one bare muscled forearm then the next was exposed to her view.

He began to toe off his boots when he realized that Victoria was starting to get up. He gazed at her in question. "I can't believe you can look at that cool, rippling water and not want to wade in it. Hell, I'd like to strip naked and dive in but I'm respectful that we don't know each other that well - yet." He laughed at the expression of alarm on Victoria's face.

"Come on, sit down. I'm going to wade and if you don't run away as soon as I'm in the river, I'll share some of that bottle that's in the basket I brought down here with us. I thought we'd get thirsty no matter what we were doing." He grinned up at her through his sun-bleached lashes before standing.

Staring, she watched him walk down the bank into

the clear river, letting his trouser legs get wet in the process. Victoria felt foolish standing there on the blanket fully clothed, yearning to be wading, too. She felt she was denying herself a true pleasure so lifted her skirt high enough to roll down her stockings and removed them along with her shoes. She scampered down the bank to the welcoming river. Holding her skirt up, she plunged her feet into the stream only to lose her breath as the water, feeling icy, hit her heated skin.

"Yikes! Why didn't you warn me? This is freezing, I swear, Mason." She glared at him accusingly.

"If I had said how cold it was you wouldn't have come in. Anyway, you'll get used to it and then it's not so bad. Even refreshing if you think about it." He smiled like a young boy at her.

"If you say so but I'm going back to the blanket when I think my lips are turning blue."

"I'll let you know when that happens. I have a sure-fire cure for them. Warms you up right away, in fact," he teased, again watching her for any interest she may show in him as a man.

Victoria shook her head, trying to ignore him as she became accustomed to the river's cold water rushing past her legs and continuing toward the town. Finally, she had her fill of walking along the river's edge and scooped up a handful of free-flowing water as it moved past her. And it was sweet. She was glad. She didn't know why that was and she took another handful and sipped its refreshing coldness.

She headed for the blanket with Mason right behind her, his legs wet to the knees. Kneeling down on the blanket next to Victoria, he said, "I'm not sure, but your lips do have a little tinge of blue to them. Would you like me to make them their usual cherry red?"

"I, um, if you think it will work." She smiled up at him inviting him to warm her.

"I think it will work just fine."

He leaned over her, helping Victoria lay back on the blanket without her awareness of ever doing so. Mason covered her mouth with his own and made a low groan as he finally got to what he had craved since the night in the jail. He sucked the bottom lip as he left her mouth just to cover it again and drink of her sweetness. His tongue asked permission to enter, he needed to become a part of her, even in a small way and she acquiesced.

Opening her mouth in response, Victoria was pleasantly surprised by the feelings that raced through her body. She put both hands on Mason's head, holding him to her lips and stroking his sun streaked hair, loving the feel of its softness as he evoked all sorts of erotic thoughts. Thoughts she never had before about a man and a woman, how they could enjoy each other, how they could pleasure each other.

How did she not understand there was more between them before this? She knew Matthew touched Abby all the time, even with Victoria watching in the same room - as if he couldn't prevent himself. Now it seemed to be the same with Mason. Did that mean he thought of her as Matthew thought of Abby or was he getting something from merely kissing her? Were the pleasant feelings traveling through her body the same as the ones traveling through his?

She relaxed into the kiss, pushed her body full length against his, wanted to feel more, have his weight on her, his hands travel over her body like they had in the jail. She wanted him to dominate her as he had that night. Take away her choice as to what he could and couldn't do.

Mason could feel a change come over Victoria and as much as he wanted more from her, he wasn't sure this was the right time. How would she feel later, when he had to drop her off at Abby's, after he had to let her go? He tried to slow things down but Vicki had her arms around his back, pressing her breasts into his chest and it felt so good to feel wanted, to think that this beautiful woman desired him, even if for a moment.

Placing his hand tentatively over one breast, Mason waited for any sign of denial but there wasn't any. If anything, Vicki arched into his palm, increasing the pressure on his back to remain close to her. He cupped then palmed the soft orb until he felt the pebbled hardness of her nipple through her clothes. That response was almost his undoing, his erection so hard he moved to accommodate the firm organ into the blanket but unwilling to give up his prize for comfort. He continued to accommodate the needy other breast and placed his mouth over the first tight bud through the thin materials between him and his reward.

Mason left the much-sought breasts to cool himself down but Vicki began to arch into his seeking mouth. She kissed his shoulder and chest the opened shirt allowed her to reach. He welcomed the advances on his person but knew this would have to end without the much-needed comfort his body, and hers, expected.

Victoria finally realized Mason was no longer participating in what they were doing as he had been earlier. He had returned her kisses but other than that he wasn't touching her. Instead had his arms on both sides of her body to hold his weight off her. She stopped kissing and Mason dropped his head to rest on her shoulder.

She felt like a fool. She had forced this onto Mason somehow and she was so stupid she hadn't even realized he didn't like it. She was mortified and tried to push him away so she could salvage her self-respect without him watching.

He held her down and whispered, "Let me recover will you, love? I'm not able to cool down as fast as you but I'll get there. Just stop wiggling under me and I'll get up in a minute." Looking at her in concern he asked, "Are you, all right?"

Victoria tried to understand what he had said, meant and what it meant to her and her emotions. "I'm fine. You're not disgusted with me? I acted so, so…I don't know what. Maybe I am bad, maybe I shouldn't be around Grace," she whispered to herself.

"Oh, Vicki, don't think those things, honey. It's my fault. You do something to me and then I can't keep control of myself. I thought I could since we weren't here after an emotional confrontation or anything but we're like fireworks and a match. It doesn't take much before we are close to conflagration." He actually laughed into her neck at his own naiveté.

She berated herself. How could she have forgotten herself to such an extent she wanted him, practically begged him, to touch her body. "I'm sorry, I shouldn't have come out here with you. I should have known better than to be alone with a man. I don't know why I let you do those things, why I wanted you to do those things."

Mason raised his head in time to see the expression of regret fill Vicki's eyes. "Don't blame yourself, honey. I brought you here and I didn't expect things to get so out of control. I planned on a little kissing, you know, allowing you to get to know me better. Maybe be more at ease around me."

"How much more at ease do you think I should be with you?" she demanded, still angry at herself for being so trusting.

He tried to explain. "Vicki, I'm so attracted to you I ache every night, an actual pain. I needed for you to learn I'm more than this badge, than the sheriff who thought you were part of a criminal gang, than a man for you to fear. I needed this afternoon more than you realize."

He wasn't sure he had made her understand. She seemed to be under some sort of thinking she had instigated his behavior. In a way, she had but his lack of control was due to his own weakness around her. His own need for them to become more to one another but now wasn't that time. There would come a time when he would be able to make her understand what was really between them but at an innocent nineteen, she had no idea.

"Will you admit that what we enjoyed together today doesn't happen between two people who aren't attracted to one another in more ways than the physical? This was all completely natural, a normal reaction between us. I want you to get to know me and learn what we can be to one another."

"I'm not sure I know what you want me to say? I felt something very strong and you were a part of that but that doesn't mean I'm attracted only to you like this," she said trying to work out what he had explained. She worried she might be turning into a woman who liked men too much. Not that she had known anyone like that but she had heard about women who couldn't stay true to their vows. As soon as their husbands had to go away from home, like to war, they brought in another man to take his place.

Mason felt as if a knife plunged into his gut at her remarks and then realized that if she hadn't been so inexperienced, she wouldn't mistake what they enjoyed today with something she would feel with any other man.

"Honey, I understand this was all new to you but believe me, what we shared today is more than what occurs between most men and women. I'll just have to hang around enough until you get used to me. Vicki, love, we have something special and I'll prove it to you if it takes me forever."

Standing up, Mason grabbed the blanket as soon as Vicki had followed him. He picked up the basket asking, "Will you come out with me again? We never even opened the wine I brought." He looked abashed at his own enthusiasm once he had gotten Vicki on the blanket and under him.

"I'll have to see. As I told you before, it's my job to take care of Grace." She wondered if she explained what had happened this afternoon to Abby, if her friend would understand what was happening between Mason and Victoria. Or would she prevent a woman with such loose morals from being anywhere near Grace? Victoria wouldn't hold it against Abby for doing that. A mother needed to protect her child from bad influences.

Both of the people riding back in the rented buggy were busy thinking their own thoughts. Mason on whether he rushed his fences and frightened Vicki of her own sexuality and Victoria on whether she had gone over the line of propriety and was unsalvageable.

Mason pulled the buggy to a stop in the middle of

the dirt road. Vicki could see the church from where they were and glanced inquisitively at the man next to her. They both spent a few minutes becoming more presentable, Mason helping Vicki straighten her hat and tucking in strands of hair that had escaped. He had rolled down his sleeves and rebuttoned the cuffs, his pants almost dry in the hot air.

"I'm afraid if I take you to Abby's I'm never going to see you again. I don't want that to be how we part. I want you to give us a chance and I don't want to have to fight Matthew to get to you." He turned to study her expression, trying to read her thoughts.

"I don't know what I should do. I knew about what happens between a man and woman but I didn't, not really. I never knew about the feelings, the strong urges and uncontrolled needs that seem to overwhelm a body. I don't know what I should do about it. I'm like a different person than when I left town a few hours ago," she whispered her confession.

"Talk to Abby, she's the best listener I know and she understands how emotions can get in the way of clear thinking. I trust her to explain everything to you. Just don't ask her to have Matthew protect you from me. I like the man but I like you a hell of a lot more." Desperation filled him as he kept glancing towards town knowing if she jumped out here, he would be seen chasing her home. "I'll fight for you if I have to until you tell me there's no hope for us as a couple. This isn't a passing fancy, Vicki. I'm willing to give you time to become used to the idea but I'll stay close by. I know you respond to me and you wouldn't do that if there weren't some feeling for me somewhere inside you. I'll wait till you know it, too."

Victoria nodded and sat back in the seat. Mason took one last glance at her then flicked the reins to urge the horse into the town center. He laid his hand over Vicki's for a moment before passing any of the houses then moved it back to the reins again.

What a mistake in judgement this trip was. What had he been thinking? Yes, he wanted to have time alone to speak openly with her but taking her all the way out to the river where he couldn't control himself…that hadn't been the best plan. And he hadn't even had time to drink the wine before he jumped her. No, he had to be honest. He hadn't exactly jumped her but pretty close. He knew she wasn't experienced and his plan was to have her warm to him little by little but it still hadn't been well thought out.

She was too innocent which he knew. Too sweet which he, also, knew. Too young for him which he wanted to ignore. Victoria was so right for him in so many other ways he was having trouble remembering she had been through a frightening experience and needed time to rethink her life plans. He simply wanted her to be sure to include him and he wanted to help those thoughts along a little.

She had thought herself ready for marriage when she decided to commit herself to Hill before realizing it had all been a hoax. So, didn't that mean she would be ready to commit to Mason? Or had her scare with choosing the wrong man once make her shy of choosing wrong again? Was time all that was needed? Maybe getting to know him better? See that he wasn't like Hill or those other men who were simply after her body?

Inhaling deeply, he decided he would bide his time. He knew they would be good together. Knew he needed her and that she would be safe with him. Knew they could make a loving marriage and have a family together. Now he needed to convince his body that waiting was the best plan. The best thing for the both of them.

CHAPTER 6

Victoria settled in with a new schedule. Matthew spent most of the next few days at home. He played with Grace and took her with him to pick up the mail or to visit friends within the town. Rebecca had come to the shop to visit as did two nice women from outside ranches. Emily and Mavis Macgregor, at least one of whom was also expecting a baby in the new year.

Victoria couldn't believe how many marriages had been held in the past few months and then how many of those resulted in the next generation for the town. She was both envious and inspired by these women who dared to come to an uncivilized territory, as it is thought of back east, to find their husbands.

Both women were open to the fact they met their husbands when they came as mail order brides, at least Mavis had. Emily came to give her friend moral support and ended up with both women marrying brothers. Victoria had heard enough of their story to know they felt lucky and blessed they found the men they had. And thankful for the people in the town of Sweetwater. That part Victoria could attest to, also. But with all the visitors and Matthew being home, Victoria had not found a time to talk with Abby about her concerns with her feelings toward Mason.

Victoria did feel more relaxed after she realized she didn't lose control around other men, even if they were young, good-looking men. It gave more credence to what Mason had told her that the two of them set each other into that frenzy of emotional conflagration as he called it. It wasn't something Victoria was going to need to control all the time around men. Only something Mason awakened in her that she would need to suppress.

Mason had stopped in once but then Emily and Mavis had come in for a fitting and he had disappeared after saying good-day to the ladies. Abby smiled at him as he left then rolled her eyes saying, "That is one hungry man!"

The other ladies laughed behind their hands and told Abby to behave herself, that she was a married woman. Victoria didn't know how Abby had known Mason was hungry, he hadn't said anything about food.

With Matthew home, there was less for Victoria to do. He liked to take Grace with him or even lay down and take naps with both Abby and the baby. Victoria still milked the goat and fed the chickens, gathering the eggs as she did so. The laundry was now done a little more often since there was Matthew's things to wash, too, but the work was completed by noon with the clothes hanging on the line. Victoria did the ironing as the clothes dried and again, by early afternoon in the hot dry air, everything was ironed, folded and put away even on her busiest days.

When the family rested upstairs, Victoria had begun to walk the length of the town, as far as the church at the northern most end of Main Street and back. She visited the churchyard but hadn't gotten up enough nerve to call on Miss Lily. Victoria didn't want to run into men visiting the ladies at Miss Lily's and have them get any misconceptions as to why she was there.

Sometimes she met Rebecca traveling between her home next to the little white church and the midwife's house across the street from the church that was used for

Rebecca's practice, a very busy practice if the number of women visiting Rebecca was anything to go by.

It was during one of these walks that as Victoria passed the livery, Bob Hill jumped out, grabbed her arm, and pulled her to him as he snarled, "Gotcha now, missy."

When he saw Victoria look toward the sheriff's office he laughed and sneered, "I seen your boyfriend set out earlier on his horse. Told the boy in the stable he'd be gone all day so now what'cha gonna do for help? Tell that fancy-pants gent that lives with you and your friend?"

Victoria whimpered as the hold on her arm tightened and Hill shook her so he could make sure she was paying him attention. "Now you're gonna go back to that lady shop and tell them you've decided to leave this here Sweetwater and go back home. If you don't, somethin' bad will happen to that bastard brat you care about."

"Grace isn't a bastard. She's perfect. Leave her out of this," Victoria said, getting frightened for Grace and Abby since both would be endangered if Hill decided to come to the shop after her. Matthew had gone out to his sister's ranch earlier and wasn't expected home till dinner.

"And be convincing about it. If that woman or her man comes after us, I'll make sure they both live to regret it. Got it straight?" With each word he gripped her arm tighter and gave her body a shake.

She could only nod, agreeing to anything Hill said to be free of him and to get to Abby and warn her to run, to hide and protect Grace. When Hill finally let go of her arm, Victoria almost collapsed to the boardwalk. Catching her balance, she rubbed her arm then turned to head toward the shop while Hill laughed. She could hear him talking to one of his hangers-on, telling them they'd be ready to leave any time now.

Victoria, dry-eyed, entered the shop and didn't even hear the chiming bell there was such a buzzing in her ears. She was having a difficult time focusing on what she had to do first. Abby came through the curtain with a giggling Grace on her hip.

She was about to tease Victoria about taking such a long walk when she looked at her friend and asked immediately, "What's wrong, Victoria?"

"Take the baby and go somewhere safe, go away - now." Victoria was gathering diapers and sunbonnet and pushing them into Abby's hands. "Go, I've got to go with him. He'll come here if I don't hurry so leave out the backdoor and travel down the alley. Go now, Abby, go."

Victoria threw her few clothes hanging on the wall hook in her cubical into her flour sack and turned to find Abby still standing there.

"Abby, please, you have to leave, now. Hill said he'd hurt you and Grace and Matthew. Go now. He won't hunt for you if I go with him."

Finally realizing she wasn't going to be able to talk Victoria out of leaving, Abby said, "I'm going. I'll get Matthew."

"No, Hill is real mean and he said he'd harm Matthew, too. He knows about us, that I've been living here and he told me you would all be sorry. I have to go, please don't tell Matthew. I don't want him hurt or killed trying to stop Hill. Mason is out of town so please go where you'll be safe. Don't tell me where you're going so I won't be able to tell Hill."

Desperate, she pleaded, "Leave now. I'll try to send

word to you later. I loved being here." She patted Grace's hair, turned and fled the shop.

Victoria walked slowly but with determination back towards the livery. She didn't know what her life was going to be like but she knew as long as she was with Hill, she would keep him from going after Abby or Grace. The man she dreaded the most in the world was waiting just inside the stable. No one else was in sight until the door closed behind her and then the same two wormy cronies of his came out of the depths of darkness.

The two men leered at her as Hill ordered her to lie down in the back of a buckboard while he threw gritty feedbags over her. She tried not to breath in the dust that shook out of the bags and found herself coughing as the men seemed to argue about something more.

She could hear Hill saying, "I wanna git outta here as soon as we kin. Just askin' for problems if we stay to maybe make a little extra but other than the mercantile nobody has much cash."

The shorter of the two worms, Victoria knew his whinny voice easily, argued, "But the dress shop sells all 'em 'spensive stuff. We could take 'em and sell 'em in Preston or pawn 'em if you don't want to waste time on 'em."

"Naw, I wanna be gone so we can be back afore nightfall. Besides, one of us would have to stay here so she don't run off agin. I promised Louise this young girl and she made it clear if I don't bring her soon, I'll be missin' my man parts. I know she's done it afore and I'm not gonna be next," Hill told the others sounding worried.

The wagon tilted as at least one man climbed onto the seat. "Now open them doors and I'll drive outta here just slick as shit."

Victoria heard the doors creak open and the reins slapped against the horses' haunches.

There was a grunt and another jostle to the wagon as it began to move when Victoria heard what could only be fists hitting face. Aggressive grunts sounded above her.

The shortest worm protested loudly, "Damn it, ya gotta help me, Hill. This guy's gonna kil…" Smack, slap and something was thrown hard against the side of the buckboard making it rock.

The wagon sped up. It must be free of the stable and heading south out of town travelling as fast as two horses can pull a wagon. Victoria bounced along the floorboards trying to keep from slamming against the side of the wagon as the wheels hit ruts and ridges in the road. She put out her hands to brace herself but found nothing to hold on to. Her body protested the rough jostling as she tried to keep her head from hitting the boards with too much force.

Bouncing along at the fast pace, Victoria wondered if she could uncover herself and possibly leap to safety from the wagon now they were out of town a little way. She could hide if she didn't break anything jumping in the first place. Possibly make her way to the train and try to get a ride anywhere. Except Preston, she would stay away from there no matter what.

Pushing the burlap bags up slightly, she took in deep gulps of fresh air. The air felt cooler on her face after being under the feedbags for so long. She tried to brace herself better but the wagon was veering all over the road. Her body was already bruised and scraped raw by the rough boards she was being thrown about on.

She wasn't sure how long she had been riding in the wagon, it could have been minutes or hours. Time seemed to lose itself as she tried to keep from being hurt. The horses were starting to tire and Victoria could tell the wagon wasn't going as fast as it had when they left Sweetwater.

Suddenly there was a loud roar and the wagon dipped and bounced as the weight shifted once more. Again, sounds of fists hitting home could be deciphered through her covering. Victoria thought if the men had become involved in a fight between themselves, this may be a good chance to jump and run for whatever cover she could find.

Pushing off the bags completely, she glanced quickly to the front in time to see two men fighting in the twilight. Without thinking too long about the execution of her plan, she made a dash to the rear of the wagon where she was thrown-out as the wheels hit a large rut and downed branches.

She landed on grass that the buckboard was now being dragged across by the two frightened horses, their reins flapping between the team's legs. As soon as she caught her breath, she jumped up and ran perpendicular to the direction the wagon was going, looking for some kind of cover but finding little.

She didn't glance back afraid the men would notice she was no longer in the wagon. Running as fast and as long as she could, she collapsed beside a bush, reminding her of the bushes along the Sweetwater River. Unwilling to stay anywhere near her abductors, Victoria got up and ran again, trying to stay on a route, running away from her captors. Then she heard it, the rushing of water and saw the bushes and small trees that grew along its banks.

Now she knew how to get home, how to get back to Sweetwater. Cupping her hands to drink the fresh sweet water, she sucked it in between gasping breaths of air before following the river home.

CHAPTER 7

Victoria thought she heard her name being called and she immediately hid, hoping Hill hadn't discovered where she was or where she was going. She prayed Mason was back in town so she could turn to him for help. Have Hill arrested for what he threatened to do to Abby and Grace. She stayed quiet, hoping the man would continue on but then she heard it, not her name but "Vicki!"

Only one person had ever called her Vicki and she listened again, hoping she hadn't simply wished the voice she was so desirous of hearing. When it came again, closer and from the direction she had come, she called out for Mason, trying to find him in the dusk. The darkness she had hoped to hide in was now causing her to stumble as she tried to reach the man calling for her. Leaving the river heading back through the overgrowth toward the sound of his voice, she called out Mason's name.

Mason came running to her shouts, grabbing her and holding her close. It hurt but she was too happy to have him find her that she didn't complain. She let him hold her before he finally set her from him to look her over. His hands skimmed over her body trying to find any wounds or blood. When he did, he cursed and lifted her in his arms to carry her back the way he had come.

"Put me down, Mason. I can walk. I would rather walk. I hurt in too many places, please put me down. We have to get back to Sweetwater to help Abby. Hill will go back to hurt her and Grace now that I jumped out of the wagon. We have to warn her and Matthew then find Hill," Victoria told him, knowing he could protect her friends.

He lowered her to the uneven ground. "Hill's been taken care of and so have his buddies, all of them hog-tied and ready for the Marshal. They'll be put away for a long time. Maybe hung if I have any say in it. Now save your strength and we'll catch up to Matthew and the buckboard in a few minutes. Are you sure you can make it? I don't mind carrying you," Mason offered.

"No, I'll walk. It's not so bad if I don't need to worry about Hill finding me," she answered truthfully.

Mason called out, whistling several times and soon a buckboard could be heard approaching.

Matthew pulled up on the dark road sounding relieved. "You found her. Are you all right, Victoria? Should we take you to the doctor or...."

"She's going to see the doctor, no matter what she says. I think she's got a broken rib, maybe only cracked. She jumped from this moving wagon somewhere along the way and I want her checked over completely," Mason told Matthew as if she no longer had a say in the matter.

Matthew nodded in what moonlight shown on the deserted road. "I agree. We'll take her there right away. Abby will nurse her until she's up and about."

"Abby won't need to do that. I can take care of myself and get back to work. I'm just a little sore. I'll be ready after a little rest and maybe something to put on these scrapes," she explained to Matthew.

Mason raised his voice. "You're hurt more than you're letting on, Vicki. Come on, I'll try to brace you a little but we need to get you back to town and the ride is going to be rocky."

"It can't be any rockier than the ride out of town. I wish I had Hill here and I'd kick him in his privates," she said bravely now that these two large men were there for protection.

Both men glanced at each other grinning, then Mason said, "He's hog-tied and thrown in the wagon back there. I'll give you a few minutes alone with him when we hit town if you're still of the same mind."

"What about the others, there's two more," she informed them.

"Matthew got the other two before they left the stable. Hill took the opportunity to take off with you only we didn't know that for sure until I ran into the stable lad coming back from Preston. Let's talk about this later. I want to concentrate on getting home and then Hill will be put into jail with the other two," Mason explained, making sure he kept her from bouncing too much.

Victoria thought that was fine with her. She realized she was too emotional to keep reliving the experience. Leaning against Mason, she tried deriving some strength from him.

She had missed her mother before but never so deeply as she did at that moment. All the thoughts that went through her mind, the fear of having those men touch her in that way, to possibly being taken to a brothel where she would be kept until she no longer had a will to do anything else. All the horrors compounded and she couldn't seem to let them go. Remembering the night the woman who meant everything to her passed, kept her thoughts from those that were tormenting her the most. Remembering the years she had with her ma as the happy, vital mother of the large brood of children. Even though they never had very much, her mother made it seem as if there wasn't anything holding them back. There was always a meal on the table and clothes, even if they were someone else's hand-me-downs. She kept them all clean and well mended so everyone went to school knowing they were loved. And there was always a bread and jam sandwich in the lunch box for each of them.

Then when Tommy was born Ma never fully recovered. It was as if the few hours she was in labor drained her of more than the energy it took to push him out. Always before, she was up and making the next meal with the newborn resting on her shoulder. With Tommy, the little tyke lay there crying for hours until Victoria came home from school and took him up. That was the last day she attended school. That was the day she admitted her mother wasn't the same and would need more care.

Not that she resented giving the help in any way. Where they lived, she had no other expectations other than to someday marry a local boy and have children of her own. Live in a small two- or three-room cabin that always seemed to need paint and wishing for a window that opened in the summer and extra firewood in the winter.

Victoria would have gone on forever taking care of her mother and her mother's house but one morning her mother wasn't there. Her body was, of course, but her ma was gone. She seemed to be the only one who mourned her. The younger ones looked to her for their meals and their clean clothes and help with their homework the same as always. Her pa ate his meals and worked the small plot of rocky ground the same as always.

She seemed to be the only one who missed the

woman they all owed their lives to. Maybe she had done too good of job replacing the woman in the other's lives. Maybe she learned too well how to run the house and the family.

Then Pa brought home a new wife, a new mother for the children who were all getting older and able to do without some of the niceties their mother and then Victoria always made sure were there. Fresh jam from the wild berries. Honey collected from the secret hive only she and her mother had known about. Fried bread when there wasn't anything else to eat.

The new wife wasn't mean but she wasn't pleasant either. Victoria never remembered her ma complaining about the condition of the house or not having money for a new hat. The woman seemed discontent with everything and sniped at Victoria and the older boys as if her lack of things were their fault. And the woman didn't like the way Victoria kept house which was spotless. Instead, she complained that Victoria was acting too uppity and wanted her to move on. Find a husband among the boys of the small town they lived near.

So, Victoria went from tending children to tending the small plot of tobacco which was their only cash crop. She also hired out to the neighboring farms during harvest and soon earned the reputation as a hard worker and quick with any job given her. But it wasn't enough for her stepmother. After all, Victoria still came home each night and the other children still turned to her for help with their homework or to mend a torn shirt.

The last ruckus, in front of the whole family, had her father siding with his new wife and Victoria searching through newspapers and flyers reading advertisements for mail-order-brides. That's when her need to find a new home brought her into contact with the men responsible for her last few hours of terror.

She couldn't believe she was unharmed and the two new men in her life had saved her.

Giving her a little kiss, Mason said, "We're here, Vicki."

Victoria opened her eyes to see the steeple of the little white church.

Mason lifted her down from the wagon and carried her up to the porch and through the front door of the white house. Rebecca was there saying, "The doctor's out on one of the ranches setting a broken leg. I'll take care of her, though. You know where the room is, don't you?"

The backroom off the kitchen was well lighted, several lamps burning, making the whole room glow. Mason set Victoria down on a raised cot and then searched her obvious wounds and injuries before letting a hissing sound out between his teeth.

Rebecca said, "Out with you, Mason. I'll call if I need you or when she's ready to make a statement for you."

Turning to Victoria as soon as the door was closed behind Mason, Rebecca smiled then sat on the nearby chair. She started by saying, "You've had a very stressful day, I hear. Is there anything you need to tell me? Anything that maybe doesn't show on the outside?"

Hearing the soft female voice, Victoria burst into racking sobs shaking her head and thinking about how much worst the day could have been, how close her life, as she knew it, could have ended.

Re-entering the room, Mason looked worriedly at

Rebecca before going directly to Victoria who put her arms around his sturdy body and held on like a limpet.

Standing, Rebecca said, "I'm going to leave her with you for a while. Her injuries can be cleaned up later. She needs to be held by a strong man who cares about her." Tipping her head like a brown wren, she asked, "You're that man, aren't you?"

"I'll take care of her, Ma'am. Can I take her into the other room and settle her? I think she's overly tired. She ran a long way before I found her," Mason told the midwife.

"Sure, no one will bother you. I'll be back in the morning. There's a nightgown in the dresser that she can wear," she instructed.

"I'll tell her. I won't leave her alone," Mason vowed.

"I didn't expect you would." Rebecca patted him on the shoulder leaving for the parsonage through the side door.

Mason carried a still weeping Victoria into the dim bedroom allowing her feet to touch the rug. "Vicki, love, I need to take this dress off you. It's filthy. I have a nightgown for you to wear and then I can get you comfortable in a nice clean bed."

Victoria stood but made no effort to undress or help Mason do so. He started unbuttoning the shirtwaist, now torn as well as dirty and again that hiss as he carefully pulled it off her arms, disclosing a long bruise along one arm. Purple bruises in the shape of fingers on the other. He found the buttons for her skirt and that ended on the floor next to the other garment. Victoria shivered, standing there in only her camisole and stockings, her shoes left in the back room.

Mason said, "All right, honey, now lift your arms just one more time and we'll be able to slip this gown on and you'll feel much better." As he lifted the camisole up and off, he viewed the damage that jumping out of a moving wagon could create. He noted the entire side of her breast, ribs and hip was already a bright reddish-purple but there was no fresh blood.

Hissing again, he lifted the clean gown over her head pulling it down to cover her nudity. Coaxing her to the edge of the bed, he had her sit down so he could unroll her stockings, now mostly in tatters with holes worn though the bottoms from running and hiding from her assailants.

Settling Victoria into the bed, he covered her with the light blanket. Turning to go back to the parlor area to wait while she slept, Vicki wouldn't let go of the hand she had grabbed as he put her into the bed.

Sighing, he said, "I'll just lay down until you feel comfortable enough to rest here for a while. I was only going to the other room. I'm not leaving you alone." Knowing it was wrong, he laid down opposite her most injured side. Soon they were both asleep, exhausted from the trials of the last day.

Mason woke up with Vicki pressed to his body, her lips kissing his chest where the shield front of his shirt opened. He said, "Hey, you're feeling better."

"I don't know all of what happened yesterday but I know you found me. I'm glad you did," she admitted to him softly.

"I had gone to Preston to check out Hill and found he had rented a buckboard that day but not a lot of other information that Matthew and I hadn't already known. On the way back, I ran into Andy, the boy who runs the stable here, riding to catch me in Preston. He didn't know who Hill was but he knew they were talking about grabbing someone and putting feed bags over them and taking them somewhere. Andy didn't know it was you but he thought I should be the one to confront them.

"I headed for Sweetwater as fast as my horse could gallop when I saw Hill on that buckboard. His friends weren't with him. I didn't see anyone with him but I jumped him from my horse as he tried to get away from me."

"Then it was you I saw fighting with him, not one of his friends?" she asked trying to understand what she had thought happened.

"I knocked him out and was putting cuffs on him when Matthew caught up with him. He had the other two tied up back here in the stable and left the reverend in charge of them. That's when we found your bag in the buckboard and my heart dropped, it really did. We started backtracking to see if you were ever in the wagon but Matthew said one of the fellas he caught told him you were with Hill." He hugged her then remembered the bruises.

"I decided to start calling for you, hoping you weren't unconscious. It was getting dark so I was about to send Matthew back to get a search party together to follow the trail all the way back to Sweetwater. Your voice answering me was the sweetest sound I ever heard, it truly was." He began to return her kisses, covering her mouth and sucking on the soft skin near her ear.

"Make love to me, Mason. I want to know what it's all about," she whispered as she continued to kiss his face, chin, jaw, lips.

Mason stopped kissing her. "Where is this coming

from? You're too injured to be thinking of anything so strenuous."

"Yesterday I came very close to having my life as I know it completely eliminated. If I don't make love with you and someone like Hill gets to me, I'll never know true lovemaking. I'll only know what's done to me after that. I want to have a good experience to hold on to," she tried to explain what she needed from him, only from him.

"I know what you're saying but I won't let anything happen to you. Hill and his pals are going to be gone a long time and that's if they don't hang for kidnapping. You're not in danger any longer," Mason told her reasonably.

"You said that once before and they came back and they could have hurt Abby and Grace, too," she said accusingly.

Mason knew she was right. He had underestimated Hill's tenacity to get Victoria to Preston. "I'll never forgive myself for not protecting you, put you up somewhere out of town where you would have been difficult to grab. But we've been watching Hill in Preston and he never indicated he was still after women. They've been having a penny-ante crime spree, robberies and pilfering, that Matthew and I have finally put an end to. I'm mad at myself for not realizing how persistent he was about getting to you. I should have put you under more protection but I thought Hill was keeping busy in Preston."

"I remember something Hill said while I was under the feedbags. I remember he said something about a woman, and if he didn't bring me to her, she would cut off his man parts. I know...." She tried to search her mind for the name, a woman she should remember, oh, yes. "Her name was, Louise. And they all seemed afraid of her," Victoria told him.

"Where do you think she was? Back in Preston?" he asked not remembering hearing of a madam in Preston with the name of Louise.

"I don't know but Hill was taking me to Preston and he said he had to get me to her," Victoria reiterated, now very sure of what she heard.

"That may help. We never had a name before but we know a woman is involved," Mason told her.

"You originally thought I was that woman, right?"

"Not for very long but, yes. You fit her general appearance and were new to the state. Then you had a sketchy story, knew no one in Sweetwater, and yet came here out of nowhere. Just had a lot of questionable history, I guess."

Victoria tried to regain Mason's attention by stroking his chest through the shirt material and leaned toward his mouth again. Mason pushed her back from him saying, "I'm not going to do anything even though I'm finding it very difficult to turn you down. You're covered with bruises and I would feel I was taking advantage of you while you're still recovering from a traumatic ordeal."

"I won't force you. I'll wait till I'm better. I'm sorry, I asked." He saw tears well in her eyes and felt rotten.

"Christ, Vicki, you make me feel like I kicked a puppy. Come on, honey, you know you're in too much pain to do anything like that. Don't make me worry you'll be asking someone else as soon as I turn my back," Mason said worriedly.

"It doesn't matter. You're not obligated to me. I was

merely there when you wanted to check me out as a possible criminal. I understand now you have Hill we'll go our separate ways," she threw the words at him like an intractable child.

"Vicki, I promise, if you're still of the same mind, I'll make love to you in two weeks. Give yourself two weeks to heal and restore yourself. Abby and Rebecca will help you regain your balance. Right now, I think your reacting to a very scary time."

"You promise if I still want you to make love with me you will in two weeks to this day?" She stared into his eyes as if daring him to deny her request.

"I promise." He kissed her on her nose and quickly swung his feet off the bed and opened the door to sneak out of the house by way of the back door.

He met Rebecca's gaze across the parlor and then said, "I was just checking on Vicki. She's still sleeping."

Rebecca gave him that look that only a mother usually can give and said straight faced, "Next time you do that, try to remember to take off your boots. They leave dirty marks on the blankets."

"Yes, Ma'am," he said feeling heat suffuse his face. "I need to send a wire to Preston. Will you stay with Vicki until I get back?"

"Go and do what you need to. Abby, Matthew and I will make sure someone is with her every moment."

"Thank you, I owe you all so much," he said sincerely.

"It's Sweetwater, we take care of our own. You don't owe us anything. Go get the bastards and we'll take care of Victoria."

CHAPTER 8

After Mason left, Rebecca went in to see if Victoria was feeling up to taking a bath. Rebecca started heating the water while Victoria sat in a chair at the table.

The midwife said, "I'll walk out to the privy with you unless you want a bed pan."

"No, I think I want to walk a little. I'll slide my shoes on and be right back."

There was a copper tub in the back room where Rebecca saw her patients. She filled it with cooler water and Epsom salt. Victoria took off the gown and Rebecca examined all the bruises and scrapes before letting her climb into the tub to sit down gently. She washed Victoria's hair and then filled the tub nearly to the top with cool water.

"This will be better for the bruises. I'm glad there were no broken ribs. I'll put some ointment on the scrapes and the bruises will heal eventually," Rebecca told her young patient.

"By two weeks?" asked Victoria, not saying why she wanted to know.

"By two weeks most of the pain will be gone. You'll be fine in a month, probably no signs of the physical injuries at all. Now what about the other. How do you feel about what happened?" Rebecca asked knowing the trauma of an attack would sneak-up on a woman after a few days. Victoria wasn't as blasé about what happened to her or the threats against Abby and Grace as she appeared to be or wanted others to think.

"I don't know. I was most scared while Hill and his

cohorts were threatening Abby, Grace and Matthew. I knew Abby would fight before she would let them near the baby so I was most worried about getting those men out of town."

"I'm sorry Matthew couldn't prevent the wagon from leaving but he was taking care of the other two and by the time he had them under control, the wagon was gone and he had to get a horse saddled to follow. He bound up his own arm until he got back last night and I could suture him."

"Matthew was hurt? Did they shoot him? He didn't say anything last night in the wagon. He even drove us back." Victoria went to change out of the clean nightgown Rebecca had pulled over her head after the bath. "I have to get to Abby."

"No, Matthew is all right. He did get cut during the knife fight but he's had worse. Doing what he does, he has needed quite a lot of medical attention in the past. Abby takes it all in stride now. She's even able to bandage most wounds. She should be able to sew him up, too, but she said she's not quite ready to do so, yet." Rebecca chuckled at her friend's squeamishness.

"I didn't know. Matthew is such a gentleman, so citified. I have a problem seeing him as a type of avenging angel," Victoria said, rethinking Matthew's role.

"But that is exactly what he is. He has saved so many women who would otherwise have been killed or committed suicide trying to get out of a life they hated."

"I knew he helped those poor women but I thought they came to him and he found them decent jobs and a place to live." Victoria felt new affection and respect for Matthew and for Abby who allowed her husband to help save these women.

"Well, he does do that but after he has taken them out from under their bosses' nose. People who feel these women belong to them because they have bought them - sometimes from the girl's own family member. Or they are stolen right off the streets and taken somewhere until they lose all fight to get back where they belong. Matthew hunts out these women and rescues them and that often means fighting his way out of a place," explained Rebecca, again opening Victoria's eyes to Matthew's life when he wasn't in Sweetwater.

"I had no idea. He is so gentle with Grace and I've never known a man to be so in love with his wife, well, that's not true. You and Daniel are in love, too. There isn't any doubt," Victoria said bringing a smile to Rebecca's lips.

"You should see Matthew's sister Callie's husband. She should be made of porcelain he's so worried about her safety. While she was expecting, I thought he was going to collapse before she delivered. He spent so much time focused on her. And all the others, too. I told you the new fathers-to-be and even the Macgregors who had barely been married brought me to Sweetwater so there would be a midwife available when their wives needed one."

"It must be very rewarding to feel so loved," said Victoria enviously.

Rebecca stared at her patient and realized Victoria was totally blind to her own good fortune. Well, it would be better for the girl to comprehend her own feelings and Mason's at another time. The way Mason worried about Victoria it wouldn't surprise Rebecca to have another wedding in the near future. Perhaps she would warn

Daniel so he wouldn't be caught off guard.

Abby knocked and struggled through the front door, holding Grace and carrying a basket. Rebecca hurried to relieve her of the basket heavy with food sent by Callie. Someone who had never met Victoria, yet, still sent the basket of delicacies.

"Oh, Abby did you carry that all the way? You shouldn't have gone to so much trouble," said Victoria worried her friend was doing too much.

"Matthew is right outside. He carried everything till I came in. He wants to talk with Mason so he'll come back for me later." She went over and hugged and kissed Victoria on her cheek bringing tears to both ladies' eyes. "I'm sorry for your ordeal. I can't believe you actually endangered yourself to protect Grace and me. You were very foolish but I am grateful for your generous spirit."

"That's all I could think of to do. Send you away," Victoria tried to explain wiping the tears from her face.

"And I was running to Matthew. Luckily, he was coming home so I sent him to the livery since that's where you indicated Hill was waiting. Then I continued on to get Daniel and I stayed with Rebecca who pulled out her arsenal."

"Daniel was involved in this, too? But he's a minister," said Victoria in amazement looking at first Abby and then Rebecca for confirmation.

"Daniel used to brawl in the streets of Kansas City before he chose the path of the church. I don't know who I'd put money on when it came to a fight between our men. I'd go with Daniel even though he hasn't had a lot of practice the last few years," said Rebecca loyally.

"Yes, but Matthew has a derringer, knife plus usually a holstered gun on his hip. And a lot of experience fighting rough thugs on the worst streets anywhere," Abby said proudly, removing Grace's hat.

"And Mason's no slouch. He only has had to throw a few drunks in the jail cell but he is a demon on the back of a horse and can roundup rustlers pretty quickly," added Rebecca making sure Victoria knew the younger man was a powerful protector as well.

"He jumped from a racing horse onto a moving buckboard. That's how he got Hill and then found me," agreed Victoria with a proud tilt to her head.

"As I said, Sweetwater takes care of its own and you are now a resident of Sweetwater, Victoria. No one is going to let anyone harm you again." Then to change the subject said, "I'm hungry. Let's get this food heated and I'll make tea. Did Callie send dessert?" asked the ever-hungry Rebecca.

Abby answered, "Yes, she said there were little cakes with frosting roses."

"I love those. Don't let me have more than two. I can't fit into some of my dresses as it is," complained Rebecca.

A silence followed her announcement and then Rebecca appeared chagrined, saying, "I'm as bad as any mother I have ever dealt with. Now I know how easy it is to let it slip. Please don't say anything or I'll have all the new husbands in a panic. Daniel and I have already discussed this possibility and he agreed with me to keep working up until I give birth. Then any expectant mothers due at the same time as me, I'll have trained another on how to deliver. Maybe one of the Mary's from Callie's ranch. And there's always Doctor Winters."

The three women thought about what was being

discussed before Abby said, "I'm happy for you and Daniel. This will make him even a better minister and husband. I know he's a great husband now but this will humanize him even more. It's humbling to know you created this little human you are now responsible for." She hugged Grace closer.

"I hope I'm ready after all the babies I've brought into the world. I know all the good and bad and Daniel is already asking about possible problems that could occur so that he is prepared. I'm more worried about him at this point. There's a fine line between knowing what will happen to one's body, in this case mine, and what all could happen. I try not to relay anything I think may have him following me around with a pillow," she said smiling at her friends, one of whom was due to give birth in a few short months.

CHAPTER 9

Mason's boots made a hallow sound with each step as he walked into the building the ranch hand told him James was in. The Macgregor ranch was a big operation and they did most things needed to keep it running on site. James, his auburn hair glinting in the setting sun, was pounding in a rivet on part of a saddle when he looked up and greeted his friend.

"Mason, what brings you out here? Problems with rustlers again?"

"No, problems with a woman," said Mason half-teasingly.

"I'm not your man for that help any more. I'm hog-tied remember?" he chuckled in return.

"I asked Mac first while he was kicking dirt waiting for your wives in town. He said everything he knew, you taught him so I thought I'd get it from the horse's mouth as it were." He plucked a piece of straw from a pile and chewed the end nervously looking anywhere but at his oldest friend.

"What exactly are you asking me, Mason?" James stopped working and stood waiting for an answer.

"I need to know how to pleasure a lady, make it nice for her, too," said the now completely embarrassed Mason.

James, shaking his head replied, "Jesus, what did you men do to get laid before you had me to talk you through it? Didn't you ever visit Miss Lily's, either?"

"I've been with women. I don't need a diagram or anything. I know where all the parts go, I just don't know how to make sure she enjoys it as much as I'm going to," Mason admitted.

"I know I'm going to regret asking this but how long has it been, you and a woman together." James waited for the answer.

Quietly Mason mumbled, "Two years or so." At James questioning look, he said louder, "Two years more or less."

"Probably more." He exhaled in one long breath. "Mason, I don't know if I'm the right fella for this. Until Mavis, I had been with a lot of women but they were worldly if you get my gist. They taught me things I never would have dreamt of on my own."

"All right, tell me some of them," Mason said, finally deciding James was going to be of some help with his problem after all.

"Look you're a horse guy so I'll try to explain it like this. I had a mare and she liked me to brush her but there was one spot that she really liked brushed most, just at the curve of her back, near the rump. Then there was a place she would kick out at me if I brushed her there. The fore leg, so I learned to look for what she enjoyed and stayed away from the things she didn't enjoy. Am I making any sense to you?"

"I should treat Vi, I mean, my lady like a mare. Try things and if she acts like she likes it to keep doing it and if she shies away, change and do something else?" questioned Mason seeing if he got the strategy correct.

"Kind of. I take it you fantasize about this woman? Have dreams, maybe even daydreams about her and you and doing things to her?" James asked without embarrassment. After all it wasn't his first rodeo.

Mason looked up at James as if James could read his

223

mind but answered truthfully, "More and more lately."

"Well, start with some of those dreams. If she likes what you're doing she's going to let you know and if she doesn't, she'll let you know that, too." Then he looked directly at his friend and said, "And Mason, it sometimes takes a little practice together so don't expect perfection the first time. Especially since she doesn't have much experience, either."

"I didn't say that," blustered Mason.

"You didn't need to." James picked up the hammer again but said before he started on the stirrup he was repairing, "I'll expect an invitation to the wedding."

Mason smiled and replied, "Sooner rather than later. This woman is killing me."

CHAPTER 10

Mason came through the shop door as usual just to speak to whomever was there. Abby usually but today Victoria made sure she was the one to greet the tall, lean sheriff. He grinned when he saw her and asked, "Everything all right in here?"

Victoria walked over to him and answered, "Everything's fine just as it's been the last fourteen days you've visited here. That's two weeks, Mason, to the day." She continued to watch him expectantly.

Mason flushed and jammed his hands into his front pockets, "You sure, Vicki?" he asked quietly so only she would hear. At her decisive nod, he asked, "When did you want to do, er, meet up or…."

"Today is two weeks to the day and you promised." She continued to stand there staring up at him with anticipation.

After clearing his throat twice, Mason asked, "Would you care to accompany me for an afternoon drive, Miss Victoria? Maybe go out to see the river?"

Victoria smiled and answered, "That sounds lovely, Mason. About one o'clock then?"

He seemed to find speaking difficult and merely nodded in agreement and left, the little chime announcing his departure.

Abby came in and asked, "Wasn't that, Mason? Didn't stay long. Did you offer him some of Miss Lily's cookies?"

"Yes, but he said he had things to do. He's taking me for a drive this afternoon, though," she added knowing the white lie was the least of her sins lately. She had just coerced a man into showing her what making love was all about.

"That's nice. You've been cooped up in this shop for far too long if you ask me. And I think you're out of danger with Hill and those other two in the fort's prison waiting for trial. Matthew said they may not live long enough to even get a trial." After seeing Victoria's shiver, she added, "Mason won't let anything happen to you today. You'll be in safe hands."

"That's what I thought, too," she answered honestly and went to change clothes.

Mason pulled up in front of the dress shop and Victoria met him on the boardwalk, smiling and looking for all purposes like a young lady going for a country drive, not a young lady going intent on becoming a woman. At least in her own mind. Mason appeared more like a man facing an execution rather than a man who was going to enjoy a clandestine meeting with a woman he finds definitely tantalizing.

Trying to smile normally, he found he wasn't relaxed in any sense of the word. He kept thinking this was going to be a disaster - for Victoria, at least, and he would blame himself for her disappointment. He was supposed to make sure she enjoyed being with him. After remembering little things said about first times and such, he wasn't sure he was the right man for this. But at the same time, he couldn't even think of her with anyone else so it fell back on him to make sure Vicki enjoyed the experience and wanted to repeat it - with him.

Victoria was going over in her mind what she planned on doing once they reached the riverbank. She approved Mason's choice of setting, the weather looked wonderful, and she had peered at herself in the mirror in the fitting room and didn't think she looked too bad. She wasn't sure how to make herself more attractive to Mason. She didn't have any of those frilly underthings that were supposed to excite the male of the species into a sexual frenzy or so the advertisements indicated. She would simply have to be enough. The last time he seemed to enjoy her so she was probably worrying needlessly.

With both of the occupants of the rented buggy deep in their own thoughts, there wasn't much conversation on the drive and soon Mason was pulling off the road. Victoria recognized the area as the same as when they had waded in the river. She waited for Mason to tie up the horses and then help her down. She enjoyed his hands on her waist and the way he slid her down his long torso. He held her in front of him for just a second before reaching behind the seat for a blanket and basket.

Victoria, her newly sewn skirt lifted slightly to keep the grass from tugging on it, followed Mason as he made a path for her through the tall grasses. He held up a few branches so she could go under them and found herself on the open bank of the river, her river - her Sweetwater.

Mason tried to break down the grass to get a flat spot for the blanket then finally turned to help Victoria sit. She had been taking the pin out of her hat and was setting it on one corner of the blanket, bending to remove her shoes. She hadn't worn stockings since she wanted less clothes between her and Mason.

Following her lead, he toed off his boots then pulled off his socks after placing his Stetson on another corner of the blanket. He removed his shirt and belt, placing his gun as he always did and unbuttoned his trousers letting them hang open on his lean hips.

Finally, he said seriously, "Victoria, I won't be upset if this isn't how or what you want. We can sit and talk or wade or whatever."

"I think I like the whatever." She smiled over at him shyly.

Mason smiled back and then leaned toward her and kissed her, covering her lips with a hungry mouth that sucked and returned for more. Her mouth was just as sweet, just as responsive as he had remembered, as he had dreamed about every night since he was last here with her. His hand covered a breast and massaged it through the clothing she still wore raising the nipple to an eager peak.

Remembering the last time and Mason's hot mouth sucking through her clothes, Vicki began to unbutton her shirtwaist while remaining in lip contact with him. Shrugging out of it, she unbuttoned her skirt so she could pull her camisole up and over her head. That forced Mason and Vicki apart but only for a moment.

As Vicki raised her hands to finally be rid of her underclothes, her large orbed breasts came to Mason's attention. He latched on to the closest needy nipple and laved it tenderly. Then unable to hold himself back, suckled it and then its twin, bringing Victoria into a sweet swoon. Her hands went to his head, pushing her fingers through his sun kissed hair and holding him to her breasts. She tried to define the feeling going through her body and culminating in the lowest section, making her aware of the female parts she usually paid no attention to.

But Mason seemed to want to. He pushed her skirt down and it was now puddling around her knees while his hand went to the downy curls. He found the hidden womanly part waiting there, waiting to gain his notice, his touch. And it did.

Mason pushed Vicki back so she was laying down alongside him. He looked at the yellowish green blotches still covering most of her one side. He kissed them from her shoulder down her ribs and then to her hip. He nuzzled the downy covering then pressed his lips to the warm core of her.

Vicki tightened her thighs together but Mason gently stroked her there. Relaxing, she enjoyed Mason paying her such intimate attention. Feeling the warm strokes of his tongue, she noted little tornados of sensations spiraling and peaking before starting all over again. She held her breath as one began and then expelled that air when she reached a peak. Mason seemed to become more and more excited as Vicki kept reaching these pinnacles. Soon she was pulling Mason up to lie on her, to place his strong erection near the mound he had recently been attending.

"Are you sure?" Mason panted, kissing every area he could reach as Vicki nodded eagerly. Pulling him to her, she urged him to fulfill his promise. Mason was too involved at this point to question much of anything. Vicki's responsiveness to his ministration had him almost beyond control, everything he'd been told fled from his mind. The only thing that mattered was the here and now, making Vicki his, claiming what no other man could after today. Hoping it would be enough to make her want to stay with him, be his wife, have his children.

Thrusting into Vicki, he held her hips as he began to retreat and then Vicki's hips came up to meet him with that little shiver of desire that stirred him so thoroughly.

She was warm and welcoming and womanly. She pushed her hips up to him and just that small movement sent Mason into a spiral of climatic spasms followed by Vicki's stronger internal muscles clenching him, sending Mason over the edge.

He collapsed onto Vicki while she hugged him to her, both trying to catch their breaths from a sensual rapture that had wound them into an erotic frenzy. Naked, Mason rolled off of Vicki but kept his arm under her. Vicki rolled toward Mason and lay there twining her fingers in his chest hair, analyzing what had occurred between them, knowing it was the two of them that had been needed to have the resulting culmination of sensations.

"That was wonderful, Mason. Thank you," she said still trying to calm her breathing and heartbeats.

Mason leaned up on his elbow. "Don't thank me, honey. I didn't know it could get so, so explosive. I have to think it was because I was with you."

"I don't have a way of knowing. Do you think we can do it again to find out if it will always be like this between us?" She looked up through her lashes to find Mason gazing at her with passion, then lower to see the desire showing in his manhood as it indicated interest in repeating the lovemaking.

"Can I touch it? You, I mean?" asked Vicki as she looked for the first time upon the wondrous body that had made her world turn over.

"Yeah, I guess," said Mason unsure of where this would take them. He never thought about Vicki wanting to touch him like he wanted to touch her. He laid back and tried not to show his rising excitement.

"It's so strong yet silky." She softly petted the

growing erection. Mason couldn't prevent a hiss from escaping.

Vicki pulled her hand back quickly. "Did that hurt? Did I do something wrong?"

"No, to both. Its...I'm just a little...I don't know, touchy right now. I never noticed it before but you didn't hurt me. I like it quite a lot." Leaning toward her, he kissed her waiting mouth.

Vicki looked back to where her hand had been unconsciously stroking the firm warm rod and placed her finger over the velvety top. Finding a bead of liquid, she spread it around feeling small tremors go through Mason. Leaning down, she kissed the soft tip and then sucked it into her warm mouth, encompassing the entire top.

"Oh Vicki, oh, honey. You don't have to do that." He tried to stop her actions but was intrigued with the feeling of her mouth on him.

"Don't you like it?" she asked innocently, still stroking the side of his overly aroused manhood.

"I like it just fine, maybe too much," he answered honestly while fingering her closest breast.

"It's something I would like to do. I'll stop in a little while," she told him and Mason remembered James' instructions to find something she liked and then do it. Mason thought it must be the same with this and he wasn't disliking it himself. Mason moaned on that thought and tried to focus on anything but what she was doing to him.

Vicki had become very decisive in her role of lovemaking and felt she had been too passive the first time. She was beginning to understand Mason's reactions a little more as she experimented and finally decided to take full initiative. She threw her leg over his body and placed the now well-tended penis where it belonged and pushed down, settling herself around him.

Mason's hips came right off the blanket, meeting her as she welcomed him into her womanly warmth once again. Holding her hips, Mason helped set the rhythm. He felt the small tremors begin and recede in Vicki until he felt her inner muscles convulse around his stiff member. During that reciprocating muscle tightening, he found a euphoric release of his own once again. Vicki stayed lying on top of him as both caught their breath.

Stroking Vicki's back, Mason tried to think of a way to tie her to him so he would never fear she would leave him.

Victoria was thinking about how she wished she was tied to him in some way that would insure she never had to leave him. But she had to acknowledge a Tennessee sod farmer's daughter wasn't what a sheriff of a growing town needed. She had no experience with town living or what was expected of a sheriff's wife but she couldn't think it was a woman with only a sixth-grade education. People would expect more of her and she feared Mason would, too, once the newness of their relationship wore off.

Once again, she would be inspected and come up wanting. Not smart enough, not fashionable enough, not the right background. She wasn't completely ignorant of how town politics worked. She had run into the mayor's wife, Mrs. Thompson, in the Mercantile and been ignored as if she weren't standing there with Helen, the owner. Although she had tried to learn proper speech and manners from Abby, she knew she wasn't anywhere near what Mason needed as a wife. Her accent had been mentioned more than once as sounding uneducated.

Not in Sweetwater, most of the people she met here were kind enough not to comment but Hill and his friends had been very dismissive of her. Even saying if she had complaints, no one would take her seriously. That she sounded too ignorant and they could tell the authorities she wasn't fully capable of taking care of herself, a 'half-wit' they said. She hadn't understood at the time they meant when they kept her captive at the hotel while they took their time with her. No, she wasn't a woman that men who had ambition tied themselves to.

Mason pulled Vicki's body against his own so he could place kisses on her face and neck and breasts. "Vicki, honey, we have to make some decisions. You could be with child even now. Tell me you'll marry me and I won't have to worry about your safety anymore. I love what you do to me, the way you make me feel, even the ache when you're not with me."

"Mason, I loved what we did, how you made me feel, but I don't want what happened to me with Hill to define my life. I don't want to make this decision right after we've been together like this. It's too emotional for me," Victoria explained not wanting Mason to feel obligated to tying himself to her merely because she forced him into having sex with her.

"But if you're pregnant, you'll marry me?" he asked hopefully.

"I don't think we need to worry about that. I spoke to Rebecca." At his wary expression, she continued, "Not about this, not about our lovemaking. I merely asked about how to keep from getting with child and she told me about this method of counting days. I'm not near the days I would get pregnant. That won't be an issue."

She assured him to his disappointment.

Mason looked at her, hurt in his eyes, "So this was a onetime thing for us? No real feelings or commitment between us, just a way to be rid of your virginity?"

"Not exactly. I didn't want my first time to be tied to a bed with a bunch of strangers. I needed to know a little love, a little tenderness. I didn't mean to make you feel, I don't know …"

"Used? I would have made love to you no matter what reason, Vicki. I guess I thought there was more emotion between us besides desire. I'm glad I was the first. I'm glad I made it pleasant for you," he said confused, reaching for his trousers and tugging them on.

"Oh, Mason. It was more than pleasant. It was explosive and I don't know how to thank you," Victoria began as if she were acknowledging a dance at a social event.

"Maybe you can bake me some cookies as an expression of gratitude," he muttered as he rose to gather the rest of his clothes which he took down to the river with him.

Why had he even thought she would consent to marry a man like him? He was sheriff in a Podunk town even if he thought it had potential. Originally, she had planned on living in Preston which was a much larger town and the county seat. More excitement happened in Preston even if that brought more crime and criminal elements to the area. And there were more activities there. Things she probably had missed out on before but could see and attend as a grown woman. Sweetwater couldn't compete with a city like Preston. He couldn't compete with a man living in such a city, either.

Victoria sat up watching him leave, unsure of what

she had said that had turned Mason from a loving man to a morose stranger. She, too, put her clothes back on but didn't go near the river. After a few minutes, Mason returned to fold the blanket and pick up the untouched basket. He helped Victoria return to the buggy.

Now what is a man supposed to say to a woman who basically told him she wasn't interested in him other than for a little sport?

CHAPTER 11

Victoria hadn't seen Mason in a couple of weeks. Not since he brought her back from the riverbank and helped her down from the buggy out front. Abby had said that was a good thing since Mason wouldn't have stayed away unless he felt the danger was over. Matthew had taken a few overnight trips to other towns on his route but never stayed away longer than one night. Possibly that would change now, too, if Mason felt Hill and his gang were contained completely.

Deciding she would return to her daily walks, Victoria planned to stop in at the Mercantile, visit with Helen then collect any mail for Abby. She'd continue walking to the end of town and return on the other side of the street back to Abby's shop. The exercise was invigorating and she wanted to return to the life she had before Hill and his thugs tried to take her from her adopted town.

Pinning on the hat she and Abby had made together, she checked her appearance in the mirror. "Abby, while you and Grace rest, is there anything you need while I'm out?" She pulled on her gloves, saying, "I may take a little longer than usual. I think I owe Miss Lily a visit in return for all those visits and cookies she's brought me."

"Be forewarned, Miss Lily loves to get hold of your hair and give you a new style. She's very good but it takes her hours to get it just right. I'd have her do mine more often but I don't want to spend that much time away from Grace and Matthew."

"I'll keep her talking and not take off my hat. I think

I can escape with my scalp." Both women laughed.

"If I don't see you by supper, I'll send Matthew out to rescue you," Abby teased.

Walking down the boardwalk, she looked into the windows of the various stores, even the meat shop. It seemed like so long since she had done these simple things. Crossing over to the Mercantile, she spoke with Helen a while but then an order was brought in by a ranch hand that had to be filled so the two ladies parted ways.

Victoria said her goodbye and continued on towards Miss Lily's which would have her walk right past the sheriff's office. She was hoping Mason would be there and she could talk to him. Unhappy with how they had left things after their time by the river, she was sorry she hadn't made her thoughts plain to him.

A pretty woman, several years older than Victoria approached on the boardwalk. Victoria looked enviously at her dark green dress with a high bustle swept up in back and the way the tight waisted top skimmed her thin figure. There were little black buttons shining all the way down the bodice ending at the waist and then again at each wrist to the elbow. A very exotic hat was nestled in her massive hair style of trailing curls.

As the woman got closer, she smiled at Victoria and Victoria smiled in return. The woman stopped and asked pleasantly, "You're Victoria Watkins, aren't you?"

Victoria stopped and said graciously, "Yes, I am. Have we met, Miss, er, Mrs...?"

Still smiling the stranger said rather menacingly, "We haven't met but you know several of my acquaintances, Bob Hill, for one."

Victoria started to push past the woman but a small gun appeared in the woman's gloved hand. Evidently, she had been hiding it in the matching reticule she carried.

"Now Hill said you were a smart girl so let's see if he was right about that, at least. We're going to turn around and head back to the livery where we will get into my buggy and take a little ride. Do we understand each other." She poked the gun into Victoria's ribs in case Victoria wasn't sure about going with her.

"I'll be missed. There are people looking out for me," bluffed Victoria. Right now, all those watching over her think she's in a safe place and it may be hours before she's missed. Victoria tried to slow her pace but then realized they would still have to pass Mason's office. She started to pray he was sitting in his office looking out the window.

A man appeared to their left, dressed in a grey suit and wide ribbon tie. His dark hair was topped with a grey derby and he had a mustache and goatee that tried to hide his weak upper lip and chin. Carrying a gold headed black cane, he searched the street furtively.

"This way, Louise. I don't want to pass that damn office and have this all blow up in our faces," he snarled.

"Look, Carl, I know what I'm doing. I've planned this all out so simply follow what I told you. Is the buggy still ready to go? You didn't let that boy unhitch the team or anything?" she snapped at her cohort.

"No, I paid the hostler and told him to take off for a while. We'll be gone by the time he returns," said the man called Carl still searching the street with his gaze for anyone paying attention to them.

They were going down the narrow space between the hotel and the building that housed the sheriff's office. The man led the way followed by Victoria with Louise and her gun bringing up the rear. Victoria thought if Mason heard her voice, he would come out to investigate.

Fairly loudly Victoria asked, "Where are we going? Where are you taking me?"

Louise shoved the gun into her back saying, "Shut up, you bitch. I'll shoot you and then put a bullet into that damn sheriff if he shows up. No one ever suspects a woman of having a gun."

They were behind the jail and coming up on the back of the livery. Victoria thought she saw a curtain move in an upstairs' window in the house behind them. Miss Lily's, Victoria thought, but wasn't sure. The ladies there would recognize her, would possibly think it odd she was with two strangers, even if one was a woman and both dressed so well.

Victoria decided her best chance of living through this kidnapping would be to go along with Louise and wait for Mason or Matthew to follow them and get her back. She had strength knowing that whatever happened when this was over, she would always have the memories of Mason and her on the riverbank. Those could never be taken from her.

The three entered the darkened stable empty of any human presence. Louise pushed Victoria up the buggy steps and into the back seat then climbed in behind her. It was *de'ja vu*, as Carl opened the double doors before climbing into the front seat. Taking the reins, he slapped them gently, pulling out of the stable and leaving town quietly. They must appear like a few close friends leaving for a day trip into the countryside.

Louise never took her hand off the gun but seemed to relax as the town of Sweetwater disappeared behind them. Carl kept a constant but sedate pace and Victoria actually saw them pass two wagons going in the opposite direction but she didn't have a way to notify others of her distress.

The buggy with its three occupants continued for over two hours and then veered off the main route and traveled another half hour. Finally, Carl pulled to a stop and got down. Louise ordered Victoria to get out. As Victoria peered around, she became disheartened to realize they were outside a small desolate looking cabin, not the city center she had expected. There wasn't any sign there were others around, no sound of a neighing horse or smoke coming from any chimney.

Victoria went where Louise directed, up the wooden steps, stepping over a broken porch board and then through a door that had seen better days. The cabin's interior wasn't any better. Dust covered what little furniture was left in a room that appeared ransacked. All but a long box on the top of the tattered mattress which Victoria thought incongruent with the rest of the room. There wasn't even a stove, merely a hole that used to house the chimney, and a bat hanging in the corner.

Louise ordered, "Open the box and put on the clothes. Everything, corset and all."

Victoria opened the box worrying about Carl coming in while she was undressed and was surprised when the box contained a duplicate of the very dress she had admired on Louise as she walked toward her on the boardwalk. Picking up the garment, she held it out to verify what she was seeing. The dresses were identical, right down to the black shiny buttons on the bodice and wrists.

"Put it on, damn you. I don't want to stay here all

night. It's getting late." She waved the gun towards Victoria.

Victoria felt she should rush to remove her clothing leaving her stockings on for the moment and pulling the lacy camisole over her head. Then she put on the corset, tied in front for easier wearing and cinched in the waist. She had only seen such fine underthings at Abby's shop but they had been too dear for her to accept them as a gift even from Abby.

"Tighter, you fat cow. The dress has to fit you and you'd never fit into it without cinching it up tighter. Hold onto this post and I'll pull them. I can't believe you don't know how to wear a proper corset. What kind of a clodhopper, are you?" As she saw Victoria glance over at the gun now resting on the mattress, Louise snapped, "Don't get any ideas. I can shoot you and cinch this up afterwards, if I need to."

The woman tied off the strings now making breathing nearly impossible. Victoria stepped into the dress and pulled it up, listening to Louise complain that the dress was all dusty.

Carl entered then. "It won't matter, my dear. By the time they find her it's going to look a lot worse than that. Is she about done?" He had come in carrying another box, the kind one gets when one buys an expensive hat or boots and set it on the wobbly table. "I've watered the horses and gave them a little feed. They'll be rested enough for us to continue."

Turning away from the door, Victoria quickly buttoned up the dress and finished fastening the cuffs. She took some pleasure that the dress was actually too loose around her waist but didn't mention it aloud. Turning back, she saw Louise open the hat box and remove what had to be hair pieces, already curled and coiffed. She approached Victoria while Carl held the gun pointed toward them both. Louise pinned the hairpieces into Victoria's own hair, matching identically. Then added the twin to the hat Louise was wearing.

"All right, now change into the silk stockings. Make sure you don't put a run in them. I have never worn a stocking with a snag or run in it in my life. Then put on the shoes."

Orders came fast and furious as Victoria took on her new appearance.

Carl said, "Stop worrying about the little things. I told you by the time she's found she'll look enough like you to make even your own mother say she was you. Did you check that she had a birthmark?"

"Yes, I'm glad the telegraph operator at Preston caught that wire the sheriff sent to Topeka that she had a birthmark after we let that little hint slip about me. Not that I actually have one but no one knows that but my closest friends." The couple chuckled together. "I'm glad Hill passed that information on to me. It's the little things that make sure this all goes over like it was planned. If Hill had brought her to me when he was supposed to, I wouldn't be under such a time constraint now. I'll go and make sure everyone sees me wearing this dress and after that I'll disappear and change my appearance. I've always wanted to be a redhead and cutting it short might be a nice change. What do you think?" she asked pirouetting for Carl's approval.

"You look lovely no matter what the color of your hair. You could be bald and you would still be the most beautiful woman." He poured compliments and admiration onto Louise's head until she was quite giddy with them.

"All right, now let's tie her up and get into Preston before it gets dark. You can come back tomorrow and get rid of her. I don't want to do it now in case something interferes with my escape. We can't have her come up dead ahead of my becoming missing."

Carl pulled a length of rough twine, very sturdy stuff, from his pocket and snarled, "Get onto this chair and put your hands behind your back. No, put them closer." He tied Victoria's hands together and then to the back of the chair. Next, he tied her feet together and then to one of the chair legs. He tested the knots grunting with approval.

Gathering up the boxes and paper the clothing was brought in along with Victoria's clothing and shoes, he searched the room for any damning evidence. Victoria hadn't said anything once she understood she wasn't needed alive, that her value to them was as a dead copy of Louise. Hill had never wanted her for prostitution, he wanted to sell her as a doppelganger for Louise.

Once that man saw Victoria get off the train in Preston, the idea to sell her to Louise must have formed and was probably more profitable in the long run. Taking Victoria and raping her then turning her over to Louise would have been like killing two birds with one stone. After all, selling a virgin was profitable and that had been their original plans for her, Victoria was sure now. Just as Mason had warned her about in the jail that day. She should have paid more attention, that there was more to Hill's plans than simply taking her to the hotel for the night.

Victoria didn't try to cry out or draw attention when the two left her in the darkening cabin. She sat there, trying to work her hands loose but stopped when she finally heard the buggy draw away from the cabin. Victoria actually felt calmer now she was alone.

Time to worry, of course, but time to hope she had been missed and for someone to put two and two together. For someone to know to follow her toward Preston, to take the turn off, to know she was left in this cabin. Tears rolled down her cheeks as regrets filled her. Regrets that she hadn't told Mason how much he meant to her, how much she loved him, how much she wanted to be with him at that very moment.

Why hadn't she made herself find him so she could explain herself? Why had she thought there was time, so much more time, when, in fact, there was none. Feeling she owed Abby so much, Victoria had planned to stay with Abby until she gave birth and perhaps a few months more. By then, Abby would decide whether to keep the shop open or sell it and become a full-time mother. She had heard Abby and Matthew discussing him staying closer to Sweetwater and selling his sales route. Victoria thought she had time and now it was too late.

Mason would never know how much he meant to her. How he saved her in so many ways and she was grateful for each time. She wished she had written it down, all the personal feelings and emotions he brought out of her. All the ways she wanted to apologize for hurting him when that was the last thing she wanted to do. She simply didn't want him to feel obligated to marry her. He had only done what she requested and he had done so reluctantly. He even offered to marry her once he thought about the possible consequences.

But she wasn't with child and he had no reason to feel he owed her anything. If she had it to do all over again, she would make sure he understood her reasons for turning his proposal down. That she didn't want to saddle him with a wife with so little to offer a husband. Mason deserved more, so much more, than Victoria could provide. She hadn't even gone through the sixth grade although she kept reading everything, she could lay her hands on. But that didn't count. A sheriff needed a better wife than she could be. A better choice than a tobacco picker out of Tennessee.

She didn't want to be found crying or with red eyes. She didn't want to give Carl the satisfaction that she had succumbed to melancholy. She would continue to hope. Hope the ropes would finally give way to allow her hands to slip through. Hope that something stopped their plans of switching her body for Louis's. Hope that somehow Mason would find her by some magical means. Hope that she got one more chance to say she loved him.

And then he was there, kneeling in front of her, kissing her tear stained face, cussing at his inability to untie the tight little knots. Taking out a switch blade, he finally cut through the string undoing the twine that had kept Victoria tied to the chair. Once her arms were free, she wrapped them around Mason's neck and cried silently into his shirt.

Picking her up, he held her close to his chest. "Please don't cry, love. It's breaking my heart and I blame myself for all this already. But I swear we were right behind you the whole way. We thought they were taking you to one of their hideouts, one of their houses. We should never have used you like that but you were already with them. I didn't think they would hurt you. I've been just outside. I would have thrown the whole plan to the winds if I thought they would harm you. I didn't dare take on the man and have you in here with Louise and a gun."

"I want to go home. I want to go back to Sweetwater," she said, little hiccups escaping between words.

"We can ride double on my horse. We'll just need to take it slowly. You ready now?" At her nod, Mason led Vicki out to the woods surrounding the cabin. Placing her up front, he mounted behind and urged the horse on. It took almost an hour to get to the main road and then turned toward Sweetwater.

They had been on that road, in the dark, and no one passed them in either direction. The going was slow due to having two people on the horse and the moonlight blocked by clouds as they moved across the sky.

Mason listened and then knew he heard a wagon or buggy coming from Sweetwater. Laying his hand on his gun, he prepared to fight off any attack but as the buggy got closer, he called out in recognition, "Daniel, we're over here."

The buggy pulled to a stop a couple of yards from the horse and riders. "Someone has been saying their prayers. I received a wire from Matthew to get a buggy on this road leading to Preston. It wasn't too plain about a cut off road, if I was supposed to try to find it or not. In this darkness I'm glad I didn't need to try."

As Daniel was speaking, Mason dismounted and lifted Vicki down helping her to the buggy.

"I'll ride back in the buggy, too, if you don't mind. This horse has done a lot of hard work today and I'll give him a rest as we take him home." Mason tied the horse to the back of the buggy and then got in next to Vicki.

Daniel said, "We won't be fast, but I can turn here. It's wide enough and we'll be home in an hour or so."

"I don't care how long it takes. I just want to get back. Thank you for coming for us, Reverend," Victoria said as she settled into the bench seat between the two men.

There wasn't much conversation. Vicki was too tired. Mason had his own thoughts and Daniel was busy trying to keep the buggy on the road and out of the ditches in the dark. It didn't seem very long before the few lights still lit in Sweetwater started to show. Daniel drove the buggy right up to the stable then turned the rig over to Andy.

Mason helped Vicki down saying, "We're going to stay at the midwife's house. I want to watch you and it's late to be waking up Abby and Grace."

Daniel asked, "Do you want me to send Becca over to you? I know she won't have gone to sleep until she knew you were safely home."

"No, Vicki's not going to be alone and, Daniel, I really appreciate your coming out and picking us up," Mason told the older man.

"All part of my duties, as they say. Good night, all." He walked toward the rectory next to the church yard.

Mason looked at Vicki and asked, "You want me to carry you or do you want to walk?"

"I'm fine. I can make it easily even if these shoes don't fit. I wasn't hurt. Just frightened and then I kept hoping someone must have seen me with those two. I prayed, wanting you or Matthew to show up. I was relieved when you came because by then I wasn't sure anyone would realize we turned off the main road. Once I learned they weren't selling me to a brothel, I did wonder if I was going to die right then."

They climbed the steps to the white porch together and Mason opened the front door into the parlor. He lit a lamp then turned to Vicki. "I'm sorry you had to go through all that. I never thought they would come for you after Hill got caught. Women don't bring that high of price, even virgins, at a brothel. I couldn't see where it would pay to come all this way to get you. But once I heard they were here again and abducted you, I was terrified."

"They wanted me as a double for that woman, Louise. I was to be sent over a cliff or something for my mangled body to be found later. Everyone would stop looking for her once her body was found. They even used the fact I have a birthmark on my hip which Hill or one of his cohorts must have seen when I was trying to get away from him in Preston. They knew the authorities were close to finding her, I think."

Trying to lighten the mood between them, Vicki said teasingly, "It's hard to believe you terrified. You and Matthew always seem to have everything covered so easily. Always controlled."

Mason leaned down and kissed Vicki's upturned face saying, "I'm never under control when you're around, woman. This has to stop or I'll be useless as a sheriff. I don't think I can go chasing after you one more time. Marry me so I can sleep next to you every night and know where you are all the time." He continued to kiss Vicki's neck and lips.

"Come on and help me undress. I don't think I'll be able to get this corset untied without help. Then I need to comb out my hair, I feel like I must look a mess," she told him without giving him the answer he was waiting for, hoping for.

"Actually, I find that dress quite fetching and the hat is one of the most elegant I've ever seen in any big city. I think you should keep it. You've earned it after what Wilson and her gang put you through," he told her honestly, following Vicki into the bedroom they had shared before.

Vicki removed the hat and the long hatpin as well as the hairpieces, placing all on the dresser top. She quickly undid the buttons down the front of the dress to the waist and then both wrists were dealt with. Pushing the dress down, she daintily stepped out of it.

Mason's throat went dry as he watched more and more of Vicki's skin become available to his sight. He finally moved when she asked him to untie the tight corset strings and he did so, finally getting them loose and freeing her. She kicked the pretty pink contraption aside and then pulled the lace trimmed camisole over her head, standing in front of Mason in all her womanly glory.

Reaching into the dresser drawer, he took out a clean nightgown and pulled it over her head then pulled her hands through the sleeves as if dressing a young child. He tried to think of her as a child who needed his assistance. Tried to remember all that she had already been through that day. How frightened she must have been.

"You're still wearing too many clothes," Victoria said coaxingly, unbuttoning Mason's shirt and pulling it out of his trousers. "Come to bed with me, Mason. I need your strength and your comfort." Kissing his now bared chest, loving the feel of the crisp hairs covering it against her face.

Mason held Vicki away from his clothing saying gently, "I think it's time you went to bed and got some sleep. I'll stay right here in the parlor. I won't leave you alone." He tried to steer her to the side of the bed.

"I need you. I need to feel you in me, on me. Please Mason, no one is coming for me here. You don't need to protect me. You need to make love to me," Vicki pleaded.

"Vicki, honey, listen to me. You always want me when you're frightened or have had a traumatic experience which is what happened today. I understand your need for comfort but I feel I'd be taking advantage of you like this." As Vicki made an attempt to tug her hands free and pull him to her, he told her, "I love you, I want to marry you and the next time I make love it will be with my wife."

"We did it before. You didn't mind before," she wheedled sounding as if he were reneging on a promise. Changing tactics, she needed to hear him admit the truth. "Mason, I'm not good enough for you. No matter how much we love one another the difference between us is too great. I'd understand if you wanted to simply sleep with me."

"And that was wonderful but I never meant it to be our only relationship. I never meant us to meet up and slip away somewhere when you had an itch to scratch. I've always been serious about us, as a permanent couple, a married couple."

"But you never really asked me," she accused. "You didn't."

"You're right, I'm sorry, but I never thought of us as anything else. It's been clear to me from nearly the beginning." He got down on one knee continuing,

"Vicki, I'm not much of a man in the long run but I have a good job that pays me and an apartment here in town. I own the livery and half of the hotel plus I have a ranch that is leased out and brings in rent every month. Will you do me the honor of becoming my wife?"

"Oh, Mason, how long have you been practicing that speech? You sounded like you were applying for a loan at the bank." But she was smiling so Mason didn't take any offence at her words.

"Is that a, yes, then?" he asked worriedly.

"It's a yes. But only because I know you love me and I love you. You have always come for me when I needed you most. That's what really matters." Gazing into his upturned face she needed his answer, too. "I feel I owe Abby so much. Can you agree to let me keep helping her?" At the nod of his head, she asked, "Now, will you come to bed with me?"

"I'll sleep on top of the blanket again, like last time but I'll take off my boots. I don't want Rebecca to scold me. After all, her husband is to perform the ceremony this afternoon." He covered his intended with the sheet. Going to the other side of the bed, he lay down after removing his gun belt and boots.

Vicki tried to pull him closer as he said, "I told you the next time I make love to you it will be as my wife. I was talking to Daniel about it when Andy brought me news of Wilson being in town. I went to the shop thinking to get Matthew to help protect you only to find you had gone out. That's when we decided to follow rather than jump the buggy and maybe get you shot."

"I'm glad you were there, both of you, but I never doubted you. Go to sleep, I'm not going to worry any more tonight."

CHAPTER 12

A few hours later Mason leaned over a sleeping Vicki whispering, "Daniel is here and I have to send a wire to find out if Matthew's back yet. If he is, we'll plan on the wedding this afternoon if that's still all right with you."

"That sounds fine. I hope Matthew is back. I find I'm looking forward to being married, especially to the local sheriff." She kissed him sleepily.

Daniel was in the kitchen as Mason entered. He looked up from the coffee pot he was filling, "Sorry to have woken you but Matthew's back and is looking to talk with you. Sounds like it all went well, though. No one was hurt, in the posse, at least. I guess Wilson's accomplice was shot. Matthew will fill you in."

Mason looked toward Daniel and motioned toward the bedroom, "You're all right with this? With me being here?"

Daniel smiled. "All man's emotions are part of God's plan. Our earthly rules and politics don't really matter in the scheme of things, only what we do. Nothing you're doing is against His will."

"Thanks for the thoughts, Reverend, but we're not doing all that much. Will you stay until I get back or someone else gets here?"

"I won't let her out of my sight," Then blushing, he said, "Well, you know what I mean. I've got my revolver with me."

"I don't think we have to worry about Wilson any longer. Now that everyone knows her plan it won't work out, so no one should be looking for Vicki again." He left through the side door in search of Matthew.

Rebecca came in the same way a few minutes later and kissed her husband on the mouth, he looked into her eyes and felt that heart-swell he was finally getting used to every time he saw her. "I brought some clothes for Victoria from Abby's. I passed Mason. He sure looks worn out. I don't think he slept much last night."

Daniel sat on the kitchen chair pulling his wife unto his lap. "Not for the reason you're thinking, though. I think it's simple worry and as soon as we get them married the better for everyone. He'll calm down some when he knows where she is all the time." Becca put her arms around Daniel's neck and let him nuzzle into her breasts, enjoying the familiarity.

"I'm glad we finally realized we needed to be together." She kissed him again feeling cherished and desired.

"I'm glad I finally realized what a poor minister I was becoming."

"That's not true. You were hardest on yourself. I've forgiven you, now forgive yourself," Becca told him, no, ordered him.

Daniel placed his hand on her abdomen. "I do. I think I'm finally over myself. I've got you and a baby on the way. It's all the proof I need to know I took the right path."

"We both did. I did, when I came to Sweetwater in the first place and you when you chose it as your ministry. It was all guided, the good and the bad, all part of a plan." They sealed their troth once more with a kiss.

Victoria interrupted, calling out from the bedroom, "Is Mason here? I only have a blanket to cover myself with and I don't want to startle anyone out there."

"It's only Daniel and me here right now." Rebecca got off Daniel's lap and headed to the bedroom with the bag. "Abby sent some things to wear after your bath but then she has a surprise she's bringing over a little later."

Daniel stood straightening his trousers. "I'll take that as my cue to leave. I'll just be across the street. Do you remember where the rifle is, Becca?"

"I do and it's loaded. We'll be fine. Go on and work on your sermon or something."

Once in the bedroom, she hugged Victoria asking, "Are you really, all right? I couldn't believe it was happening all over again and after I teased Mason about watching you so closely. I feel maybe we all should have kept a closer watch."

"I spent most of my days with Abby and Matthew. I rarely went out without everyone knowing where I was. It was just my bad luck to be out when Wilson came to look for me again. At least they didn't come to the shop to find me. I don't know what they would have done to Abby and Grace." Victoria said earnestly, "They didn't have good plans for me."

"I'm glad they're all in jail and the Marshall has them." Rebecca shook her head as if to clear away the bad thoughts. "I want to concentrate on getting you ready for your wedding. Now I see Daniel started some water boiling so I'll start filling the tub."

"I'll help, too. I didn't get any new bruises this time, well, I don't think so anyway. I was lucky Mason and Matthew followed so closely."

Miss Lily arrived as Victoria and Rebecca emptied the tub, bringing in a basket of cookies and muffins, then 'oohed' and 'aahed' over Victoria's long hair. Finally,

Victoria felt sorry for the older woman saying, "All right, I'll let you dress my hair if you let me pay you for doing so. I feel like such a fraud having you all do these things for me. I'm not actually hurt or anything."

"I enjoy working with such beautiful hair. I don't usually charge my female clients, just the men." At the other two lady's expression of interest, she added blushing, "Oh, for cutting their hair, I mean."

"That's all right, too, Miss Lily. I would love to have you style my hair for today," Victoria added.

"Will you be wearing a hat, my dear, or a veil perhaps? It makes a little difference to how I place the ringlets and such," said Miss Lily seriously studying Victoria's hair, fingering it for fineness and curl.

Abby knocked on the front door and came through, carrying Grace with Andy behind her bringing in a couple of boxes. Abby thanked him and slipped him a coin, which he tried to return.

"Don't be silly, Andy. It saved Matthew from having to walk down here with me. You deserve more for helping so much yesterday. Go on, take it." She practically pushed him back out the door once he had set the boxes down.

Abby turned to the three women in the kitchen. "Oh, good, you're here already, Miss Lily. I was worried Victoria would put up a resistance and I wasn't going to be able to talk her into anything on my own," she said breathlessly removing her own hat after placing Grace onto Victoria's lap. "I want to unbox this as soon as possible to let the fabric breath and then we won't need to press it at all."

All female eyes were faceted on the long dress box as Abby untied the ribbon holding the lid on and pulled out a lovely soft, grey dress with double bustle. The material shimmered and caught the sunlight and the three women let out their breaths in sighs at the same time.

Rebecca said, "Oh, Abby its breathtaking, absolutely breathtaking,"

Miss Lily concurred, "I haven't seen anything like it as a day dress. It is ideal for a wedding. I will have to think of the perfect hair style to compliment the neckline."

"It has a matching jacket, trimmed out in lavender like the sleeves and underskirt. It's really a flounce so the dress isn't too hot for summer wear, but it appears as an underdress," Abby proudly explained her design methods.

"What's in the other box?" asked Rebecca excitedly.

Placing the dress over the chair, Abby opened the smaller box. She took out a grey hat with a wide band of lavender ribbon, and a white turtledove made of real feathers nesting in its crown. White netting that could be pulled down was rolled up along the brim of the hat.

Miss Lily's eyes glittered with excitement. "Oh, I can work with this, Abby. How lovely an ensemble. It really is."

Soon each lady had taken on a project and Victoria was being turned into the perfect bride. Nails buffed, hair coiffed, brows plucked and she was finally ready for the clothes and hat. When all was done to everyone's satisfaction, Victoria looked like an elegant young woman, dressed better than the most citified debutant.

The other ladies hurried to their homes to ready themselves as Victoria watched the wedding guests arrive across the street. She was surprised so many people found the time to attend at such short notice but it only proved how well known and liked by Sweetwater Mason was.

Matthew, dressed in a dark suit and white shirt, a top hat on his head came across the street to escort Victoria after he had dropped Abby and Grace at the church. Victoria evidently was the only one not in her proper place. She gave a nervous smile at Matthew, her best friend's husband, and took the arm he offered.

As they entered the church the organist burst into Mendelssohn's wedding march and Victoria's heart swelled with love as she first saw Mason waiting for her next to the minister and a tall good-looking stranger, she knew was James Macgregor. Mason looked as she had never seen him. A grey suit with grey striped vest, white shirt with black tie and his shoes polished. His best man, wearing a darker suit, was a couple of inches taller but just as distinguished. She walked beside Matthew down the aisle between the pews filled with guests, most of whom she didn't know, and then he placed her hand into Mason's as they stood before Reverend Walters.

Miss Lily was the organist at the wedding as well as sang them a lovely romantic song. The ceremony didn't take much time. Daniel said the solemn words that had been said over couples for centuries of marriages. 'Dearly beloved' and ending 'Let no man put asunder.' Mason leaned in to the kiss, chaste by their standards and then they turned to greet what appeared to be the whole town of Sweetwater.

They all followed the couple out of church and some climbed into buggies and wagons while others began the walk to the hotel's restaurant where the newlyweds would greet their guests at a reception of sorts. Matthew had brought Champaign and his sister, Callie, had sent a wedding cake, beautifully decorated with edible roses and leaves on vines. A spun sugared star to represent Mason's badge was standing on the top of the three tiers.

Victoria was moved by such a show of affection from people she had never met. She had trouble keeping the tears out of her eyes. Abby misted up a couple of times but then she was expecting so it was natural for her to be more emotional than most. After all, this marriage meant Victoria was going to be a part of Sweetwater forever, just as she had hoped all those weeks ago.

After much of the food and cake had been disbursed Mason made a brash announcement. "Ladies and Gentlemen and Grace, thank you for attending and witnessing our marriage today. Please stay and enjoy yourselves as long as you want but you will have to excuse me and my new wife. We are about to begin our married life in the privacy I have been yearning for since I said, I do."

Then he swept his beautifully dressed wife up into his arms and carried her out through the double doors to whoops of catcalls and whistles. He didn't put her down as Victoria expected. She enjoyed the ride as he continued to carry her out to the rear door and over to another pushing it open with his shoulder.

Mason let Victoria slide down his body as he set her feet on the floor of his apartment in the rear of the hotel. She looked around noting the sparse amount of furniture and décor although what was there was of good quality. The window curtains were very nice as was the nickel-plated decorative stove and patterned carpet on the parlor floor.

"I haven't had time to fix it up much. I hoped you would enjoy doing that," he explained hesitantly.

"You haven't had time? But I thought you've lived here for years," she said smiling at her new husband.

"I have but it was good enough for me then. I mean, I haven't had time since I planned on marrying you. I meant to but things kept happening." His gaze moved around the room seeing it as she was. "I picked up a Montgomery Ward's catalog but that's as far as I got."

"I don't mind, Mason. I was teasing you. We've both had a lot of things on our minds. My mind, for example, thinks we both have on too many clothes." She began to unbutton his shirtfront working toward his belt buckle.

Mason sucked in his breath saying, "I agree with that, love. How do I unwrap you? You look prettier than a Christmas present and tastier than that wedding cake." Leaning, he covered Vicki's mouth with his own.

After a few minutes, Vicki pushed Mason away. "Help me out of this dress and then I'll help you."

Mason's fingers trembled a little as he unbuttoned the front of the grey and lavender dress as she found the hatpin and removed her bonnet. She laid it down on the nearby table and finished the buttons much faster than Mason was able to do.

Helping to pull the dress over her head, he placed it on a chair. Then sucked in his breath again before letting it out in a long hiss as he saw his bride wearing only the pink corset over a very see-through lacy camisole and pink stockings tied with pink ribbon.

"See, just like presents on Christmas morning," he told her on a drawn-out sigh. He began by untying the corset and kissing Vicki's neck as he did so.

"I can't get to you if you keep bending over to kiss me, Mason. Play fair," she complained.

"I think this is fair. You naked and me enjoying the scenery." He continued to kiss her neck, edging toward her mouth, his hands cupping the weight of her now available breasts.

"No more until I get your coat off, at least," she bargained. Mason tore off his coat, tossing it toward a sofa and returned to sucking on Vicki's breasts and neck.

His hot breath was tickling her and she again said, "You have on too many clothes. Let's make a deal. I'll let you do anything you want as long as you're undressed as much as I am."

A light glittered in Mason's eyes as he ripped his shirt off and hopped around trying to yank off his shoes. Then socks and trousers and drawers followed, leaving him as naked as Vicki.

She pulled his head back down to hers whispering, "Now I call that fair."

Vicki's hand went down to hold his manhood, urgently trying to wedge itself between them. Mason moaned his encouragement as his mouth left her lips to fasten gently unto one of her engorged nipples.

Sweeping his wife up into his arms, Mason carried her into a room with a large bed set in the center, the shades already drawn against the setting sun. He lay her on the opened sheets and crawled in next to her.

"I've been fantasizing about you sharing this bed with me. I had to start sleeping other places in the house to keep from reaching for you in my dreams, they seemed so real. Now I have you here I don't know what to do first." He stroked her body with one hand while the other held her in place.

"I'm here, Mason. You don't have to be afraid I'm going to disappear. Not anymore. But these dreams, these fantasies…show some of them to me and I'll show you some of mine." She again placed her hand on his erection trying to sooth it's trembling.

"I don't think that's going to help, love. Let me see if this helps us both." He slid down the bed so he could nestle against her curls. Then placed his tongue and mouth where he had dreamt of them being so often.

Vicki tensed then relaxed, letting Mason have this first fantasy fulfilled. She'd have the next. She held his head to her, stroking his hair as he rhythmically stroked her, making little spirals of euphoric sensations tremble through her body. Soon, too soon, Vicki had reached the maximum point of sensation as she convulsed around Mason's fingers and tongue.

Mason returned to cover her breast with his mouth and rub the now tingling aftermath from her quivering thighs. Placing the still trembling male appendage at her warm entrance, he mutely asked for entry which was granted eagerly.

Vicki kissed the warm chest and hugged Mason to her hips, loving the feel and weight of him on her, joining with her and knowing he was receiving the same sort of enjoyment he had pleasured her with. His urgency became almost frantic but soon the cataclysmic spasms were announcing his release and Vicki held him tighter as he found relief in her body.

"I don't remember it feeling that good. Maybe James was right. It takes a while to get it perfected." He rolled to the side holding Vicki close but no longer trembling.

"You spoke to James about our lovemaking?" she asked quietly, not believing the handsome man who acted as witness in the church should know such intimate details about her and Mason.

"Not us precisely. I mean, it was about us, but he didn't know who," he tried to explain.

"Well, he probably does now," Vicki pointed out trying to find a way to ever look that man in the eye again.

"I know stuff about him so it's all right. Anyway, he wasn't a great lot of help. I figured out most of it. Well, with your participation I did." He kissed her lips quickly as if trying to take her mind off thinking about his confession.

"You did quite well. Now I think it's time for my fantasy. You're not the only one having long lonely nights you know. There's something I've been dreaming of doing again only better," she said as she slid lower in the bed.

Mason, a contented grin on his face said, "James did say it gets better with practice."

A word about the author...

Author Susan Payne has always loved to read which meant she often found herself reading books she was too young to fully understand. That didn't stop her. She found a dictionary and looked up anything that she questioned. She still thinks reading a thesaurus is a good way to spend an afternoon.

Raising a family of five children kept her busy but also allowed her time to read. Often more than fifty books a month with her children playing at her feet. That's where her love of history met her love of words as she read the new historical romance genre.

In her forties, she decided to try her hand at writing but became discouraged when she never reached the conclusion to the many stories she began. She 'retired' even after joining the local chapter of Romance Writers of America and saw how many of them seemed to write with ease.

Later, Susan found her mind filled with characters all clamoring to tell her their stories. All wanting to be heard. All wanting her to tell the world how happy they were with their chosen partners. How they had gotten through loss and survived as well as thrived.

At over eighty manuscripts, Susan is still hurrying to get the words down so that she can write the next. All stories of men and women who made their mark on life and then moved on.

Highland lairds, Berserkers from northern Europe, Georgian and Regency then on to the western US. The stories keep coming and the couples keep finding their happy-ever-after.

Thank you for purchasing
this publication of The Wild Rose Press, Inc.

For questions or more information
contact us at
info@thewildrosepress.com.

The Wild Rose Press, Inc.
www.thewildrosepress.com